RANGER MCINTYRE:
THE DUNRAVEN HOARD
MURDERS

JAMES C. WORK

FIVE STAR
A part of Gale, a Cengage Company

GALE
A Cengage Company

LIBRARY OF CONGRESS CATALOGING-IN-PUBLICATION DATA

Names: Work, James C., author.
Title: The Dunraven Hoard murders / James C. Work.
Other titles: At head of title: Ranger McIntyre
Description: First edition. | Waterville, Maine : Five Star, a part of Gale, a Cengage Company, [2020] | Series: Ranger McIntyre
Identifiers: LCCN 2019018318 (print) | ISBN 9781432859480 (hardcover : acid-free paper)
Subjects: LCSH: Park rangers—Fiction. | Murder—Investigation—Fiction. | GSAFD: Mystery fiction.
Classification: LCC PS3573.O6925 D86 2020 (print) | DDC 813/.54—dc23
LC record available at https://lccn.loc.gov/2019018318

First Edition. First Printing: February 2020
Find us on Facebook—https://www.facebook.com/FiveStarCengage
Visit our website—http://www.gale.cengage.com/fivestar
Contact Five Star Publishing at FiveStar@cengage.com

Printed in Mexico
Print Number: 01   Print Year: 2020

HISTORY NOTE

Lord Dunraven, born Windham Thomas Wyndham-Quin, was the Fourth Earl of Dunraven. He ruled a vast estate in Ireland, including the village of Adare where his impressive mansion can still be visited. An avid adventurer and traveler, Lord Dunraven came to the Colorado Rockies in 1872. Taken in by the wide meadows and trout-rich streams of Estes Park, he set his sights on acquiring the entire valley for a hunting and sport reserve. In 1877 friends and associates of Dunraven built the English Hotel on the east edge of the park. By the end of the 1879 season, however, Dunraven and his principal cohorts had decided not to return to Estes Park. The hotel changed hands and continued to operate until 1911 when it burned down.

Roads into Estes Park in those days were primitive. Winters were harsh. In mid-September the hotel and Dunraven's cottage were locked and boarded up and would sit dark and empty until spring. Growing up in Estes Park, I heard the rumor that the Irish aristocrats had cached their valuables each winter—coins, silverware, paintings, lamps, etc.—and that when Dunraven's party failed to return to the valley in 1880 the cache was forgotten. If the story was true, then the Dunraven Hoard lay undisturbed somewhere in our valley or the mountains surrounding it.

CHAPTER ONE:
THIS RANGER FOR HIRE

"Take off your trousers," she said.

There was no point in protesting, there was nowhere to run: empty except for a three-legged stool and a wobbly table, the cubicle had no windows and only one door, which she was guarding. There was an eye-level opening in the concrete wall, but it was only eight inches square. She already had his boots and tunic; his revolver was in the pickup truck outside.

He slid the suspenders off his shoulders and stepped out of his trousers.

"All right," he said.

Her hand appeared around the edge of the half-open door, holding a different pair of trousers.

"Put these on."

"What's this square hole in the wall for?" he asked as he pulled up the trousers and fumbled with the buttons. The light bulb hanging from the center of the ceiling didn't provide very much light.

"I'm not sure," she said. "Mike must have had some use in mind when he built the room. Then he put in the hydroelectric plant and we got an electric freezer and didn't need a cold room to keep things on ice. Maybe he was going to run a vent pipe from that hole through the kitchen wall to the outdoors. Come on out here."

Minnie March looked Ranger McIntyre up and down. She gave his waistband a tug.

7

"I'll look around for the black suspenders," she said. "I think I know where they are."

"The fit feels perfect," McIntyre said. "I didn't know you were a tailor, too."

"You mean besides being a pretty face?"

"No. A good cook."

"Turn around, wise guy," she snapped. "And count yourself lucky I don't kick you square in your behind."

Minnie held the dinner jacket for McIntyre. He put his arms in the sleeves then drew it up over his shoulders.

"Looks perfect," she said.

"Mike had expensive tastes," McIntyre observed, stroking the satin lapels.

"Always bought the best he could afford. Always said there was no money saved in buying cheap clothes. He'd be proud to see you in his dinner jacket. We never went anywhere he could wear it, but he was proud of it. Let's go in the dining room. Cook and I have your place all set up."

Ranger McIntyre followed Minnie. According to Emily Post's new etiquette book, in a formal dinner situation the ladies precede the gentlemen into the dining room. He had also read that the gentlemen wait at the doorway while the ladies find their place cards. The hostess gives a signal when all the ladies are in place, at which point the gentlemen enter and take their places.

Minnie led the way to one of the tables where a full formal place setting had been laid out.

"C'mon over here, Tim," she said. "You must be awful sweet on that Denver FBI lady, going to all this trouble just for a dinner party."

"Guilty," he confessed. "I do like her. Besides, it's something different to do with my two-week vacation. I can't afford to go anywhere. Plus, this invitation to a Denver dinner party is a little puzzling. I love a puzzle."

"How's it a puzzle?" Minnie asked, pulling his chair out for him. "Sit here. Remember to keep your spine or shoulders from touching the back of the chair. No slumping, not that you could. Where'd you learn to hold yourself that straight? Army?"

"Partly the army. Mostly my mother. She was a fanatic about posture."

"And what's the puzzle you mentioned?"

"Miss Coteau has a rich acquaintance who's throwing this dinner party. Very influential. His son goes to college up at Boulder. The son and a couple of his chums were hunting for treasure somewhere near the national park and one of the boys ended up dead. You probably read about it."

"Accident, the newspaper said. Said he fell head-down into an ore bucket at one of the old mine shafts."

"That's the one. Apparently, the wealthy man's son thinks it was murder. He also thinks that he was the intended victim. Somehow this rich guy knows Miss Coteau at the Denver FBI office and told her what his son had said and she told him she knew a guy who knows the area and who has a couple of weeks off. That's why she's taking me to dinner at his mansion. Says I need to meet him."

"Possible murder, attempted murder, wrong victim!" Minnie exclaimed. "Right up your alley, I'd say. You're acquiring quite a reputation as a sleuth even though you're just a tree cop. Maybe I should stick around this winter and find out how you solve it! Right now, though, we need to see what you've learned from Post's book. Honest to God, Timothy, going to all this trouble just to impress Miss Coteau! You'd think you'd be married long ago. Did you actually read that whole book?"

"Sure. Well, I did skip some parts, like how to conduct oneself during a steamship voyage. That voyage back from France after the war pretty much put me off the idea of making the crossing ever again."

"Can't say as I blame you. Now, look at your place setting and tell me what you found out from Post."

Ranger McIntyre sat straight as a ramrod at the table in the empty dining room and surveyed the formal place setting before him.

"Okay," he said. "Hands in lap. Never fuss with the plates, never adjust the silverware. If something's missing or out of place or if a knife has a smudge on it, signal the server to fix it. Remember to keep your eye on what the hostess is doing. Don't unfold the napkin or touch anything on the table until she does. If an appetizer or salad is served, don't make a move toward it until you see the hostess pick up her fork."

"Good," Minnie said. "Now tell me about the layout."

"Your largest plate is called the service plate, the small one is the bread plate. Between each course the server will either remove the service plate or put another plate on top of it. Don't touch it, don't put any food on it."

"What about the drinking glasses?"

McIntyre began to recite the Emily Post book like a schoolboy doing his multiplication tables.

"That tall one on the left is for water. The fat one next to it is for red wine, the straight one is for white wine, and that little short one is for sherry. Except with prohibition going on, there won't be any wine."

"Say!" Minnie exclaimed. "What if they did serve wine! With an FBI employee and a federal park ranger sitting at the table? Wouldn't one of you have to arrest the host?"

"Not my jurisdiction. I can only make an arrest if I catch a ground squirrel or a bear drinking bathtub gin. Besides, I'm on vacation and don't have to arrest anybody. Besides which, I think it's legal to drink booze you already own. You just can't buy it. Or sell it."

"What about your eating tools?"

McIntyre pointed to each eating utensil in turn, left to right.

"Left side of the serving plate you've got your salad fork, fish fork, and dinner fork. On the other side there's a dinner knife, a teaspoon . . . and what's that next one?"

"Demitasse spoon."

"What's it for?"

"See the little coffee cup to the right of your other cup and saucer? That's a demitasse. In case you want a little bit of strong dark coffee after dinner."

"Oh. The spoon is for putting sugar in your demitasse."

"Never! The server will ask if you want sugar, and he will put it in your cup for you. The spoon is for you to stir with."

"Holy cow," McIntyre said. "Anyway, next to the itty-bitty spoon comes the soup spoon and finally the seafood fork. At the top of the plate I've got my cake fork and my dessert spoon. I'm ready for any kind of food they might throw my way."

"Let's hope they don't throw food at this shindig. What about that small bread plate?" Minnie said, pointing.

"Bread plate and butter knife. Always break bread or rolls with your fingers, don't use the knife. If you use the knife for butter, don't lick the knife afterward."

"You're such a gent," Minnie said.

"What are those last two little gadgets?" McIntyre asked.

Minnie pointed to the tiny bowl and miniature spoon, then to a little crystal block the size of a pack of Black Jack chewing gum.

"That little bowl's for your personal salt. Or they might have a teeny-tiny salt shaker there instead. But never reach for the salt. In fact, don't ever use it. Bad manners to salt your food."

"Then why have it there?"

"In case you want it."

"Oh."

"The little square thing is your knife rest where you put your butter knife to keep butter off the linen tablecloth."

"Good idea. I guess I'm ready to eat without embarrassing myself too much. What's next?"

"Let's go find black shiny shoes and an overcoat and you'll be all set to wow the ladies."

"I don't know how to thank you," Ranger McIntyre said as he stood up and followed Minnie out of the dining room. "I know Mike would have been happy to loan me his tux and all, but for you to tailor it for me and go to all that trouble . . ."

"Shush!" Minnie said. "It's the least I can do to pay you back for watching over the lodge all winter while I'm with my sister in Kansas."

"I don't mind. I enjoy checking the place once a week or so. It gives me something to do after the tourists have all gone home."

"Weird, isn't it?" Minnie said. "One day there's so many people in the park that you couldn't swing a cat, then along comes Labor Day and the schools reopen and you could shoot a cannon down the village main street and not hit anybody. But I'll be worried about you."

"Me? Why me?"

"With all the lodges closed for the season, where will you eat breakfast? And fishing season will close, too. You'll have nothing to do."

"I might work. You know, be a park ranger?"

"Well, yes, you might try it. But I hope you'll ease into it real gradual-like. I wouldn't want you to hurt yourself."

There were no two ways about it: Vi Coteau was a stunner. If the Hollywood filmmakers ever made a film about the life of a glamorous FBI "secretary" they would have to hire Miss Clara Bow for the part. In her everyday clothes—usually a tight-fitting skirt, tailored jacket, and cute cloche hat—Vi could cause men's heads to snap around at a hundred yards. The sight of her in this evening's slinky floor-length satin gown and fur-trimmed long cape made other women want to lie down in front of an oncoming bus.

When Ranger McIntyre saw her coming through the lobby of his hotel toward him looking classy and refined, he almost regretted having planned a little joke on her, which was that he had parked his pickup truck at the curb and was going to tell her that they would drive it to the dinner party. It was the pickup that the owner of Small Delights Lodge had given McIntyre, the truck with "Small Delights" stenciled on both doors.

"I thought we'd drive to the dinner in my truck," McIntyre told her.

"Here's a nickel," Vi replied, pretending to hand him a coin. "Go buy yourself another thought. I have a cab waiting. Where's your hat?"

"Don't have one. My head's bigger than Mike March's was."

"You know what, Ranger? I'm not even going to ask you what that's supposed to mean. C'mon."

All through dinner Ranger McIntyre had the distinct feeling that his tailored dinner jacket, waistcoat, and tie were making a good impression on the ladies, including Vi Coteau. Several times he looked across the table and caught her looking back at him in a way that he found gratifying. He admitted it to himself: he was enjoying the attention. He was not likely to ever attend a formal dinner again as long as he lived, but for now he liked it. It reminded him of being in uniform on parade and having all those lovely French women throwing kisses as the squadron marched by.

Finally, the ordeal of formal dining was over. The hostess put aside her dessert fork and announced that the ladies would adjourn to the parlor, the gentlemen to the library. Her husband, Mr. William Leup, signaled for his son, Richard, and Ranger McIntyre to follow him to his private study. Mr. Leup's personal secretary handed around the cigar box and McIntyre graciously accepted. When the cigars had been trimmed and lit and the first few appreciative puffs had been duly performed, Mr. Leup offered chairs and got to the point.

"We've rather a mess going on, I'm afraid," Leup began. "As you know, son Richard here had a friend, Winston Dole, who died while the boys were up in the mountains. The Dole family is anxious to learn more details about the death; Richard has convinced himself that it was not accidental. Not only was it not accidental, but Winston was not the intended victim. Richard thinks that he himself was the target. I want more information. I want someone to look into it and bring me the facts of the matter. Unfortunately, it took place outside the jurisdiction of the Denver police. I have several important friends there. The county sheriff's office is woefully undermanned. I could hire a private detective to find the perpetrator—and I firmly believe there is a perpetrator—but none of them know the mountains. City boys."

"I see," McIntyre said.

"I have been on the phone to the FBI. The director is a friend of mine, as is the local FBI agent. As you know, Miss Vi Coteau works for him. She is a friend of Richard's sister. She suggested to me that she knew a forest ranger who has a proven knack for investigating and solving crimes, such as the death of young Winston. If it was a crime. I spoke with your Supervisor Nicholson and had a word with my friend, the Secretary of the Interior, and Supervisor Nicholson indicated that you would be willing to undertake to look into it for me, even though the incident technically took place outside the national park. Nicholson also indicated willingness to extend your vacation time, if necessary, in view of the fact that the tourist season is over and things have quieted down in the park."

Whew, thought McIntyre. *What a speech. It's easy to see him in politics.*

"I'd be happy to help, if I can," he replied. "Maybe Richard could tell me more about where and how this incident took place. The newspaper wasn't very specific."

He was going to add "and I don't have anything else to do for a couple of weeks" but thought better of it.

CHAPTER TWO:
CONFLICTING OPINIONS

When Richard opened his mouth to speak, his father held up a fat hand to silence him. The gesture as well as Richard's reaction seemed automatic as if it happened on a frequent, if not constant, basis.

Richard slumped back in the oversized wingback chair, crossed his arms on his chest, and glared at the fireplace like a college boy when the coach tells him he can't play in Saturday's game against State. His resentment of his father was palpable: it seemed to hang in the room like the tobacco smoke, making for an awkward silence. McIntyre turned his head from father and son and pretended to take an interest in the framed coin collection hanging on the wall.

"What happened is this," Mr. Leup began, studying the ash on his cigar, "young Richard and his friends Winston Dole and Charles Monde, instead of tending to their studies at the university, went off on a treasure-hunting lark. You know the closed-down gold mines, the ones at Big Horse Park on the Rocky Mountain National Park boundary? Of course, you do. How long have you been with the park, anyway? Probably it doesn't matter. As I said, these three boys took it into their stupid heads to go larking about among the old tunnels and mine buildings instead of studying their books like they should. They became separated, each one wandering off in a different direction to search for this treasure or whatever. Late in the day, it started to turn cold and dark. Being a bright little college boy,

Richard decided they should be returning to the fraternity house. Except they couldn't find Winston anywhere. Charles and Richard searched and searched and finally ended up driving to the nearest telephone to call for help.

"Well, it was a dark night. By the time a search party had been organized, there was not much use in trying to find anything. They set out again at first light the following morning and found him within two hours. He had hiked over a hill and down a long gulch to the May Day Mine."

"And he was dead by then," Ranger McIntyre put in.

"Of course. Would you care for coffee?"

Mr. Leup pressed a button on his desk and a servant appeared in the doorway.

"Coffee," Mr. Leup said. He waved the servant away again.

"Dead as a rat in a rain barrel," he continued. "Headfirst down into an old ore bucket, just his feet showing above the rim. Good thing one of the searchers spotted those boots sticking up or else Winston could've hung there until the trump of doom."

McIntyre turned to Richard, who was still glowering at the fire.

"Hung?" McIntyre said. "He was hanging?"

Richard stared back at the ranger as if he were the stupidest man he had ever deigned to speak to.

"No. Not 'hanging.' You're not listening. He was stuck headfirst down into an old ore bucket. The bucket was hanging. On a heavy chain from the old headframe. And before you ask, the doctor said he probably died of asphyxiation from being upside down in there. There was no way he was going to get himself out again. Even the men who came to get him couldn't haul him up and out. Luckily one of them finally thought to unhook the chain and lay the ore bucket on the ground so they could pull him out that way."

"This ore bucket," McIntyre said. "It wasn't suspended over the shaft? You said it hung on the headframe."

"No, of course not," Richard snapped. "Not over the shaft. Off to the side, by the old shed. Maybe headframe isn't the right term. I wouldn't know. A thick beam, two thick upright posts. Like a doorframe, only much, much heavier, you know? No, like a goalpost on a football field. That's what it looks like, a football goalpost. The chain went around the beam. The ore bucket—you must have seen one somewhere, if you know the area as well as what's-her-name, Miss Coteau, says. It has an oversized swinging handle on it, with a loop at the top. That's where the chain was."

It wasn't natural at all. McIntyre knew the old May Day Mine site and had seen the rusted ore bucket lying on its side against the framework. He didn't remember seeing any chain on the bucket, although there was some in a pile of metal junk nearby. Thick chains, iron rods, bent pulleys, broken angle braces, anything that the miners had thrown aside and was too heavy for hikers to carry away. How, he wondered, had that ore bucket ended up hanging from that gantry? One man alone might be able to stand it on end and then work it into position under the frame. Maybe. He'd either have to be very strong or very clever at physics to hang it up.

"That wouldn't be the headframe," McIntyre explained. "More likely to be a gantry. Maybe the miners built it to hoist heavy equipment into wagons. But what were you and Winston and Charles looking for? Your father said you were hunting for treasure?"

"They were playing hooky," Mr. Leup replied, speaking for his son. "Less than two weeks into the college semester and these three decide it's too nice a day to sit in a classroom. Everyone knows there is nothing of value to be found in those old mines, not even enough gold ore to turn a profit."

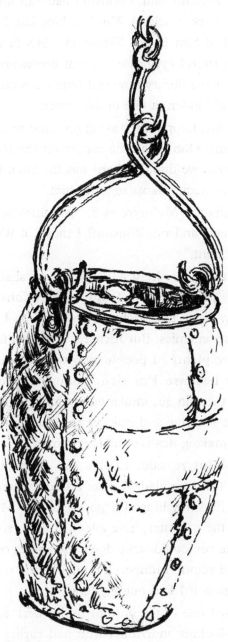

Ore Bucket

"Actually," Richard said, "Winston had run into a fellow we used to know, back in school. Weird looking kid. Didn't like him much. We called him Beeky. Skinny kid. His face was nothing but nose and round eyeglasses. A real bookworm, you know? Beeky works at the library now and found something in a book about a 'hoard' hidden at one of the mines."

"Yes, yes," Mr. Leup said, waving his hand to silence his son. "Not important. Don't lead the ranger off the track. The issue is, Mr. McIntyre, we think Richard was the intended victim. It's possible that someone wants to harm him."

"Harm Richard?" McIntyre said. "You think someone meant to harm Richard and not Winston? I mean, if Winston's death wasn't an accident."

"Yes. Winston is . . . he was . . . a boy of, shall we say, little promise. Few prospects. No family connections, certainly no family money. None too bright, in my opinion. I can't imagine him having any enemies. But Richard, on the other hand, is my son. There are plenty of people who would love to cause me grief simply because I'm rich. Some believe that I took advantage of them in accumulating my fortune. It's none of my fault that I'm smarter and quicker to seize opportunities. I'm very good at making deals, at making money."

"I see," McIntyre said. Leup's ego seemed to know no bounds. "Well, I'd be glad to poke around where it happened and see if I find anything. I'll go up to the May Day Mine tomorrow or the day after, have a look around, and report back to you. Maybe you could write down the names of the boys and addresses and phone numbers for me. Yours, too. That way I can let you know if I find out anything."

Leup pressed one of the buttons on his desk to summon the tall, nervous-looking individual who had earlier proffered the box of cigars.

"My secretary," Leup explained. "I don't write things down. He does."

"Okay," McIntyre said. "I'd also like the names and addresses of anyone who could tell me more about the young man who died. I want to look into his story of a treasure hoard."

"Nonsense," Leup said. "Fraternity hijinks, one of those infantile things they play at. I don't know this 'Beeky' person, but I wouldn't put it past him to make up such a story just to gain attention. Hijinks, that's all the treasure nonsense is. I once had to bail Richard out of the police station because some frat brother told them a certain bathroom window at a sorority house had no curtain. The police caught half a dozen boys climbing a tree outside the place one night. Another reason I don't like my son socializing with boys like Winston and Charles. Not good for his career, not good."

"Winston was okay," Richard ventured to say. "And he seemed pretty certain there was something to find. Look here, Ranger . . . what was the name? MacTyre? You make sure you don't go spreading the word about there being a treasure hoard up there. If it shows up in the papers there'll be idiots tramping all over the place looking for gold."

"Poppycock," his father said. "There's no treasure hoard. Now put down that cigar and go with Means into his office. Help him make out this list the ranger wants."

The boy and the secretary left the room. Mr. Leup turned his attention to Ranger McIntyre, a broad smile on his face.

"Cigar to your liking?" he said. "Now tell me, and be as candid as you wish, do you think that this new national park will make land more valuable in that little village of yours? I'm thinking of investment, of course. Another hotel near the village could make money, no doubt, but it would take years to realize a profit. However, if a man knew the territory and he spotted a bit of land . . . some location that would double or triple in value as the Rocky Mountain National Park took off as a tourist spot . . . well, sir, that man and his investors might turn a very tidy profit indeed."

The taxi made its exit through the pretentious gateway of the Leup mansion and went chugging along the empty streets of Denver. The taxi driver was mentally adding up the fare and the tip. The two people in the back seat were what is known as a "handsome couple" in their expensive clothes. Better yet, the good-looking young man in the tailored tux and overcoat seemed bent on making a favorable impression on the glamorous lady, which meant he'd probably leave a hefty tip. The hotel they had asked for was in the medium price range, but at least it wasn't cheap. Yessir, this fare could make his evening worthwhile.

In the back seat, Ranger Timothy Grayson McIntyre was also doing some mental calculations. He was trying to remember if he had enough cash left for the taxi fare back to the hotel. What was he going to say when he opened his wallet and discovered he was a couple of dollars short? Vi Coteau hugged her silver fur cape around her against the chill in the air and smiled at him.

"Penny for your thoughts?" she said.

"Might need more than that," he said. He was still thinking about the taxi fare.

"What?"

"Never mind. Interesting friends you have back there."

"I wouldn't say 'friends.' I scarcely know Mr. Leup. His daughter and I have been thrown together on various occasions. We've had some long chats, that's all. Mostly about fashion and food."

"The dinner was very good, I thought," he said.

"Yes, very."

"No egg salad sandwiches." He was remembering their first lunch at a Woolworth's lunch counter, and a mountain meadow picnic a few weeks later. She had told him that egg salad was one of her three weaknesses.

"No," she said.

"I feel awkward," Ranger McIntyre confessed.

"You? You feel awkward? Listen, friend, you were wonderful back there. You handled every course of the meal from soup to nuts. One of the girls whispered to me that you probably dined that way all the time. Our hostess couldn't keep her eyes off you. Neither could the other women. They all asked me who you were and where I found you. That tux fits like a dream, you've got the posture of a drill sergeant, and you don't have a hair out of place. You're a beautiful man to look at, Ranger. So there!"

"Boy, you really know how to hurt a guy. Never been called beautiful before. I was starting to feel really, really awkward even before you said it. What I meant was, here I am in the back seat of a taxi with a gorgeous lady and I can't think of anything brilliant to talk about. Besides that, I feel like I should kiss you and don't quite know where to begin."

"Oh, I see!" Vi Coteau's laugh caused the driver to take a look in his mirror. "Then let's change the subject. Are you going to help Mr. Leup get to the bottom of young Winston Dole's death?"

"I guess I will," the ranger said, relaxing against the seat again. "Only I have a feeling Mr. Leup wants me to discover that it was an accident and the kid was being stupid when it happened. I think he's afraid that his son, Richard, will be suspected of being involved somehow. Because it would reflect badly on himself, see? On the other hand, I also got a feeling while we were chatting over our cigars that Richard—let's see, how to put this? That Richard wouldn't be surprised to find out his father had something to do with Winston's accident."

"Jeepers!" Vi said. "You don't take many steps before leaping to your conclusions, do you?"

"Think of a jigsaw puzzle," the ranger explained. "There's always a few pieces lying in the jumble that you notice out of the corner of your eye. Your eye catches something about those particular pieces. You almost automatically know where they belong. Know what I mean?"

"Jigsaw puzzles?" Vi said with a sweet smile. "My life's never dull enough that I need to do jigsaw puzzles. I wouldn't allow it to be. What specifically are you going to do about the Winston accident?"

"Tomorrow or the next day I'm going to drive up to the May Day Mine and poke around. I want to take a look at that ore bucket and gantry."

"I'd love to come along," she said, watching for his reaction. His eyes widened with interest and that very small smile of his creased one corner of his mouth. "But I can't," she continued. "I'm a working girl, after all. Maybe I can drive up this weekend. We could have another picnic while I help you solve the case."

"It might be too chilly for a picnic," he said. "Most of the lodges and restaurants are already closing down for the season."

"Well, at least we could take a hike together and visit the death scene. Afterward we could go see your little ranger cabin and you could show me your jigsaw puzzle collection."

McIntyre was still working on his snappy comeback when the taxi brakes squealed and the taxi came to a stop at his hotel.

The taxi driver was none too pleased to learn that the man was going to disembark at the hotel, not the woman. It meant the man would either hand him some money—never enough—and tell him where to drive the woman, or he would give the woman the money for the fare. Women never tipped as good as men did.

24

Ranger McIntyre's Man Mood Dial was set to "Awkward" again. Vi Coteau, however, handled the awkward moment with her customary classiness. When he reached for the door handle, she didn't stop him but allowed him to step out. From outside, peering in the door to say good night, there was no suggestion that he should kiss her. As for the other bit of awkwardness, "I won't come in," she said sweetly. "I have to be at the office early, you know. Besides, with this prohibition nonsense we would have to stick to lemonade. And that's no fun."

He began to reach into his pocket for his wallet.

"No, no," she said. "My treat. It was my idea, you're my guest, so it's my treat. Good night, Ranger."

"Good night. And thanks! I enjoyed it. Give me a phone call when you can come up to the park."

She told the driver her address and off they went, the driver more certain than ever that the size of his tip would barely be enough for a cup of java. If he was lucky, maybe a stale sinker to dunk in it.

CHAPTER THREE:
CRIME SCENE? OR ACCIDENT
WAITING TO HAPPEN?

Starting the week it opened for business, villagers called Kitty's place "that all-night diner" where night owls and early risers could find a day-old sandwich or a dry sinker of a doughnut and cup of strong coffee, but officially it was named Kitty's Café. That's where McIntyre went just after sunrise. He had climbed out of his warm bed when it was still dark outside, poured Brownie her morning bucket of grain by lantern light, and by the time he got to the village, he was hungry enough to go into Kitty's. He needed nourishment for the drive south past Blue Spruce Lake to the eastern edge of the national park. That's where the abandoned mines were. His favorite breakfast spot in the village, the Pioneer Inn, wouldn't open for another hour. One of Kitty's breakfast "specials" would have to do.

"Hiya, Ranger!" Kitty greeted him. "Grab a stool! What'll it be this morning? Say . . . you're outa uniform! Whatsamatta, y' been fired finally? Ah, hell, there's other jobs. In fact, I could use a dishwasher if you're interested. What'd you say you're havin'? Lemme pour your orange juice and you can tell me all about it."

McIntyre suspected that Kitty was born with some part of her brain missing, the part that lets people sleep. He had known a guy like that at the aerodrome in France, during the war. A pilot like himself, but never seemed to sleep. Any time during the night you might find him polishing a boot or cooking an egg or reading a book. Speaking of eggs, Kitty kept her own chickens

26

and eggs were one of the few things she could cook without spoiling.

"I'll have three over easy, Kitty. And toast. Are there any hash browns?"

"Oh, piles of them! Tiny hasn't been in yet this morning, so there's plenty. Oh, boy, can that guy eat hash browns!"

She turned to the stove and spoke over her shoulder. McIntyre rested his elbows on the counter and sipped at the orange juice.

"What's up with the civvies, Ranger?"

"I'm on vacation, Kitty, that's all."

"Off to do some fishin' then. Reggie was in here yesterday, brought me a couple of nice ones he pulled outa the Thompson River. Down by the old diversion dam, he said. 'Course you know Reggie, he won't tell his real hot spots. Keeps those to hisself. Where you off to this early, anyway? Willow Creek, maybe."

"No fishing," McIntyre said. "I thought I'd drive down toward the mines and look around."

"The May Day Mine," she said. "Where that kid got himself dead? Yeah, I don't guess you'd be able to keep your pokey nose outa that one. Ask me, I'd say he was after the Dunraven treasure."

"You know about it?" McIntyre asked.

"Sure. It's been a local rumor as long as I can remember. Them three college boys was in here last month and was all excited talking about it. One of them was showing the others a sheet of paper, something he'd copied outa a book. You need ketchup?"

Ranger McIntyre had finished half his breakfast when the door to Kitty's Café opened wide. The doorway and seemingly half the room was filled with the jolly ponderousness of "Tiny" Brown, proprietor of Beaver Point Store out on the Moraine

Park road. Every couple of days he drove into town to have breakfast at Kitty's. No one knew why.

"Morning, Ranger!" Tiny's bass voice could rattle dishes off the shelves. "How are you this fine morning? Going fishing, are you?"

Tiny took the stool next to McIntyre. More like two stools next to McIntyre.

"No, just doing some annual vacation time."

"He's investigating the death at the May Day Mine," Kitty volunteered.

"Say, I heard about that!" Tiny said. "Pretty strange accident, if you ask me. Right up your alley, as the folks say down in the flatlands where they have alleys."

"Me and the ranger were just now talkin' about the Dunraven treasure, Tiny," Kitty said.

"Yeah," McIntyre said. "What do you know about it, Tiny?"

Tiny Brown was not only the best sandwich maker in the valley, he was also the best amateur historian. More than a hobbyist historian, he was a walking repository of facts about the region.

"Dunraven's treasure hoard," he said. "That's a mysterious one for sure. Well, the short version begins in the 1870s when Lord Dunraven and his associates closed down the English Hotel for the season to go back to Ireland and were fearful of leaving anything that might tempt thieves to break into the place. According to the rumor, they locked all the more expensive furniture in a secure room. But anything like gold or silver . . . or fine art, such as little statuettes . . . they took to a hidden cache. One old boy, Ambrose Sharpy, he bought the land after the English Hotel burned down and spent years digging holes all over it. That's why you see all those young pine trees where the hotel used to be. Sharpy disturbed the soil everywhere. Ponderosas love to drop seeds in freshly turned earth."

"What would it have to do with the old gold mines?"

"That, I couldn't say. For a long time, people did believe that there was a root cellar somewhere up the mountain from the English Hotel. Some even swore they had seen the cellar entrance, supposedly made out of extra-heavy timbers with a padlock on the door. Maybe that root cellar, if it existed, looked like a mine tunnel? Could you pass the ketchup?"

McIntyre slid the ketchup bottle along the counter. "Tell me more about this English Hotel."

"Sure," Tiny said. "So, you already know how Lord Dunraven came from Ireland in 1873 and decided to make this whole valley into an American hunting preserve for himself and his friends. Their diaries and letters tell about how they would kill hundreds of elk and deer every season, catch thousands of trout, kill deer and mountain lions. They had a great ol' time here. Well sir, a bunch of them organized a development company, put up a sawmill, and built the English Hotel. Grand place, for the time. Three floors! Fancy dining room, a ritzy saloon, the whole shebang. Had a wide covered front porch across the front of the building with a view of Longs Peak. It opened in the summer and closed for the winters. One winter Dunraven and his cronies went home to Ireland and never came back. That's when another bunch of investors took over. Burned down more than ten years ago. In 1911."

"Too bad. There's days when I could use a good saloon."

"Not legal. Prohibition, remember?"

"Hard to forget. Lord Dunraven lived there? In the hotel?"

"No. He built himself a fancy cottage. It's still there. You know the place. They still call it the Dunraven Cottage."

"Right," McIntyre said. "Where would a 'hoard' come into the picture?"

"Not sure," Tiny said. "Like I said, nobody wintered in the valley in those days except for a few hardy pioneer families. Maybe the original English Hotel owners did hide their valuables somewhere. Maybe money, too. They would have used British coin, see? Pretty heavy to haul back and forth across the ocean. Maybe Lord Dunraven took a pile of heavy coins, maybe his fancy hunting guns and stuff such as that, and cached them before he went back to Ireland. Then never made it back here again. I think his last trip was 1877 or thereabouts. It would make sense for him to have a secret cellar room at his cottage, or some kind of root cellar or hidden hole."

"Or a hiding place in an old mine," McIntyre said.

"Or in an old mine," Tiny agreed. "Mines were all over the place. Back then prospectors were always digging holes looking for gold. It took a long time before they figured out there isn't much gold in this part of the Rockies. But, yeah, a mine would make sense. Maybe that old tunnel up at the May Day Mine."

"Long ways from the cottage, though."

"That's the beauty of it," Tiny explained. "If you're going to hide your treasures, don't do it next to your house or in your backyard where people might come snooping around. No, find a spooky old hole where nobody would think to look. But I don't know what mine tunnels there were in 1877."

"It might not matter," McIntyre said. "Whether it was real or not. What matters is whether they thought it was. Those three college boys were poking around looking for some hoard they heard about, that's what made them go there. Anyway, I'm headed down toward the May Day Mine today to have a look around. Kitty, how much do I owe you here?"

McIntyre drove lazily, one hand draped over the steering wheel. The road leading out of the village was deserted; the morning was crisp and clear; he was in civvies and on vacation. Having a puzzling incident to figure out was icing on his cake, so to speak, especially since there wasn't any pressure on him to do anything about it. The college kid had died of asphyxiation, the medical examiner said. Nobody had any reason to harm him, Richard Leup said. The only real question to figure out was why he ended up with his body jammed into a rusted ore bucket. It was a gruesome death, according to the examiner. Winston's fingernails were broken off and his fingertips bloody and raw from clawing at the sides of the bucket; blood-caked wounds on both sides of his head showed that he had thrashed back and forth, hitting his head over and over on the bucket before he passed out.

As it happened, the route to the abandoned May Day Mine crossed Meadow Creek. McIntyre crossed the bridge, pulled off the road, and parked the truck. He couldn't resist. He had to assemble his fly rod and make at least a few casts into the stream. The first time he went to lunch with the lovely Vi Coteau, she had told him there were three things she could not resist—egg salad sandwiches, nonpareils candy, and a third one she wouldn't tell him about. McIntyre's own list of irresistible things included an unhurried breakfast, preferably with sausages and pancakes, and a private stretch of trout stream. He retrieved the fishing vest he kept behind the seat, put it on, joined the sections of the fly rod together, and threaded the line through the guides. The abandoned mine had been there for fifty years or more. It could wait a few minutes.

McIntyre made his approach cautiously, creeping lightly upstream, keeping the willows between him and the water. At this time of year, with the water low and clear in the creeks, the trout could see a predator's shadow fifty feet away and could feel the slightest vibration of a footstep on the bank. He hunkered down behind a wild rose bush and selected his dry fly from the fly wallet, a little #16 Ginger Quill. Slowly, slowly he stood up. He made the first cast with as little arm movement as possible, holding his breath. The little dry fly arched through the air to alight on the surface ten, maybe fifteen yards upstream. He watched it float down the current along the far bank.

He had to repeat this careful procedure half a dozen times before a cutthroat trout came to the Ginger Quill. The water was so smooth and clear that the fly seemed to be lying on a sheet of plate glass; the trout rose from the streambed with lazy movements of its tail, as if it didn't care whether it caught the bug or not.

He released the fish since he had no way to keep it fresh all day. The stretch of stream was now spooked, thanks to the short battle between McIntyre's fly rod and the cutthroat. It would be a quarter of an hour before another one would take a fly from the surface. The ranger reeled in his line and smiled his broad smile and drank lungsful of the heady mountain air. All things, in that moment, were in place: he loved his quiet, pine-scented world. Too bad he needed to poke around one of the ruined places, a mining dump where a young man had died. Or been killed.

Something was puzzling him about Winston's death at the old mine. McIntyre had been told that the young man was discovered head-down in the ore bucket hanging from a gantry. Apparently, the bottom of the bucket was no more than a foot off of the ground. How had he gotten into it? For that matter, what was it doing, hanging from the beam like that? The hanging bucket wasn't right. McIntyre was comparing it to his fly fishing: the Ginger Quill had to look natural and behave naturally, had to look like an insect that would be found on the water during that season and during that time of day, floating the weaving currents as if it was not tied to a line. From a trout's perspective every piece of the picture, no matter how small, had to look normal and natural. But McIntyre had seen that ore bucket several times—it was the only ore bucket remaining from the deserted May Day—and each time it had been lying in the same place, on its side, next to the old mine shack. Why was it hanging from a beam? Who hung it, and why?

There was another thing that didn't seem natural, and it was Mr. Leup himself, the wealthy gentleman with many busy business and political pursuits. Why was he interested in the young man who was killed? It was pretty clear that he hadn't liked Winston. His only contact with the grieving family was to make certain they wouldn't blame Richard or stir up publicity involving the Leup family. Leup told McIntyre that he didn't much like Richard hanging out with "those empty-headed frat boys," so why bother himself about the death of one of them? Had it been young Richard who was killed, then the elder Mr. Leup's involvement would seem natural. But like the old ore bucket, it seemed to be out of place. Like a jigsaw puzzle piece where the shape is right but the color is all wrong. Perhaps Leup didn't trust Richard's account of what had happened. Perhaps he suspected that his son was more involved than it appeared. For reasons known only to himself, he wanted to find out more information without involving the usual law enforcement people. Protect the family name, maybe. Covering his tracks—or Richard's—except there didn't seem to be any tracks.

As McIntyre wiped his fly line dry and stowed his vest and rod behind the truck seat, his imagination went into high gear. Maybe Richard Leup's association with Winston Dole was somehow more of a threat to the family name than anyone had thought. Maybe Mr. Leup arranged for somebody to frighten Winston away, to give the kid such a scare that he would leave Richard alone. And maybe, McIntyre thought, maybe the intimidation went wrong and Winston ended up dead and Richard ended up looking like he might know something about it, which would stir up considerable interest among the newspapers. Let's bring in a naïve local forest ranger, one with no authority and no connection to the newspapers, and let him find any evidence that might have been left behind. Then we can clean it up if need be.

McIntyre parked below the mine site. The narrow dirt track continued on up and around a hairpin curve to the buildings, but the road bed looked very unstable where it crossed the tailings pile. The tailings were loose, unpredictable, could slide down into the valley along with his recently acquired pickup truck. It would be better to park and walk.

The mine itself looked like a quarry carved out of the side of the mountain. The wide level spot was devoid of vegetation, being mostly crushed rock. There was the timber skeleton of the old headframe where a steam engine once raised and lowered the ore buckets, but the engine was gone, the buckets were gone, and the cable was gone. A single ore bucket remained. McIntyre remembered it as lying against the side of the mine shack, but now it was lying under a thick beam that was supported by thick posts, like a frame that could hold a kid's swing. A heavy chain and hook hung from the center of the beam. The ore bucket had an ominous, nasty look about it, probably because that was where the unfortunate Winston Dole had died. The bucket was about five feet long—the searchers had seen Dole's feet sticking out the top—and the width of a man's shoulders. It wasn't a perfect cylinder. Like most buckets used to lift ore up a narrow mine shaft, it had a bulge in the center to help keep it from becoming stuck. It had a steel lifting loop like the handle of a milk bucket, only much bulkier. McIntyre could see where the rust had rubbed off. Rust had also rubbed away on the chain's hook.

There was no way to tell how heavy the thing was. Could a man manage to stand it on end and hook it to the chain? Mc-

Intyre studied the terrain before trying to raise the bucket. The open end, where the lifting loop was, was downhill; therefore, it would be easier to try lifting the bottom end. It didn't matter which end he picked up, since all he wanted to know was whether a man could do it. McIntyre squatted at the bottom of the ore bucket, got a good grip with both hands, and then used his legs to do the lifting. The iron was heavy, but not immovable. The open end dug into the ground, the bottom end came up as he heaved. McIntyre got the bucket's base up to shoulder height before deciding that he had sufficient information about the weight of the damn thing and let it drop. A determined guy could stand it on end, though. And with a little common sense about levers and lifting he could methodically rock it back and forth, sticking bits of old wood cribbing underneath, until he had elevated it high enough to fasten the chain. There was plenty of cribbing lying about, mostly short pieces of mine timber. McIntyre gathered up three pieces and jammed them under the ore bucket to prevent it from rolling away down the slope. While kicking the third block of wood into place, he saw sun glinting off the ground, reflecting from an object that wasn't there before. It must have fallen out of the ore bucket when he tilted it up.

A heavy coin. Copper, recently polished with coarse material that scratched it, as if someone had rubbed it in the sand to make it gleam. Doing what any other curious human would do, McIntyre got down on his knees and peered into the dark bucket to see if there were any more coins, but the copper coin was the only one. It was larger than a penny, almost the size of a quarter. According to the date stamped on the back, 1822, it was a hundred years old. The design was a harp with the word "Hibernia" or "Liber_ia" above it; the front of the coin showed a man's head wearing one of those Roman ivy wreaths and the words "Gorgeous" or "Geo_iius IV" and "D:C: Rey" or "Rex."

Here was an interesting twist to the puzzle and no doubt about it. McIntyre sat down on the ore bucket and took out his notebook. Writing down details always helped him think, just as pushing jigsaw puzzle pieces into various patterns on a table helped him to see various possible ways they could fit into the whole picture.

Call it an accident, he said. First assume it happened unexpectedly. Winston Dole was probably in a lighthearted mood, skipping classes to go treasure hunting with his chums. They decide to search in one direction. He says he'll look around the other way. Then for some reason he starts walking very fast, goes much further than the rescue searchers assumed he would, apparently heading directly for the old May Day mining site. He must not have wasted too much time looking here and there, but instead went to the ore bucket, which was hanging from the gantry. He wanted to have a look inside . . .

The ranger poked around in the dirt and rust that had fallen out of the ore bucket along with the old coin. Sure enough: the stubs of three burnt wooden matches.

Assume that Winston stuck his head down inside the ore bucket and lit matches to see what was in there. Saw the coin. Tried to reach it. Fell in so far that he couldn't wiggle out again. Eventually asphyxiated. Clawed at the sides until his fingernails were torn off and bleeding, banged his head on the bucket to attract attention. But how did he manage to look down inside it in the first place, if the bucket was hanging by the chain? And why would he lose his balance and topple in?

That bunch of wooden cribbing might be the answer to the last question. Look at the pattern, McIntyre said to himself. *It looks like it was stacked next to the gantry and then somebody kicked it down. Look how it fell.* So far it was natural to imagine that Winston found the bucket hanging there, that he stacked up some cribbing in order to climb up and look inside, that he lit some

36

matches to see in the dark.

And then he fell into the bucket, or was deliberately tipped in.

Call it deliberate. Assume another person besides Winston was here. Assume they had a reason to harm the kid. Lay a trap. Hang the bucket open end up. Stack cribbing next to it. Drop a shiny coin inside. Then go find Winston, tell him Dunraven's Hoard may be hidden at the old May Day Mine because you think you saw a penny in the old ore bucket but you couldn't reach it. Winston makes a beeline for the place, climbs up the cribbing, lights matches, sees the gleam, and tries to reach it. Once he's halfway in you take hold of his feet and shove him the rest of the way into the bucket. Then you kick down the stack of wood and walk away. Maybe you want him to die, maybe you just want to frighten him and you figure his friends will find him before it's too late.

Then again, McIntyre thought, Winston might have found the coin elsewhere, had it in the pocket of his shirt or jacket, and it fell out when he went headfirst into the bucket. Once in a while, the simple answer is the right answer. Sometimes a simple dry fly pattern such as a Gray Dunn works better than a fancy Silver Doctor. A simple breakfast of scrambled eggs and sausage can be more enjoyable than a fancy omelet—and boy! could he murder a plate of the Pioneer Inn scramble just now. With a couple of slabs of toast and jam.

The ranger's imaginary breakfast was interrupted by a voice behind him.

"Hey there!"

CHAPTER FOUR:
EXPERTS AND THEORIES

The man coming toward him was middle-aged, quite fit and athletic-looking in tan jodhpurs, knee-high boots, and a white shirt and broad brim hat. He had a rucksack on his back, a pair of field glasses slung around his neck, and he carried a clipboard. McIntyre recognized the deliberate stride of an experienced mountain hiker. His entire physical attitude, the way he carried himself, was more than simply a statement of confidence and self-assurance. His posture announced to the world that here was a man who was accustomed to being right. About anything and everything.

McIntyre slipped the copper coin into his pocket and stood up.

"Nice day!" the man said. He looked McIntyre straight in the eye as if daring him to disagree.

"Sure is," McIntyre replied. He pointed at the stranger's clipboard. "Looks like you're working, though. Still, it's good to be outdoors on a day like this."

"Yes, it is. It will rain later this afternoon. But I will not let it interfere with my work. I enjoy being outdoors whatever the weather. Part of the job. Mining engineer. Name's Beauchamp, John Beauchamp. And you are?"

"Tim McIntyre," the ranger replied. "I'm on vacation. I guess you'd call it a busman's holiday. I'm with the Park Service."

"Park Service? I saw a truck down below and assumed you were connected with the lodge on Blue Spruce Lake. The truck with 'Small Delights' on the door. Assumed it was yours. The lodge has closed."

Small Delights again, McIntyre thought. One of these days he needed to repaint those pickup doors.

"It's my truck, all right," he replied. "Got it from the owner when he moved away. I parked down there because I didn't want to take a chance driving up over the slag pile."

"Good thinking," Beauchamp said. "I parked my car down there for the same reason. Safety. That's what I'm here for. I'm attached to the School of Mines, making a safety survey of mine sites. Kind of an inventory, mainly structures. I go around and report on hazardous conditions at abandoned mine sites. Would you believe it, there's more than fifty abandoned mining sites in and around the new national park? Some of them go way back to the early 1800s."

"I know a few of the old mines," McIntyre said. "Had no idea there were that many."

"There are. Half of them no more than shallow tunnels dug into a cliff. Some are caved-in holes on a mountainside. My main concern is the ones that still have old machinery, like that headframe over there."

He indicated the nearby framework of heavy timbers, high as a two-story house and with an enormous iron wheel at the top.

"I'll have to check to see if that lumber is rotten, or if there's any dangling cables or chains that ought to be taken down. Anything hazardous. Then a crew comes to do the work. I'll have them close off that road, too. Can't have any automobiles sliding off the mountain. That ore bucket you were sitting on when I arrived . . . is that the one I read about in the newspapers?"

"Probably," McIntyre answered. "It's the one where that kid died."

Beauchamp got down on his knees and peered into the dark opening.

"The newspaper reported he got stuck in here," Beauchamp said. "Wedged in, I guess. Terrible thing. Apparently one of his pals was in the area but he couldn't find him. Not in time, anyway. Frankly, I thought the story in the papers made it sound suspicious, how that second college boy said he couldn't find the one who was stuck in the ore bucket. Couldn't find him? When you're with somebody hunting or hiking in the mountains, you must make it a point to know where they are at all times. Even if you can't see them."

The engineer took off his rucksack and pulled out a flashlight to peer into the ore bucket.

"He had no reason to go in there, none that I can see."

"That's what I was thinking," McIntyre said.

"I wonder if the sheriff asked the right questions when he talked to the two companions," the engineer went on. As he spoke, he continued searching the inside of the rusty bucket. "Somebody ought to find out what was said in that interview. I think there's more to this so-called 'accident' than meets the eye, that's what I think. I wonder where they are now. I bet they went back to college like nothing happened, that's my guess."

Beauchamp finished his inspection of the ore bucket and stood up, switching off his flashlight. He looked at the wooden blocks that were holding the bucket in place.

"It's been chocked with pieces of cribbing. Recently."

"That was me," McIntyre said. "Didn't want the bucket to go rolling down the hill."

"Not a bad idea," Beauchamp said. "In fact, if it was up to me, I'd wrestle the thing over to the mine shaft and let it drop in. That way, nobody would be tempted to roll it down the mountain or climb inside it to see what they could find. I'll make a note for the crew to do that. What did you say you were doing up here?"

"Just poking around," McIntyre said. It was the truth, but not all of the truth. "I was checking out the fishing stream and thought I might come up here. Morbid curiosity, I suppose. And I'm always watching out for interesting mineral specimens or artifacts. Back at the cabin, I use a mine relic for a doorstop. It's a cam wheel from an old stamping mill. Cast iron. Shaped like a three-leaf clover."

"From the mine at Big Horse Park where the old stamping mill is still standing. It has clover leaf cams."

"No, I found this one up at the Betsy Mine. Where the old boiler is."

"Yes. I know that place, too. Well, I need to be doing my survey."

"Sure. I guess I'll drive down and finish examining the trout situation. Say! I just had a weird thought! I bet those college boys parked their car the same place I did. That's kind of spooky, huh?"

It was a ploy, kind of a false cast to see if there was anything in the pool, and it seemed to work. John Beauchamp took three steps toward him, chest swelling importantly, like a male prairie chicken flaring his feathers. His attitude betrayed what he was thinking: he found McIntyre's ignorance impossible to overlook.

"You didn't read the newspaper account," he said accusingly. "Not carefully, at least. There was no one parked here. The place was deserted. Those boys parked their car way over that ridge behind us, over there where the road comes to a dead end at Lantern Creek. There are two old mine tunnels there. Nothing more than exploratory holes, really. Okay? Now, Winston Dole wandered away from the other two. He came hiking over the ridge and ended up here."

"I wonder why."

"What?"

Why you know so much about it, McIntyre thought.

"Why come in this particular direction?" McIntyre said. "Why come this far? And without telling his friends? In the newspaper account, the boys were looking for treasure, or thought they were. Mostly larking around, skipping class, playing hooky. One of them abruptly leaves the others and hikes straight for this particular place? Alone? Seems awful sudden and deliberate."

"In other words," Beauchamp said, "you think he might have had a spontaneous motive to go off on his own. A thought hit him, maybe, or maybe he spotted what he thought was a clue."

"Could be," McIntyre replied. "Then again—come to think of it—I've been on any number of search and rescue missions. It's pretty common, when you find the missing person, to wonder why the heck or how the heck they got to where they were. Often they don't know themselves."

"This is one of those situations, probably," Beauchamp said. "We'll never know. At any rate, they didn't have a car here. Nobody was here."

"What about this for a theory?" McIntyre asked. "What if maybe Winston ran into somebody over there by Lantern Creek and they told him to come here. He could have. You know how it goes, meeting other people on a trail. They stop and chat, he says he and his pals are looking at old gold mine sites, the stranger says 'there's one over the hill there' and off he goes to find it. Ever run into somebody while you're fishing and they tell you there's a really good spot a little ways upstream?"

"Nothing about any stranger in the papers," Beauchamp said. "Would've been a witness."

The disdain in his voice told McIntyre that Beauchamp was through with the conversation. "I need to get on with my inspection," he said.

"It wouldn't be in the papers because the other two boys didn't know. If Winston was alone and came across another hiker, Winston's the only one who would know about it. Maybe the person told him not to say anything. Told him finding a clue to the treasure would be a surprise for his two buddies, maybe. And then led him off to the mine."

"I wouldn't know," Beauchamp snapped.

"Me neither," McIntyre agreed. "Be seeing you."

McIntyre walked down the mine road and across the unstable part of the waste dump. He didn't expect to see the door of his pickup standing wide open, nor did he expect to see a dark-skinned, leathery-faced individual sitting in his truck holding an ancient shotgun. McIntyre kept on walking toward the pickup, telling himself he really needed to get into the habit of strapping on his revolver whenever he went outside. The guy examining the dashboard looked up when he heard McIntyre's steps on the gravel.

"This your truck?"

"That's right," McIntyre said.

"Wanna sell it?"

"No, I don't. I just got it."

"I need me a truck like this. How much you reckon it can haul?"

"No idea," McIntyre said. "Quarter of a ton, half a ton maybe."

"Yeah. Anyhow, I need me a truck. What'll you take for it?"

"What do you need it for?" McIntyre asked.

"Nosy, ain't you? Listen, I don't like folks pokin' around my mountain here and I really don't like 'em stealin' stuff they come across up to the mines and I especially don't like 'em sticking their noses in where they don't belong."

Speaking of noses, McIntyre thought. The guy's sunbaked leathery face featured a nose that jutted forward like a beak. It made McIntyre think about those puffin birds in the *National Geographic*. This fellow's nose wasn't that colorful, but the shape was the same. Sun and wind had not been kind to it, either. Between the weathering of the skin and the loose-fitting old clothes it was impossible to tell how old he was.

"You own the mountain?" McIntyre asked. "And the mines?"

"No, but I got me a claim, back in the canyon. I got first dibs on any equipment and such that might be lyin' around. What I can't use, I can sell for scrap and that's why I'm buying your truck. To take scrap down to Longmont. First thing I'm gonna do is paint out those silly Small Delights signs on the doors."

"Like I said," McIntyre replied, "I only got my pickup a few months ago myself and I don't want to sell it."

The guy unfolded his lanky legs from under the steering column and got out of the truck cab.

"You're damn annoying to do business with, you know that?" he said.

"Sorry," McIntyre replied. "But tell me: did you hear about the boy who got killed here at the May Day Mine?"

"Heard about it. Never saw it. Apparently, the daffy little bastard hung up that ol' ore bucket on a crossbeam and crawled inside t' die. That there's another reason I keep runnin' people off the mountain. Dangerous places, these ol' mines."

"You didn't see him alive?"

"Nah. But I seen his two buddies when they was out lookin' for him. 'Way yonder across the hill. I was about to run 'em off but she was gettin' dark and they left anyhow. Damn kids. Listen, I'm too busy t' stand here jawin' with a man what don't want to do business. You decide to sell that truck of yours, you lemme know."

"How do I find you?" McIntyre asked.

"Prob'ly you don't. You poke around up here, I'll find you. I'd know you even if you was wearin' your fancy green uniform."

The man walked away. His back seemed crooked and his shoulders seemed to droop like those of an ancient creature.

The long shotgun swung from one hand as if it weighed no more than a lady's purse. McIntyre watched him go, wondering how this character knew he was a ranger. Then again, any reasonably observant person might notice the boots, dusty but showing they were polished regularly, the pressed crease in the khaki work pants, the cleanly shaven chin. Or maybe he had seen McIntyre in uniform before, only McIntyre had not seen him. It might be worthwhile to come back and talk with him.

It was early the following morning. Ranger McIntyre hurried into his cabin when he heard the phone ringing, pulling off his mittens as he went. The cabin was still dark—it always seemed dark in the little log cabin—and he had to fumble around a moment before picking up the phone and unhooking the earpiece.

"Fall River Station," he said. "Ranger McIntyre speaking." The phrase was automatic. Being on vacation, he should have just said "hello?"

"My! You sound very formal!" came the velvety female voice. "Could it be possible that his tailored tuxedo has turned our rough ranger all sophisticated?"

"Good morning, Miss Coteau," he said, unbuttoning his sheepskin and sitting down at the desk.

"What are you up to this morning?" Vi Coteau asked.

"The usual. Got up, built a fire in the stove, gave Brownie a bucket of grain, and put down fresh bedding for her. I checked the rat trap under the meat cache. A couple of squirrels were chewing pine cone seeds and scattering the shells everywhere. I arrested them for littering. The judge might let them off with a fine."

"You're a silly ranger, you know that? Do you want to know why I called, or not?"

"If you want to tell me. I assume you had a dream about how fantastic I look in my tux and you had to hear my voice again."

"I'll say it again. You're a silly ranger. I called to tell you what I found out about that coin."

"Wow, that was quick!"

"I had to go to the library yesterday afternoon anyway, so I took your description with me and shared it with Mr. Pipple."

"Pipple? There's actually a person named 'Pipple'?"

"Yes, and he's a genius at finding things in the library. Photographic memory. Knows every reference book that ever existed. He's helped me dozens of times, a lovely little guy. Round glasses covering half his face, but a mind like a steel trap. And for your information, he likes me."

McIntyre's imagination treated his mind to several quick images of the lovely Vi Coteau. They were like slides in a magic lantern show, pictures of her in evening dress, or in pleated white skirt and sailor blouse, or business suit and silk stockings. What was not to like?

"Okay, what did Mr. Pipple say?"

"Mr. Pipple says it's a hundred-year old Irish penny. To a coin collector it might be worth as much as two dollars, in fine condition."

"It's not very fine. The lettering is hard to read. Plus, it's been polished with sand and it's scratched. Did he have any idea as to what it might be doing at an abandoned mine?"

"None at all. He did say that such coins were not uncommon in the Old West. Irish laborers carried them for luck. Or to put on their eyes when they died. Apparently, any family in the Old West, if they had Irish roots, would have an Irish penny or two kicking around the house."

"From the way I discovered this one, I've got the feeling it was inside the ore bucket and young Mr. Winston Dole got stuck when he tried to reach it. To him it might have looked like a clue to the whereabouts of the Dunraven Hoard. See? Maybe the coin suggested that the hoard was cached at that mine. Or it could've been planted there to make somebody assume the hoard was nearby. Then whoever planted it told Winston, then tipped him into the bucket when he tried to reach for it. It might have been a killer who didn't want Winston and the boys to find the hoard. That's my guess. Or they were out to kill Winston for personal reasons."

"Did you think of the third possibility?"

Vi had a habit of thinking in threes.

"What's that?"

"Winston found it and realized it could be a clue to the hoard's hiding place. Then he made the mistake of telling the wrong person. Maybe showed them the penny. They took it from him and tossed it into the ore bucket. When he went to retrieve it, they tipped him in."

"Maybe," McIntyre agreed. "But that would mean the murder wasn't planned. If it was murder. I'm all but convinced it was a murder. I think it was planned. Remember my telling you about the ore bucket, how it was hanging from a wooden beam?"

"Yes."

"It was hung there recently. It used to be lying on the ground. They collected enough scraps of cribbing to raise it and hook it to the chain, then stacked the cribbing where Winston Dole could stand on it to look down into the bucket. The killer might say 'I saw something shiny down in this old ore bucket. Looks like a coin, but I can't reach it. See if you can. I'll hold your legs.' "

"But why kill the boy and then leave the coin behind? Wouldn't it be evidence?"

"Maybe by mistake? He'd have to take the bucket down to retrieve the coin. But with the body inside the ore bucket, it would be too heavy for him to unhook from the gantry. He realized that too late. And if he did put the bucket on the ground,

Winston might have regained consciousness before suffocating."

"Could be," Vi said. "Your theory is sure a swell theory, as theories go. It might be worth following up. Oh, I did have one more interesting tidbit to tell you. About my library visit. Surprising coincidence, is what it is. I was talking to Mr. Pipple about the circumstances and he told me that Winston Dole, Richard Leup, and the third frat boy, Charles Monde, had been in the library at least twice and had spent more than an hour searching the biography section. After Winston's death, Richard Leup came back and did the same thing. Mr. Pipple asked if he could help him find anything but Richard said no, he was just looking around."

"After his friend was killed, Richard Leup came all the way from the university just to poke around in the city library?"

"Odd, isn't it. The interesting part is this. Mr. Pipple said he was sorry to learn of Winston's accident and Richard more or less shrugged it off. You know, as if it didn't mean much to him. 'A callous young man, if you ask me,' Mr. Pipple said."

"Son of a gun. Odd behavior. One more thing to think about. I'd better go to town and have breakfast so my brain will work better."

"I suppose it's too chilly up there to have a picnic," Vi suggested. "I'd like to see your crime scene, if it was a crime. We could pick up a couple of those good sandwiches at Tiny's store. You could show me more of your national park. And show me where you live."

McIntyre looked around his gloomy little log cabin. Before showing it to Vi Coteau, he would need to clean the place up. The logs needed to be wiped with linseed oil. He ought to whitewash the walls in the cooking area. He'd been meaning to do it for a year or more, and hammer a few nails in the wall to hang up the pots and pans that were now precariously stacked on the porcelain topped table. The curtains, such as they were, needed washing. He had two armchairs near the fireplace and needed to repair the broken leg on one of them. The chunk of firewood holding it up didn't look very attractive. That was just the inside of the place. He would need to spruce up the outhouse and give Brownie a good brushing.

"Maybe in a week or two?" he suggested, mentally kicking his own backside for not keeping his place spick and span all the time.

Vi Coteau sounded disappointed, but perhaps it was only McIntyre's imagination. Where Miss Vi was concerned, he had plenty of imagination.

"Well, all right," she said. "Fine. Maybe the weather will warm up by then, hmmm? Meanwhile, why don't I see if I can chat with the Leup family. Perhaps I can catch Richard at home this weekend and find out what he was doing at the library. I'll be subtle, of course."

"Okay. If you happen to be at the library yourself, you might ask Mr. Pipple if there is any way to know which books the boys were interested in."

"I'll do that. In fact, I'll phone him and ask him. First thing Monday morning."

She rang off with a velvety-voiced suggestion that the ranger might keep an eye on the weather during the coming week—or two—and as he hung up the earpiece, McIntyre once again surveyed his bachelor lodgings and began a mental list of things he needed to do before entertaining a lady. First, however, he wanted to study the lay of the land around the May Day Mine and work up a clearer picture of what had gone on there the day Winston Dole died. He reached into the dark corner behind his reading chair and dragged out a tall wicker basket containing more than a dozen maps rolled up and tied with lengths of Christmas ribbon. The old basket was a catchall: in addition to the rolled maps it held a scuffed, stained softball, a fly fishing reel he intended to repair, several magazines containing articles he wanted to save but had forgotten why, a watch cap he had been looking for last winter, and a really boring book written by one of the village pioneers. The corner of page fifteen was still turned down where he had stopped reading.

The ranger selected a map, untied the Christmas ribbon, unrolled the map and looked at it, then rolled it up and put it back again. He did the same with the second one. The third map turned out to be the one he wanted. It showed the eastern edge of the park and the area to the east of that, including the roads leading to the towns of Longmont and Loveland and all the various private cottages and private roads along the way. More to his purpose, it showed the old timber claims, water claims, and mining claims, and the roads connecting them.

He spread the map on the table he always kept cleared off for jigsaw puzzles and weighted it down by putting the oil lamp on one corner and the unread book, the unrepaired fishing reel, and a magazine on the other corners.

Opening a box of revolver ammunition and dumping out a half-dozen of the heavy .45 cartridges, he placed one on the site of the English Hotel, one on the May Day Mine, one cartridge on the end of the Lantern Creek road where the college boys had parked their car that fateful day, one on the Betsy Mine and one on the Big Horse Park Mine. Studying the overview, it didn't take the ranger long to realize these would be the most likely locations for the Dunraven Hoard, if there was such a thing. Dunraven and his employees from the English Hotel could have driven their valuables on the wagon road up along Fish Creek to the Lantern Creek road, then one of three side roads to one of the other mines. It would be the most logical thing for them to do, if they were hauling boxes of coins and crates of statuettes and artwork. To go to any of the other mining sites they would have to use packhorses or mules.

Whether any of those three mines really existed at the time didn't matter when it came to figuring out how the boy had died: whether the hoard was real or not, Winston Dole was looking for it when for some reason, he walked up to the May Day Mine.

The question really was, what caused three college boys to go looking for treasure in that particular area? He suspected that Winston Dole had met somebody in the woods, somebody who told him to go to the May Day Mine. And now McIntyre began to suspect the same person had told the trio to go look around Lantern Creek for the hoard. Lure the three boys there, wait until they separated, find Winston alone, lead him to the May Day. It wouldn't be difficult, but who would do it, and why?

Hunting for his box of thumbtacks and then tacking the map to the log wall, Ranger McIntyre mentally took apart the Winston Dole puzzle and stirred the pieces. Maybe the whole incident was an accident after all. Some safety-conscious citizen hung the ore bucket on the gantry to prevent it from rolling down the hill. It could have happened that Winston and his pals were looking for treasure when Winston simply remembered that the old May Day Mine was there. It might have been Winston who stacked the cribbing and stood on it to look down into the bucket; his hands slipped, he fell in, end of story. In the library, the boys found a book they thought was a clue to the treasure and went looking for it. By lunchtime McIntyre had nearly convinced himself that Winston's death had been pure accident. As for the mysterious Irish penny, it could have dropped out of Winston's shirt pocket. No way to know where he found it.

Worrying about it wasn't going to get him anywhere. What he needed to do instead was start sprucing up the cabin before Vi Coteau saw it. He might drive over to the maintenance shops for some white paint. And starting first thing tomorrow . . . he'd go to town and treat himself to breakfast at the Pioneer Inn.

CHAPTER FIVE:
A PERFECT DAY TO
HAVE NOTHING HAPPEN

From its hillside vantage point above the village, the Pioneer Inn's view of the Rockies was like something you'd see in a railroad brochure or on a colored postcard. Beyond the green carpeted mountains squeezing the village into its narrow valley, Longs Peak jutted its gray granite East Face into the crystal blue sky. South of Longs and stretching far away to the north, the other peaks of the jagged Front Range made a daunting barrier of cliffs, crevices, and snowfields.

McIntyre always sat at one particular table in the Pioneer dining room because it had the most sweeping view of those Rocky Mountains. There he loved to linger over his coffee, watching the play of light and shadow among the titanic rock formations. That magnificent wilderness of mountains was where he worked and where he lived, where he watched over the visitors, monitored the plants and the animals, cared for hundreds of small details of road and trail. Once in a while it was very good to take a step back like this, sip his coffee, and lose himself in the view of the whole range, the sweep of nature's stage on which he acted out his own small part. Occasionally, sitting at his table at the Pioneer, he was reminded of flying his biplane over France where he looked down on the embattled, ruined fields. From up in the air he could take it all in at once, set free for a few moments from the oppressive details, the racket of gunfire and the smell of men and blood and mud.

On this particular morning, McIntyre went to his favorite

table, took off his hat, sat down, and picked up the menu. Ordinarily he would go to the buffet; however, today he was on vacation and was giving himself a treat. He would order off the menu.

"Good morning, Ranger McIntyre," the waitress said. "Not in uniform today?"

"Good morning, Mari. Nope, I'm officially on vacation. The green suit stays in the closet for a couple of weeks."

"Too bad," she said with a smile. "I always like seeing you in uniform."

"I did consider wearing my new tuxedo to breakfast, but I knew it would make me look too darn irresistible."

"You're awfully considerate," Mari said. "The sight of you in a tux probably drives girls wild. Orange juice or tomato? And are you ready to order?"

"Tomato. What's the morning special?"

"Same as yesterday morning."

"I wasn't here yesterday."

"Well," she said, smiling again, "in that case it'll be even more special for you. I'll bring your juice."

This is it, McIntyre thought as he watched Mari walk away, *this is what living is about. If they had told me we needed to annihilate the Kaiser's entire army in order to save the world for mornings like this, I would have said "hand me a gun."*

He sipped his juice and gazed at his beloved Rocky Mountains. Peaceful as they looked at a distance, those canyons and pine forests harbored countless predators and victims, all of them playing out the eternal drama of bloodshed. At this very moment, a mountain lion was chewing into the neck of a deer, a hungry grizzly was digging a frightened marmot out of its den. Some unsuspecting insect was about to go down the throat of a rising trout and a hawk was about to fold its wings and dive on a field mouse. Patrolling those peaceful-looking mountains,

Ranger McIntyre had witnessed more of Lord Tennyson's "nature, red in tooth and claw" than Tennyson could have dreamed of. Yet, when viewed from behind the window glass, with the magic aromas of breakfast being cooked for him, McIntyre's world was all peace and beauty.

Even soaked in maple syrup, the pancakes were as light as clouds. The bacon strips were crunchy along the edges and chewy in the middle and the eggs looked so perfectly done that it seemed a shame to put the fork to them. McIntyre swirled the last morsel of pancake in the last bit of syrup, popped it into his mouth with a gratified smack of the lips, and allowed himself a contented sigh. What a morning.

"There's a phone call for you, Ranger McIntyre," Mari said. "It's Dottie over at the supervisor's office."

McIntyre looked at his watch. Sure enough, it was just gone eight o'clock.

"How did she know where to find me?" he asked.

"She probably drove by on her way to work," Mari said. "She lives just over the hill. Your little pickup truck with 'Small Delights' printed on the door is hard not to notice."

"I gotta see about painting those doors," he said.

He went to the reception desk to find the owner/manager/receptionist/cleaning lady/laundress chatting on the telephone.

"Here he is now, Dottie," Charlene Underhill said, "I'll talk to you later, okay?"

She handed McIntyre the earpiece and pushed the phone across the desk to him. He smiled his thanks, a smile that the ladies of the inn would rather have than a tip. Almost.

"Hi, Dottie," he said.

"Good morning. Enjoy your breakfast?"

"Very much. And you?"

"I have two growing boys and a working husband. Breakfast for me is a kind of blur. Listen, you'd better ask Charlene to pack you a lunch. Your lady friend from the FBI phoned this morning. Another 'accident' at another abandoned mine. You're supposed to call her, collect, right away."

"Yes, Operator. I'll accept the charges. Tim?"

"Good morning. What's up down there?"

"What's up is up where you are." Her voice sounded serious, but still had that throaty feline edge that prickled the tiny hairs on the back of his neck. "There's been another one. Mr. Leup is in a rage. The men from the Colorado Mountain Club managed to transport the body to a mortician in Longmont without anyone knowing about it, but now the news reporters have somehow found out and are clamoring for photos and interviews with Richard and the family. I'm afraid we need your help figuring out how it happened."

"Who is it? What did happen?"

"It's the other boy, Charles Monde. The fraternity brother of Winston Dole and Richard Leup. Yesterday morning the Mountain Club came across his body at the old Big Horse Mine in Big Horse Park. They were hiking out of the mountains after a camping trip."

"Let me guess. They had left their cars at the end of the Lantern Creek road?"

"That's right."

"Charles Monde. One of the three. How did he die?"

"That's part of the puzzle we hope you might be able to help with. Dottie said you're on vacation and have nothing to do?"

"Not exactly. I thought I might clean my cabin in case you were serious about wanting to come see it. Unless the trout are rising. Although somebody said fishing season was closed. I'll have to find out."

"Why don't you forget about sweeping, and fishing, and help us? I'll tell you the plan for today. You remember FBI agent

56

A.T. Canilly. My boss? He and I are going to leave almost immediately and drive to Longmont to examine the body. Monde's parents are supposed to be there, too. We hope young Richard Leup will also show up, but Mr. Leup, senior, says the boy has hidden himself away in his bedroom and is afraid to go anywhere."

"Richard thinks he was supposed to be the one who had the accident? Again?"

"It looks that way. Now, Agent Canilly is up to his ears and whiskers with a really important federal case at the moment and can't take time to do the spade work on this one himself. He and I will leave Longmont and drive to the Big Horse Mine site, might arrive there by one o'clock or thereabouts. You meet us there. Do you think the Pioneer Inn has any available rooms?"

"Lots of them. In fact, the place is empty now that the tourists have all gone home."

"Good," she said. "I'm bringing a suitcase. Agent Canilly will return to Denver. After looking at the death site you'll drive me to the village and I'll rent a room at the Pioneer. We'll have a few days to dig up whatever we can. I just pray the reporters don't find us. We can work at your cabin. All right?"

A worried grimace replaced McIntyre's smile when he hung up the phone.

"Trouble?" Charlene said. "How about we have coffee and you can tell me about it."

"While I have coffee, maybe you can pack a lunch? For two people? You remember Miss Coteau, don't you?"

"Oh, yes! The gorgeously slim lady with the clothes. That breezy little dress she wore when she stayed here, I could have murdered her for it. Is she . . . I mean, are the two of you . . . I mean you two look good together, like pie and ice cream!"

"Me?" McIntyre said. "And her? I couldn't even keep her in hats, not on my salary. No, she and I have to collaborate on a death situation, that's all. She'll need one of your rooms. Maybe for a couple of days."

"She's got it. Grab your coffee and come in the kitchen. We'll chat while I make those lunches. And you, young man, will tell me why you have such a long face. It's not like you."

McIntyre perched on a high stool and watched as Charlene bustled around the kitchen collecting bread and lunch meat and apples and salad.

"Aw," he said, "it's being a bachelor, Charlie. Vi Coteau wants to see my cabin. Wants to visit me where I live. I don't have any problem with that, other than the fact that it looks like I keep pigs in it. The logs are all dusty, the kitchen area needs paint, the curtains aren't fit to blow your nose on, my old braided rug is overdue for a wash because I'm afraid if I washed it, the whole thing would fall apart. I just been letting everything slide."

"While you went fishing," Charlene said.

"Yeah. Guilty. Now the place is a mess. I'm going to be really embarrassed to have her see it."

"Don't fret," Charlene said. "She's a sweet young lady. I'm sure she'll understand. With your personality? Heck, any woman would be tickled pink to go out with you no matter if you lived in a packing crate out in the alley."

"Oh, great!" McIntyre grumbled. "Now I'm just a personality. It's like a girl saying she likes you because you're 'a real character.' A packing crate would make a better impression than that coyote den I live in."

"Hush. Here's your box lunches. I included a couple of bottles of root beer, too."

"You're an angel," McIntyre said.

"Nice of you to notice. But I'm putting the lunches on your breakfast tab anyway."

Opening the door to leave, Ranger McIntyre overheard Charlene on the telephone asking the operator to connect her with the supervisor's office.

"Dottie?" Charlene said. "Listen, are you real busy today? Something has come up."

McIntyre slowed the truck, scanning the west side of the road for a dirt track. It would be overgrown with brush and grass and almost invisible in the pine forest. He wished he had thought to tell Vi about it when he had her on the phone. You usually drove to Big Horse Park by going up the Lantern Creek road to the trailhead, but he knew about this old unimproved road that came out at the abandoned mine. Maybe the FBI had a detailed map in its files and she could use it to find the disused road. The FBI seemed to keep records of everything.

The Big Horse Mine was much older than the May Day. It had no vertical shaft that he knew of, no headframe, no buildings left standing. In fact, there was little left to see, mostly a tunnel that went into the mountainside about fifty yards where it was blocked by a cave-in. The old miners had laboriously drilled the granite by hand and used charges of black powder to blast their way, probably following a miniscule vein of gold ore in the hope that it led to the mother lode. They must have found enough gold to give them hope for more: beside the creek they had erected a stamping mill and a sluice to crush the rock and wash the gold out of it. Now the long wooden chute of the sluice was rotten and falling apart and the stamp mill stood looking like the giant gate of an abandoned mansion. Its heavy timber frame was still solid. The iron flywheel and camshaft still turned, but never again would the thick steel rods rise and fall in rhythm, crushing chunks of granite beneath their iron shoes.

McIntyre parked his Small Delights pickup near the edge of the woods and walked toward the old mine. Vi Coteau and Agent Canilly had not yet arrived. McIntyre had all of the stillness of the mountain and forest to himself.

Stamp Mill

Or so he thought.

He was approaching the gaping mouth of the mine tunnel when the mining engineer—Beauchamp—came out of it, his hands in the air as if he intended to surrender. But McIntyre wasn't in uniform and didn't have a gun. However, the figure who followed the engineer out of the gloomy tunnel did have one. The leathery character with the puffin's beak nose had the muzzle of his large-bore shotgun pressed into the small of Beauchamp's back. The two men kept coming toward McIntyre until the one with the shotgun spoke.

"Far enough," he said.

"What's going on?" McIntyre asked.

"Still nosy as ever, eh? None of your beeswax, that's what. You decide t' sell me that truck of yourn, Mister Ranger?"

Beauchamp looked at McIntyre in surprise. "A ranger?" he said.

"Why don't you lower that shotgun? I'll tell you what I'm doing here," McIntyre said. "I don't think Mister Beauchamp meant any harm or tried to steal anything from you."

"Hah! A lot you know, Mister Nosy Pants. Weren't for me this greenhorn idiot'd be layin' under ten ton of rock inside that tunnel, that's what. I heard hammerin' comin' from in there and went in about thirty, forty feet when I seen this dumb dude hammerin' away at a support post. He wouldn't stop when I told him to. I pointed Ol' Nevermiss at him and marched him out."

"I see," said McIntyre. "Okay, I think he's safe now. Why don't we lower the hammers and point the gun somewhere else."

"Hah!"

The man had his back to the tall frame of the stamp mill. He swung the shotgun to point it at McIntyre's belt buckle.

"I don't see where you got any call t' tell me what t' do," he said, "especially seein' as how you ain't packin' no firearm."

"No," came a calm female voice from behind him. "But I am. And it's pointed at your head."

The mountain man went rigid, then stiffly, cautiously, turned around to find himself looking down the barrel of a .38 revolver being held by an attractive young woman.

"Hand it over," she said. And hand it over he did. As a rule, he did not associate with women, yet he knew enough about them to know that they are to be taken seriously when armed.

"Hiya, Ranger!" This time the voice was that of FBI agent A.T. Canilly, strolling nonchalantly out of the woods, acting as if he had just run into McIntyre on a street corner.

"Pretty good, huh?" he said. "We tossed a coin to see who got to sneak up on this character with the shotgun. Vi won. How have you been, anyway? Vi tells me you're taking a bus-man's holiday to look into this murder situation."

Without taking her eyes off the scavenger, Vi Coteau deftly

slipped the latch on the shotgun barrels and let the shells fall out onto the ground. When she handed the gun back to its owner, he grabbed it and took off running in the direction of the creek.

"Now," Ranger McIntyre said, addressing Beauchamp, "maybe you'll tell me what's going on. You were trying to bring the roof of the mine tunnel down around your ears, is that right?"

"You know better," Beauchamp replied. "You know why I'm here. I was tapping the beams with my hammer, that's all. Testing for rot and decay. I need to decide whether to send the crew up here to dynamite that old tunnel or not. Those timbers seem solid enough, though."

"Speaking of which," McIntyre said, "I stopped at the May Day site and didn't see any sign that this 'crew' of yours had been there to do anything."

"Yeah, well, they're awful busy, that's why. I need to be moving on now. Want to look at one more place before I knock off for the day."

McIntyre looked at Agent Canilly and Agent Canilly nodded his head.

"Okay," McIntyre said. "But first, why don't you write down your name and address and a phone number where I can find you. If I need expert information, see?"

He handed Beauchamp his pocket notebook and pencil.

After the mining engineer was gone, McIntyre was able to give Vi Coteau his full attention. Agent Canilly strolled off to examine the stamp mill.

"Nice outfit," McIntyre said.

"Thanks! It's new. You like it?"

She did a little pirouette. The skirt was a subtle dark tartan, the shoes sturdy and sensible for mountain walking, the tweed jacket tailored to her contours, and the beret in the same tartan as the skirt. McIntyre examined her closely from ankles to eyes and finally asked the question that any male might ask a pretty woman.

"Where did your gun go?" he said.

Vi laughed and shook her head at him.

"I can't see where you'd keep it. Ankle holster, maybe?" he said.

"You know one thing I like about you, Tim?" she answered. "I never can predict what you're about to say! If you must know . . . but no. Where a lady carries her .38 is something only she and her tailor need to know. Speaking of knowing, you might have said that you knew about a road to this old mine. We had to park down over the hill and hike up."

"Sorry," he said. "Forgot."

They walked to where Agent Canilly was taking photographs of the stamp mill and surrounding scene.

"Well, Ranger," he said, "we sure do have us a real mess here. Leup wants to pull in an out-of-state lawman he knows, Mrs. Leup is apparently in shock, young Richard has dropped out of college in midterm and is hiding at home, and that's just the Leup family. I dread the thought of interviewing the Monde family. The only good thing is that nobody has told the newshounds where the death occurred. Leup also talks about putting a team of private detectives on the case but I convinced him the thing to do, in order to keep it as quiet as possible, was to let you figure it all out. Vi can lend you a hand for a few days."

"Okay," McIntyre replied. "I'll do what I can. Tell me, how did the boy—Charles Monde?—how did he die?"

"The body is with a doctor in Longmont. Part-time coroner and medical examiner for the county. We stopped there on the way up here. According to the doctor, the kid's chest was crushed by some heavy object the size of an average book, maybe six to eight inches square. His sternum was snapped in half, lungs and heart squeezed until they burst. The doc said he'd only seen one case that was in any way similar, and that was a man who was working under a heavy truck, lying on his back with a metal tray of tools resting on his chest when the jack slipped and the truck came down on him."

"Holy cow."

"You said it. Luckily, the Mountain Club members who found the body took lots of pictures and made sketches. Now that I've seen that thing over there, I pretty much think that's the murder weapon. What we need to figure out is how it happened. C'mon, I'll show you."

Canilly led the way to the abandoned stamp mill. In its heyday it must have been a formidable piece of machinery capable of crushing several tons of ore per day. Most of the portable pieces had long ago been carried off by souvenir hunters or scavengers, but enough of the equipment remained to show how it had worked. The standing frame in the shape of an immense capital H was constructed of sawn timbers nearly two feet thick. Five long and heavy steel rods had been installed to stand upright inside the frame, but now one was missing. The tops of the rods went up through holes drilled in the cross-beam, where they had once been attached to cams the shape of clover leaves. As the horizontal camshaft turned, it lifted and dropped the iron rods in sequence.

The foot of each rod was a block of iron about eight inches square, probably weighing in the neighborhood of thirty pounds. When you added the weight of the steel-lifting rod, the whole thing would weigh over a hundred pounds. The function of the stamp mill was simplicity itself: a sloping wooden chute held heavy chunks of rock from the mine. These rolled down beneath the hammers where they were arrested by a crossbar. The five hammers rose and fell in rhythm, pounding the rocks into pieces small enough to pass under the crossbar and into the sluice box. The whole operation had been driven by a waterwheel in the stream next to it, but of the waterwheel nothing remained except two concrete pedestals.

"You're telling me they crushed him to death?" McIntyre said.

"Yup. Here, I've got one of the witness's sketches. See? They found him lying on his back in that old rotting ore chute with one of those iron hammers sitting on his chest. This wide dark stain here, that's his blood. The doc says the blood from his lungs and heart must have come out his mouth and nose."

"Did they move him?"

"No. Covered him with a tent canvas. Two of them stayed, two hiked out to tell the sheriff. And then when the sheriff got here it took four men to lift the hammer high enough to slide the body out from under it."

Ranger McIntyre looked at the sketch again.

"Marks on his wrists, ankles?"

"Like he'd been tied up, you mean. Answer is yes. He had a wound to the head, too, like he had been knocked out with a club. Knocked him out, trussed him up, put him under that hammer rod."

"Four men to raise it, you said."

"Yup. I suppose two of us could lift it, except there's nothing to take hold of, just that steel shaft. So, I think we're looking for at least two men as killers."

"Seems like it," McIntyre agreed. "Or one man pretty clever with physics."

"What do you mean?" Vi asked.

"If a killer was planning this in advance, all he needed to do would be to raise one of those hammer rods high enough to slide the victim under. And bring the victim up here to the old mine, of course. I'd be willing to bet the killer told Charles

Monde that the Big Horse Mine was where the Dunraven
Hoard could be found. Followed him here, or arranged to meet
him here, conked him with a club, tied him hand and foot,
dragged him under the stamp mill, which he had already fixed
to squash him. Or maybe it was just meant to frighten him."

"I'm not following you," she said.

"Wait a minute," McIntyre said. "What if . . . what if Winston
and Monde both knew where to look for the Dunraven Hoard?
And what if somebody wanted to frighten them into telling?
Maybe that's why young Richard Leup is so frightened for
himself. He's one of the ones who saw the book that the librarian told us about, whatever it was. Three boys look at that book
and two of them die in really strange ways. What if Winston
wasn't supposed to die, just have a terrible fright when he found
himself with his head down in that ore bucket? And what if
Charles Monde was supposed to be frightened by a stamping
hammer being lowered onto his chest? But by accident the hammer didn't come down gradually, it came down all at once and
the killer couldn't lift it again. Just like he couldn't fish the
penny out of the ore bucket."

"Let's go back a step," Agent Canilly said. "How did one
man raise the stamp hammer?"

"Physics," McIntyre replied. "Given enough time to work on
it, nothing could be simpler. I bet if we look around, we'll find a
nice long lodgepole that could be used as a lever. Or a long
steel rod. You put your fulcrum right there, see? Then you can
lever the hammer up. Probably four, five inches. Then you need
to take another purchase and do it again."

"Except if you're holding the end of the lever down, how do
you chunk something under the hammer to hold it up?"

"Easy. Look. Take this flat rock, put it next to the hammer
foot on the downhill side. Now take that round rock there and
prop it against the uphill side. See? When the hammer rises, the

rock will roll under it. The flat one keeps it from rolling too far. Now you lever up the hammer, the rock rolls under it, and you're on your way. Find a higher fulcrum, do it another few times with bigger rocks, and pretty soon the thing is high enough to put your victim under."

"And you keep it there how?" Vi asked.

"I'm guessing he would cut wedges out of green wood, then climb up on top of the frame and wedge them into the hole where the rod slides up and down. Maybe I'll climb up there and have a look. Picture this scene a minute: the assailant is sitting astraddle of the crossbeam with his hammer in his hand ready to knock the first wedge away and let the rod drop an inch or two. He's taunting poor Charles who's lying down there all trussed up with the hammer shoe against his chest. Makes a pretty picture, huh?"

McIntyre had noticed a length of timber lying near the stamp mill. He heaved up one end of it and braced it against the mill's support post at an angle. Then, like the native islander in *National Geographic* going up a coconut tree, the ranger clambered up the timber to stand on the crossbeam holding onto one of the hammer rods for balance.

"Toss me your camera," he said. Agent Canilly threw the Kodak up to the ranger.

"It looks like I'm right," McIntyre said. "There's bits of fresh wood stuck to the side of the hole around this rod. And here's a hammer mark on the beam. He must have missed the wedge while he was pounding them in. We might look around for those wedges. Down in the woods would be my bet. I bet the hammer rod dropped all at once, he went into a panic, tried to lift it, couldn't, threw the evidence into the trees down there, and lit a shuck out of here. Wait: he would also need to take the ropes off the wrists and ankles. Maybe we'll find those."

"Lit a shuck?" Vi said.

"He means 'hurried,' " Agent Canilly translated. "You can

put a ridge runner into a tuxedo, but you can't make him talk good."

"Hmmmph," retorted McIntyre. "Besides, how do you know I have a tux?"

"Are you joking?" Canilly asked. "Down at the office it's all that Vi and her girlfriends could talk about after the dinner party."

The ranger swung down from the crossbeam and dusted himself off.

"Heckuva murder weapon," he said. "Leaving a man to be crushed to death like that. It's like something out of Edgar Allen Poe. Why would a killer do it that way? And leave the body to be found? Why not just shoot him and bury him in the slag pile, or drag him into the mine tunnel and cave it in on top of him? But go to all the trouble to crush his chest?"

"Don't forget the other one, either," Vi said. "Suffocated in that old ore bucket. I think we're dealing with a deranged person. Sadistic. A person who resents young college men."

"We ought to make a careful search all around here," McIntyre said. "Whoever set this up, he spent time here doing it. He must have been here more than once. Let's hope he dropped something, some kind of clue. Up in the park, we see illegal campsites and almost every time they leave something like a matchbook or cigar band, even an envelope or grocery receipt."

"You two'll have to do it alone," Canilly said. "I'm leaving. There are other cases I need to work on. I'll phone Leup and let him know you're making progress. Coteau, you check in by phone tomorrow."

McIntyre and Vi Coteau walked down the hill with Canilly in order to retrieve Vi's long coat and her small suitcase from the car. They walked back up to the mine with the sound of Canilly's motor fading away behind them; when they could no longer hear it, the mountain silence once more wrapped around the forest like an atmosphere of looming intimacy.

CHAPTER SIX:
CLEVER CLUES AND MISSING MOTIVES

Ranger McIntyre stashed Vi's suitcase and coat in his truck.

"Now," he said, "I think we could do a better search if we split up. Why don't you look around the stamp mill? Meanwhile, I'll check and see if there's any tracks leading in or out of this place."

Vi's first discovery was easy: it was a fresh groove in the dirt. Deep and obvious, it led away from the stamp mill and into the forest. She called McIntyre over to see it.

"Good! That's exactly what we're looking for," the ranger said.

"Somebody dragging something?" Vi asked.

"Looks like it. Let's follow it a ways."

Whoever left the narrow furrow across the dirt and into the forest had taken no trouble to conceal it. Where it went across rocks it left a scratch and bits of metal. They followed it through the trees for several minutes until it led them to discover a road that looked as if it had been abandoned decades ago. The recent furrow then continued along the roadway in the general direction of another canyon they could see in the distance.

"That's enough for me," McIntyre said. "I know what it was, and who it was. What I wonder is, did he see what happened at the stamp mill?"

"Explain?" Vi said.

"The guy with the shotgun and the bird beak nose," McIntyre said. "Remember the missing hammer rod from the stamp mill? A steel rod, maybe eight feet long, two inches thick? He's the one who took it. He dragged it home to sell for scrap. I'll bet you a dollar he's squatting in some old cabin. There's another abandoned mining claim in that canyon up ahead."

"A man living like a hermit in a gloomy old cabin," Vi said. "It gives me a shudder just to think about it. We don't have to go there, do we?"

Thinking about a filthy cabin didn't give McIntyre a shudder, but Vi's remark did make him wince.

"No. I can find him when I want him. I think Bird Beak discovered those old claim shacks up Soda Canyon. He probably took one over, thinking it was on U.S. Forest Service land. He told me he goes around collecting scrap metal from other old mines. The funny thing is, and I doubt if he knows it, the Soda Canyon claim is actually inside the national park. It's illegal."

"And he took the missing steel rod."

"Right. But I don't think he's the one who managed to wrestle it out of the timber frame. I think, if it was him, he would have knocked the frame apart and salvaged all the metal parts. No, I think it was our killer who wiggled that rod loose from the frame. He needed it out of the way, see, needed a wider gap between rods to put the victim in."

"We need to work on your grammar," Vi said sweetly.

"Probably," McIntyre agreed. "The murderer likely used that loose rod as a lever to raise the hammer rod that killed the boy. Our scrap metal prospector found it lying there later and dragged it away. What I'd like to know is whether Bird Beak saw the killer. And whether he saw the body before the Mountain Club guys did. Maybe he was there even earlier and saw the mill frame with one of its rods drawn up and wedged in place. We'll find him one of these days and ask him. But it can wait. First, I want to make sure we didn't overlook anything at the mine. If there's a snowstorm, everything will get covered up."

They returned to the mine and kept searching. As McIntyre predicted, they found three hand-carved wooden wedges in the trees down the hill from the stamp frame. The wedges had been whittled from spruce branches and were about eight inches long. The thicker ends showed signs of having been hammered.

"Things are starting to make a little more sense to me," McIntyre said. "We'll take another look around before we go. Right now, it's past my feeding time. Let's go back to the truck and see what Charlene packed in the lunch boxes."

"Tell me more about Charlene," Vi Coteau said.

She and Ranger McIntyre had chosen a grassy spot beside the mountain creek. He spread his car robe on the ground and with a Sir Walter Raleigh bow and flourish bade her sit upon it. The robe being just wide enough to accommodate two picnic boxes and a lady in a tartan skirt, McIntyre elected to sit on the grass with his back to an aspen tree. He was eating a sandwich, admiring Miss Coteau, and simultaneously sizing up the possibility of catching trout in the fast-moving little creek. In fact, when she interrupted with her question, he had been thinking that a fellow might tie on a small light-colored bug, like a #18 Ginger Quill, and cast it right behind that one rock . . .

"Charlene?" he said. "Not much to tell. She's married to Claude Underhill. Awful nice lady. He's away more than a week at a time, though. He drives a heavy truck for an excavating outfit that's trying to dig a tunnel under the Rocky Mountains. He's only home once or twice a month. I'm not sure where they're from originally, but they've been in the village longer than I have. Why?"

"I thought perhaps she had set her cap for you. I have a feeling she doesn't like us having a private picnic in the woods."

"Charlene? Me? Never! Why?"

"These sandwiches. Onion and bologna?"

"I see what you mean," McIntyre said. "She usually includes pickle relish. Well, maybe she ran out."

"No, smart guy. I mean onion and bologna would not be my first choice for a romantic mountain rendezvous. Unless I wanted to sabotage it. Bad breath, you know."

McIntyre laughed. And Vi smiled at the way he laughed. An undersized trout jumped up out of the tumbling water to catch a bug and was instantly swept downstream.

Having finished his sandwich, he gallantly waited for Vi to finish hers before unwrapping the dessert brownies. McIntyre sipped his root beer. He took a crumpled piece of paper from his pocket and carefully smoothed it out.

"What do you have there?" Vi asked as she daintily licked a spot of mustard from the tip of her little finger.

"Found it next to a log, about ten yards from the stamp mill. All wadded up. It looks to be a page from a notebook. There's a sketch on it."

"Can you tell what it is?"

"Oh, yeah. Obvious. Look."

He handed her the piece of paper. It was a pencil sketch of the H-shaped stamp mill that had crushed Charles Monde's chest. On the bottom corner were printed the words "Big Horse Mine rock crusher" and along one edge was a wiggly line, maybe an attempt to show the road leading into the mine site.

"I wonder who dropped that?" she said. "Or threw it away? From the look of it, I'd say the person decided against keeping it. Maybe it wasn't a good enough drawing for them. They crumpled it up and tossed it aside."

"That's what I thought, too. Probably sat on that log to sketch it, didn't care for it, and like you said, balled it up and dropped it. And I think I know who it might have been."

"You do?"

"Beauchamp. The mining engineer who told me he's doing safety inspections of all the mines hereabouts. The first time I met him he was carrying a notebook on a clipboard. It was about this size."

"Oh. In other words, he drew a picture for his report."

"Seems that way. Notice anything about this sketch?"

"Other than it's not very well done?"

"It isn't, is it? But it shows a missing hammer rod lying on the ground. See? Right there. That thick line? Also shows one of the middle hammers already raised up. I think maybe Mister Beauchamp Mining Expert saw the stamp mill after the killer had gotten it ready to receive his victim. Maybe he even came along as the killer was preparing the mill and interrupted him. Maybe he saw who it was. Either way, my guess is that Beauchamp recognized how dangerous it would be to have that one hammer raised up and he made a sketch, intending to report it."

"Or," Vi said.

"Yeah. Or he did it himself and made a drawing of it for some reason. And for some reason wadded it up and threw it away."

The ranger offered the lady a brownie and took one himself.

"Let's have another look around and then go back to town."

Vi Coteau was on one side of the pickup truck, folding the car robe. McIntyre was on the opposite side, stashing the empty lunch boxes beneath a piece of canvas so they wouldn't fly out of the pickup bed on the way home.

"I thought of another possibility," he said.

"Like what?"

"Maybe the killer made that drawing and gave it to Charles to lure him up here. Like a treasure map, kind of. Then the killer followed him or waited for him. It could have been Charles who wadded it up and tossed it away. Maybe Charles came here, looked around, didn't find anything, and threw the drawing away. Maybe the killer walked up to Charles, like Beauchamp did to me, maybe conked him on the head, tied him under the hammer mill, let the rod down onto his chest. Didn't notice that the boy had thrown away the drawing, or forgot it. But I don't want to worry about all the what-ifs. I think we need to look at all of this differently."

"Differently how?" she asked, putting the car robe behind the seat of the pickup.

The ranger checked the cord he had used to lash her suitcase into the truck bed. Didn't want to lose it on the way back to the village.

"Instead of us trying to figure out how the Irish penny got to the May Day site or how the notebook page got to the Big Horse site, I think we need to start looking at motives. It's like when you do a jigsaw puzzle and try to find the border pieces to make a frame for the rest. I'm going to talk to the families and to young Richard Leup and try to figure out what they knew, or thought they knew, and who else knew about it, and whether there's anyone who might want them dead. Maybe they're both dead because of something they knew."

"Then you'd work backward to the question of why it was done in such a complicated way, right?"

"Right!"

"By the way," she said, "you remember Richard's sister? From the dinner party?"

"Vaguely," he said. "There was one fascinating woman at the dinner who had all my attention. I hardly noticed the others."

"You know what, Ranger? Not only are your sugary comments awfully obvious, but your timing absolutely stinks. A while ago we were alone beside a mountain stream, on a blanket. But you don't start with the sweet talk until we have a pickup truck between us. Parked next to a murder scene."

"Oops," he said. "Well, what about Richard's sister?"

"That antique Irish penny. It made something click in my mind. The other day I remembered what it was. Richard's sister told me that her father is a coin collector."

"Now that you mention it," McIntyre said, "when we were in his study, I noticed a few picture frames with coins in them. But if anybody took one of them . . . it would have to be somebody who had the run of the place . . . Mr. Leup would have noticed it missing."

He opened the truck door but took a long look around the mine site before climbing in. Vi was unfolding her long coat.

"Want me to walk all the way around there and help you put on your coat, little lady?" he said.

"Not unless you want me to poke you in the nose with my little fist," she replied, shrugging the coat up over her shoulders.

The shadows were growing long and the mountain air was turning chilly as the small pickup chugged slowly down the mountain, following the bumpy pair of ruts that had once been the road to the Big Horse Mine. Between the growling of the engine and the noisy heater fan it was nearly impossible to carry on a conversation, but neither of them minded. Vi Coteau was having an adventure, which she loved, and Ranger McIntyre had himself a puzzle, which he lived for.

"Evenings are colder now!" McIntyre shouted over the engine. "I expect we'll have snow."

"Probably!" Vi Coteau shouted back. "I think we ought to go back up to the mine tomorrow. Take more photos! Look around at least one more time before the snow covers everything."

"I was thinking the same thing," McIntyre said. "Something about that mine tunnel's been nagging at me. I can't figure out what it is."

By the time they reached the main road, the truck's cab had

warmed up. McIntyre turned down the heater. Vi relaxed on the seat.

"That road we just came down," she said. "In your theory about the Dunraven Hoard, that's one of the possible roads they might have used to move valuables from the English Hotel to a hiding place, to a cache like the Big Horse Mine?"

"If the story is true, yes. If you look at a map, you'll see it's pretty much of a straight shot from where the hotel stood. And, of course, back in those days all this area would have been unpopulated. More remote than it is now."

"It would be fun to find the hoard, wouldn't it!" she said.

"Sure. But don't raise your hopes too high. These buried treasure stories tend to be myths. And besides, if anyone actually found it, they probably wouldn't have told anyone. It could have been found and removed years ago."

"Hey," she said, "what about the guy with the hawk beak nose? Could be he's a suspect, right?"

"I wouldn't rule him out," McIntyre answered. "Except I don't think he'd leave the bodies lying around. If they were discovered it would bring newspaper reporters, cops, curiosity seekers. The guy likes his privacy too much to want people stomping all over 'his' territory. I think—if he was the killer—he would probably dump the bodies down a mine shaft or haul them out to the main road. He wouldn't go to the trouble of hanging up an ore bucket and putting a body in it. He wouldn't go jacking up a heavy stamping mill rod just to put the other one under it, either. I can tell you one thing. When we find out what really happened, we're also going to find out that the way the deaths took place is the key to it all."

It was dark when they arrived back at the village. The brightly lit windows of the Pioneer Inn were a welcome sight, promising warmth and food. Charlene wouldn't hear of the two of them sitting in a lonely corner of the chilly, empty dining room; she insisted on setting a card table in the lounge near the stone fireplace and a crackling blaze. McIntyre fetched two chairs while Vi collected a tablecloth, napkins, and utensils from the dining room sideboard. It turned out to be one of those suppers where a man doesn't think he's very hungry and ends up wolfing down everything in sight, in this case Irish stew with lots of onion in it, warm bread, a bowl of salad, and rhubarb pie for dessert.

They talked as they ate, going on and on the whole time like nervous teenagers on a first date. They laughed, they chatted, they said funny little things: they couldn't seem to quiet down to a normal conversation at all. McIntyre would start to steer the topic toward a serious analysis of the murder scene, even suggesting they find pencil and paper and begin to chart such things as motives and timeline, but in less than a minute they would be back talking about his Small Delights truck or her fast Marmon roadster or the dinner party at the Leup mansion or the possibility that a snowstorm could show up during the night and strand them in the Pioneer Inn. Wouldn't that be too bad!

Charlene sat listening awhile, sitting in a wing chair by the fire and knitting, until she announced that she had bookkeeping to do in the office. She left but then quickly returned, carrying a flat box.

"Tim," she said, "look what I have. You'll like this! One of the guests this summer was a jigsaw fanatic like you. He left this one for us, said maybe other guests would enjoy it as much as he did. Look! You can borrow it if you want, or some winter day on your day off you might want to work on it here. Pretty neat, isn't it."

The picture on the box showed a wonderfully complicated picture. It was a scene from *The Arabian Nights* with dozens and dozens of flowers and plants in the foreground, a reflecting pond (*lots of plain silvery-blue pieces in that one,* McIntyre thought), turrets, trees, ten or twelve human figures, and a wall decorated with a challenging geometric pattern.

"Let's do it!" Vi Coteau said. "Right now!"

"Do you mean it?" Ranger McIntyre said. He had done jigsaws with only two women before this. Usually he did them by himself in his little cabin. "Maybe I'll borrow it and take it with me."

"No, it'll be fun! C'mon, help me sort it out."

Vi dumped the box on the table and began flipping all the pieces right-side up. Charlene realized that she had made a mistake. She shook her head, giving McIntyre the sympathetic look you give a man who chooses to pick at his salad while a beefsteak turns cold. Her head still shaking, she returned to the office and her bookkeeping.

"Now then," McIntyre said, searching for border pieces, "while we work on this, let's talk about murder motives. I've got a theory about trout. They'll come up and grab a dry fly for lots of reasons. One, they're hungry and need food. Two, they're not hungry but that bug annoys them. Or they think they rule the pool and they don't want any other fish to have any food."

"Why are we talking about fishing?" Vi said, triumphantly seizing a corner piece together with an adjoining piece of the border.

"Two young men killed, why? To rob them? To defend a claim to that so-called treasure hoard? Did the killer maybe torture both boys, or threaten to torture them, except it went wrong, trying to make them tell where the treasure is?"

"Far-fetched," Vi said. "But go ahead."

"Might be far-fetched but it could explain the bizarre way the deaths happened. The assailant discovered the ore bucket, for instance, and thought it might be a good idea to shove Winston Dole into it headfirst and keep him there until he spilled the beans. Same with the hammer mill, just gradually lower it onto Charles Monde's chest until he talked."

"Only slightly less far-fetched," Vi said. "Hand me that border piece next to your elbow."

"Okay. Second possibility might be annoyance. Both boys could have annoyed the killer to the point of homicide. We know they annoyed Mister Bird Beak nose because he thought they were out to steal his scrap metal. And they were hanging around 'his' territory looking for something and he didn't know what."

"We know that Mr. Leup was annoyed with them, too," Vi said. "Don't forget that. He made it very clear that he didn't like his son hanging around with them. Mr. Leup is—was—afraid that Monde and Dole might involve his precious Richard in a scandal. And we know that Mr. Leup has more than enough money and influence to make people and problems disappear."

"Know what I just thought of?" McIntyre said. "There's nothing like working a jigsaw puzzle to help you think."

"That's what you thought of?" she said.

"No. What I thought was, what if the victims could have been anyone? I mean, did it have to be Monde and Dole or did they just happen to be in the wrong place at the wrong time. Maybe the killer is deranged, an insane person who likes to construct clever killing devices and wait for a victim to come strolling by. Maybe it had nothing to do with who they are or what they were searching for."

"I don't like it," Vi said. "There's a piece of that azure blue, right over there. I don't like it because it would mean the killer would have to hang out at the mine sites all the time, waiting. Besides, we know of at least two other people, that hermit and the mine inspector, who came and went and nobody killed them. No, I'm sure it was because of who the boys were."

"I'll go along with that," McIntyre said. "What next?"

"Sex," Vi said, pushing a tab into an opening with a soft click.

"Pardon?"

"Motives. The old battle of the sexes, the craving for it, the way it can make people crazy enough to kill each other."

"Oh," McIntyre said. "Probably not in this case."

"Then we're left with greed, insanity, or revenge."

"Yeah!" McIntyre said. "Revenge is good! Holy cow, even young Richard Leup might have had a grudge against his two pals. Maybe they had pulled a dirty trick on him, a gag that would land him in serious trouble. Maybe they got him into some kind of difficulty with his girlfriend. If he has one."

"Every college boy has a girlfriend. Or at least imagines he does."

"Or a professor!" McIntyre went on. "His so-called friends did something to make a professor turn against him. Therefore, he made up a treasure story to lure them to those lonely old derelict mine sites where he could frighten the bejesus out of them. That could explain why Richard is all upset and hiding in his room now. His plan went wrong."

"Could be," Vi agreed. "Or it could be that all three frat boys pulled off some serious prank and their victim, whoever it was, set out to get revenge. That would explain why Richard won't come out of the house. He knows who it is and he knows why his friends were killed and he thinks he might be next."

An hour seemed to drift by, and then another. From time to time McIntyre got up, stretched his back, and put logs into the fireplace. Toward midnight they raided the kitchen for cold pie and milk, leaving a promissory note where Charlene would find it. The mantel clock struck one o'clock before Vi Coteau said that she was too sleepy to talk any longer. Kissing McIntyre on the cheek she wished him a good night and went to her room.

Ranger McIntyre thought about the long, cold drive back to

his cabin and he thought about how cold and dark—and unkempt—his cabin would be. He looked around until he found a stack of lap robes, intended for customers who might want to sit outside. Using two lap robes and his overcoat for blankets, he lay down on one of the couches and fell asleep to the sounds of the dying fire.

Mari, the hired girl, found him still asleep when she came in the morning to start breakfast and straighten things up. There was a jigsaw puzzle on the card table, nearly finished, two plates and two milk glasses on the side table, a pile of cold ash in the fireplace. It was safe to assume that the gorgeous creature from Denver would be asleep in her room, but the noise and smell of breakfast being prepared should be enough to bring the both of them awake. Cleaning and dusting could wait: Mari had a very special assignment today. It was her job to feed the two guests and keep them busy. Charlene wanted the pair kept out of the way while she and Dottie put the finishing touches on "Project Top Secret."

Ranger McIntyre set the hand brake and turned off the engine. The Big Horse Park Mine site looked just as they had left it yesterday, empty and quiet.

"Might be snow coming," McIntyre suggested, scanning the skies.

Vi Coteau agreed. The clouds hanging above the Front Range had the cold, ominous look of wet and sticky snow to come. Together they left the truck and went over yesterday's ground once again, crisscrossing the clearing in both directions, going down into the trees below the slag dump, checking the stamping mill frame for any kind of clue.

"In Sherlock Holmes stories," McIntyre said, studying the rough, splintery timber, "this is where Sherlock discovers a single piece of silk thread snagged on the wood and deduces that it came from a certain expensive brand of smoking jacket."

"If you say so," Vi said. "Wait. What's that?"

She was pointing into the trees near the stamping mill.

"What?" McIntyre said.

"Something a lot bigger than your bit of silk thread. See the mark on that tree over there? C'mon."

The tree was a venerable ponderosa, the oldest tree for hundreds of yards around. High enough that McIntyre would have to stand on tiptoe and stretch in order to reach it. A deep V was carved into the trunk. The V, a foot long and a foot high, lay on its side and was pointing toward the mine tunnel.

"Deep into the wood," McIntyre said. "Whoever carved it wanted it to last, at least until the tree fell. Judging from the way the bark has grown into the grooves, I'd say they carved it a long time ago."

"A long time ago?" Vi said. "You're supposed to show off your woodcraft skills and tell me it was cut into the wood exactly fifty-two years and three months ago."

"You're right," he said. "I'm not at my best this morning. I spent a restless night on a couch."

"Mari said you didn't look restless when she found you," Vi said. "If anything, she said it looked like you were resting very, very well. You're very good at resting."

"What this looks like is a kind of arrow pointing at the mine tunnel," he said.

"Why so high up the tree?" Vi asked.

"Possibly where it would be less noticeable. Or more noticeable. I don't know why. It might be like some bear claw marks I saw once. My assistant ranger, Jamie Ogg? One day he dragged me to an aspen grove where he had come across bear claw marks almost eight feet up a tree. His conclusion was that we had a giant bear wandering around. But what we figured out was that the snow on the shady side of the mountain got several feet deep and didn't melt until late in spring. The bear had stood on the snow, see. This could be the same deal. A man on snowshoes maybe carved it. There could easily be three feet of snow here, in late winter."

"Okay," she said.

"Or whoever carved the V on the tree was standing in a wagon. Or on his horse. No, a wagon. Hey, maybe one of the men who hauled Dunraven's Hoard up here pulled his wagon up to this tree and cut a mark in it. You know, X marks the treasure. Let's go have another peek at that mine tunnel, since that's where the arrow points."

The ranger retrieved his flashlight from the pickup truck and he and Vi Coteau advanced cautiously into the dank blackness of the old mine. They had gone less than twenty yards when the flashlight beam revealed fresh slivers and chips of wood scattered about. McIntyre shone the light on a tunnel support.

"Here's the support beam Beauchamp was hammering on when our nosy hermit showed up," McIntyre said. "He must have been using a geologist's hammer with a point on it. Except why would he pound on an upright? Checking for rot? If he knocked down the post the whole tunnel ceiling could collapse on him."

"You'll have to ask him," Vi suggested. "He's probably in the telephone directory."

Leaving the riddle of why a man would go into a dark mine tunnel and hammer away at a support timber, they moved deeper into the tunnel.

"If I remember right," he said, "there's a cave-in a little ways ahead. Whole tunnel is blocked by it. If the Dunraven Hoard is on the other side, nobody's going to be able to reach it without doing a lot of serious excavating."

Vi Coteau's foot slipped and she grabbed McIntyre's arm to keep from falling down.

"Darn!" she said.

He shone the flashlight at her feet.

"Oh, fudge!" Vi complained. "Mud on my new walking shoes. Dang it all to heck, anyway. Shine your light over there. And over there. Why, the whole floor is mud. I vote we turn around and get out of here."

McIntyre pointed his flashlight further down the tunnel, but all there was to see was a pile of broken rock and dirt.

"There's the cave-in, anyway," he said. "Okay, let's head for the fresh air."

Once they were outside again, McIntyre had Vi Coteau put her foot up on a rock while he wiped away the mud with twists of grass. Kneeling at her feet with one hand gently gripping her slender ankle, McIntyre had a thought.

"That's kind of odd."

"Odd?" she said. "I'll have you know I have rather nice ankles. More than one shoe salesman has told me so. Odd?"

"Not you. I mean your ankle isn't odd. It's the mud. But it's probably nothing. Probably an underground spring the miners cut into while digging the tunnel."

"Why is that so strange?"

"Strange that they didn't make a way for the water to drain out. Lots of times you'll find a drainage gutter dug along one wall of a mine, leading outside. I'm going to go back and take one more quick look."

"I'll wait," she said.

Ranger McIntyre wasn't gone long. When he came back out of the mine, he had the pleased-but-puzzled look of a puppy who's just caught his first flying moth and doesn't know what to do with it.

"Anything wrong?" Vi asked.

"I dunno. It's that underground water. There is a drain gutter. The miners made a trench from where you stepped in the mud and it leads right along the wall. And there's water seeping down it, too."

"So?"

"So it seeps halfway to the mouth of the tunnel and stops. No more trench, no more water. Vanishes into the floor."

"Amazing," Vi said.

"Take a look around," McIntyre said. "See? It's totally dry here. There's nothing but dirt, grass, rocks, mine rubble. If that water had been dribbling out here all those years, we'd be looking at aspen trees, chokecherry bushes, maybe willows."

"Like over there?" Vi asked, pointing down the slope.

"Yup, just like that. The mine seepage must go down through the floor of the tunnel, where it flows underground down over the hill. You know, I bet if we dug up the floor, we'd find a hollow place underneath, like a cave."

"I'm not risking these new shoes helping you move rocks," she said.

"I didn't mean right away," McIntyre replied. "Right now, we've got a more important job to do."

"Which is?" she asked.

"Lunch," he said. "I thought we'd make a little detour on the way back to town and stop at Tiny's place for a couple of those egg salad sandwiches you're addicted to."

"Good thinking," she said with a smile. "Then we can go see your rustic ranger cabin in the Rockies. You could make us coffee to go with the sandwiches, and we could phone Mister Beauchamp and ask him why he was trying to bring the tunnel down on his head. You do have a telephone in your bachelor hut, don't you?"

"Of course," McIntyre said. "A ranger is always on call. Except when I disconnect the phone wire from the wall. I used to leave the earpiece off the hook, but did you know that when you do that, anyone on the party line can hear whatever you're doing in the room, whatever you're saying? Embarrassing."

"Talk to people in your cabin a lot, do you?"

"Only myself, mostly. The horse once in a while."

She didn't ask what the horse might be doing in the cabin.

All the way down the bumpy mine road and most of the way along the main road into town, McIntyre kept worrying about the state of his quarters. He wondered how long it would take him to straighten it up a little before letting Miss Coteau in the door. Thank goodness he had washed his pots and pans and dishes. If she'd give him a little time to tidy up the bed and hang up a few clothes . . .

"Brownie!" he said.

One perfect eyebrow arched, Vi Coteau looked at the ranger.

"Maybe after sandwiches," she said. "You don't want to spoil your lunch. Didn't your mother ever tell you that?"

"No," he said, "Brownie's my horse. Oh, boy, she's going to be hungry. She'll wonder where I was all night. I wanted to go into the cabin ahead of you and straighten it up, put away a few things, but the first thing I need to do is give Brownie her grain and turn her out into the pasture."

"One thing about being with you," Vi said.

"Which is?"

"I never know what you'll be thinking of next."

CHAPTER SEVEN:
CABIN, TO JAIL, TO JUNKYARD

The day was pleasantly warm for late autumn, without any breath of breeze to chill the skin. The sun beat down through an absolutely cloudless sky. If he had a comfortable chair on the porch and a light jacket around his shoulders, a man might doze and dream until it was time to yawn and stretch and go fish the late afternoon rise.

"Lazy day, isn't it?" Vi Coteau observed as she stepped from the pickup truck. She stretched her arms in the sunshine.

"I was just thinking the same thing," McIntyre agreed. "Warm days in September make me feel as lazy as Mrs. Ludlam's dog, as my mother used to say. Look, I've got a comfortable chair here on the porch. Why don't you relax and enjoy the sunshine? I'll just pop around to the stable and let Brownie out. And then I'd like to go inside and straighten things up a little. You understand."

"Sure," Vi said. "Maybe we'll have our sandwiches out here on the porch."

If proof was needed that haste really does make waste, it was provided by McIntyre's rush to see his horse taken care of. In too much of a hurry to hunt for his pitchfork, he scooped armloads of hay for Brownie's trough and got dust and bits of hay stuck all over his flannel shirt. When Brownie nudged him to open the pasture gate he forgot to look down and stepped in a nice fresh pile of her droppings. As he was looking down at the mess of manure on his boot, he heard the familiar squeal of a door hinge and knew that it could only mean one thing.

His cabin door was being opened.

Instead of waiting for him she was going inside. His heart sank at the thought of what she was going to see.

McIntyre slapped Brownie on the rump to urge her into the pasture, then ran—watching his step this time—to the pile of waste straw where he could wipe his boot. A handful of straw got rid of most of it, but not all. In desperation he did the unthinkable: he used Brownie's grooming brush to clean away most of the remaining manure.

Now I'll have to wash this brush before I use it again, he thought. *Great.*

How could he explain the condition of his cabin to Vi? When she opened the door, she probably thought she was looking into a hermit's den. In his mind he pictured the dim interior with all the clutter on the table, the dust on the log walls, the dirty windows, his sleeping bag rumpled on the bed. If she tried to turn on the overhead light, it wouldn't work. The bulb had burned out and he hadn't gotten around to buying a new one. It was a resigned-looking ranger who went around the cabin to the front porch, shoulders slumping and apology written on his face like a dog who has soiled the carpet.

When he stepped over the threshold, however, McIntyre's facial expression of apology changed to one of utter bewilderment. The overhead light was on. Bright sunshine was pouring through sparkling clean windows, windows where fresh flowery curtains had been hung. The logs of the walls were no longer caked in dust but rather seemed to shine with sunlight. The floor had been swept and mopped; the table had been cleared of his maps and bits of junk and polished; now it sported a vase of autumn aspen branches sitting on a square of tartan cloth.

Clearly, he had walked into the wrong cabin, although there was his rolltop desk just as cluttered as he had left it. But all of his clothes had been put away. His hats, gun belt, hiking staff, and rucksack hung neatly on pegs behind the door. The cups and plates had been stacked in the shelves above the sink. As for the bed . . . his eyes kept going back to the bed . . . the sleeping bag had been taken away and in its place was a cream-colored chenille bedspread with a pair of matching pillow covers. He hadn't seen a bed that neatly made since his days in the army. No, that wasn't right. He had seen beds as neatly made, and he had seen those chenille bedspreads before. At the Pioneer Inn.

An envelope on the table held the answer. It was addressed to him and contained a simple note.

"Dear Ranger: You're welcome. Signed, Charlene & Mari & Dottie."

Vi Coteau had already taken the blue enamel coffee pot from the shelf and was standing at the sink filling it from the pitcher pump.

"I thought we could make coffee to go with the sandwiches," she said. "It would be lovely to sit out on the porch to eat lunch, don't you think?"

"Sure," he said. McIntyre struck a match and lit one of the two burners of his kerosene stove. Vi set the coffee pot on it and looked around for the coffee canister. In no time at all his once-gloomy little log cabin was fragrant with the smells of a warm stove and fresh coffee and the presence of a woman. He would never see his cabin again without remembering those aromas and the sight of Vi Coteau standing at his small stove stirring the coffee.

"Mmmmmm!" she murmured. "Maybe it's the mountain air, but Tiny's egg salad sandwiches are especially tasty today! It's nice out here on the porch, isn't it? And look what a fantastic view you have! The little river, the meadow, the aspen trees, mountains everywhere, it's like paradise. And I do like your cabin. You said it was a mess, you liar."

"I need to make a confession," Ranger McIntyre said, taking a cautious sip of hot coffee. "It was a mess. That note I found, it was from Charlene. It seems that she and Mari and Dottie drove up here and cleaned the place for me. Or for you, more likely. They didn't want you to see it the way it was."

"Nice ladies," Vi said. "They must like you a lot."

"I like them, too," he said. "They're 'good people' as my dad used to say. But I was wondering how they got up here? Claude has the family car and won't be back for a week or more. I bet it was Dottie. She's got that Dodge sedan she drives."

"No matter how they got here, they did a very nice thing for you. C'mon, finish your sandwich and let's start organizing all our notes, determine exactly what it is we need to figure out, then perhaps rustle up supper. Maybe you've got a can of beans or the makings for stew?"

McIntyre had been assuming that he would drive her back to the Pioneer after they had discussed the two mine site murders. Now it began to sound as though she assumed she was going to stay until supper. Or maybe long after supper. Unbidden, his thoughts went drifting in through the open cabin door and seemed to hover over the chenille bedspread. Another question, however, abruptly pulled his mind back toward the investigation.

She drives a sedan, his brain was whispering. And *I'll drive her to the Pioneer. Drove up here.*

"How did Monde get to the mine?" McIntyre blurted.

"Pardon?" Vi said.

"How did Charles Monde get to the old mine at Big Horse Park? I don't recall the sheriff or anybody saying anything about a car. Logically he would have driven a car up the Lantern Creek road, like you and Agent Canilly did, and hiked over the hill to the mine. If he had a car, what the heck happened to it? If he didn't have one, then a second person must have driven him there. Except . . . who would drive him all the way from Boulder or Denver, then drop him off and drive away again? Doesn't make sense. Vi, this might be a key piece. First thing tomorrow morning, let's find out whether the kid had a car or not."

Vi Coteau had paused with a dill pickle spear halfway to her perfect red lips. "That's the *first* thing you want to do in the morning?" she asked. Her remark went unanswered: Ranger McIntyre barely had time to let it sink into his brain when the telephone rang. He went into the cabin and sat down at his desk.

"Fall River Station," he said. "Ranger McIntyre speaking."

"McIntyre. Agent Canilly. You got my secretary up there?"

"She's sitting on the porch. Hang on a minute and I'll bring her to the phone."

"No need. Listen, McIntyre. Mr. Leup has been riding my back pretty hard. It seems that son Richard is becoming a basket case over this. One minute he says he's to blame, the next minute he says he'll be their next victim, and so on and so forth. I keep telling Leup it's not a federal case but he keeps on phoning me to find out if we've made any progress. Problem is, there's been a couple of new cases crop up—and they are federal—and I need Vi back here. Now."

"Sure," McIntyre said. "We've just finished lunch. I need to stop in town for gas, then I can drive her to Denver."

"I'll save you a few hours," Canilly said. "As it happens, I need to drive north to Longmont and pick up a package of evidence from the local police chief. You know Longmont? Know where the jail is, on the outskirts of town?"

"Yes."

"Why don't you two start in the next ten minutes or so and

we'll rendezvous at the Longmont jail. Vi can ride back to Denver with me."

"Sounds good," McIntyre said. "We'll need to stop in town for her to grab her suitcase and things. Listen, while I have you on the phone, let me tell you an idea I had about Charles Monde. If he had a car . . ."

"No time," Canilly said. "I'm in a rush. You tell Vi about it, she'll tell me. Meet me in Longmont. Then you can go back to working on the Leup case, provided you still want to help. I'd appreciate it if you could manage to calm him down. He and young Richard. Both Leups are more nervous than if they'd killed those two boys themselves. I'll see you in Longmont."

McIntyre's little pickup truck purred steadily along, taking the curves gently and refusing the urge to "open up" on the straight stretches. The ranger liked driving the highway that led down to the foothills and through the foothills out onto the farming lands of the high prairie. It was a pleasant drive, a scenic drive where a man might stop anywhere along the way to take a photo or toss a rock into the river, maybe wet a fly line. In the lazy autumn days after the tourists had all gone home, it seemed almost like being a tourist himself to take the road to Longmont. The only blot on the picture on this particular autumn afternoon was an unshakable awareness of Vi Coteau riding next to him and of her small suitcase lying in the truck bed behind them.

After one of those long silences that writers like to call "awkward," she finally spoke.

"I'm sorry," she said. "I was looking forward to our evening."

"Me, too," McIntyre replied.

"Although it might have become . . . well, you know," she said. "I mean you, me, the cozy cabin. Yes?"

"Oh, believe me, I know what you mean," he said. "Lead us

not into temptation and all of that."

"McIntyre?"

"Yes?" He kept his eyes on the road.

"You need to know that I think I understand," she said. "I can feel the way you hesitate when you're with me. You hold back. You make jokes just when things are beginning to look serious. I have to tell you, Tim, there are certain girls who could find it darn annoying, the way you have to crack wise when she's feeling romantic."

"Yes," he said, making a downshift to negotiate the curve in the road ahead. "Matter of fact, there's been couple of them who have. Found me annoying, I mean."

"I talked to Dottie. And I talked to Charlene, too. They told me about your lady friend and about the car wreck. Don't be angry with them. I was the one who asked. I more or less insisted. They told me the story."

"Most everybody in town knows the story, I guess," he said.

"It must have been horrible," Vi said, putting a hand on his arm. "Losing her like that. I can see why you might not want to . . ."

"I think 'be involved again' is the polite phrase they use nowadays," he said. The road straightened and he pushed in the clutch and pulled the shift lever into fourth.

"Involved" was the word, all right. Newspapers used it frequently during the war, saying "Troop A Artillery Battery was yesterday involved in an artillery duel with a German artillery position" instead of saying "twelve unlucky doughboys with torn eardrums frantically wrestled with explosive shells in the filthy mud while waiting without breathing for a German round to hit their position and blow them all to Hell." *Involved*, they called it.

McIntyre liked this woman who was riding beside him. He liked her a lot. He felt a need to be with her, needed her bright eyes flashing at him, needed the way she could seem ready to smile even when her lips were in a straight line and her brow was trying to frown. He needed her to work a jigsaw with him or watch him while he caught a few trout for supper. He needed her to sniff the air and send him outside to finish cleaning Brownie's droppings off his boot. At the same time, however, he wanted to be alone. Not to let his emotions wallow in the loss of the one real love he had known and had lost, not to become a self-pitying hermit. For a while he just wanted to be alone.

"Could probably blame the tourists," he said. "Heck, we blame them for everything else!"

"What are you talking about?" she asked.

"Not wanting to be involved. For feeling that urge to merge, like the youngsters say. I'll tell you how I think the tourists might have an effect on local love life. Up in the park, see, we spend three months doing nothing but herding tourists, seeing tourists, worrying about tourists, talking to tourists, getting ready for them or getting over them. We don't feel that we have any personal time at all. Even if you take time off to do a little fishing, you're likely to run into a family of tourists having a picnic next to your favorite fishing spot."

"And?"

"September finally comes and they all go home. One fine morning the roads look deserted, the various resort cabins are empty. Everything's quiet again. You look around and say 'now, what was I doing before they came?' and you experience a kind of euphoria from realizing your life is private again. Nobody asking anything of you! And then . . . you could ask Jamie Ogg to verify this from personal experience . . . you walk into the local café and there's this girl you know? She looks a lot prettier than you remember and it's like you're seeing her for the first time. And you realize she's not a tourist girl who's merely passing through. It's a relief to see somebody who isn't demanding your attention. You start a conversation about how nice it is to have the season over with and before you know it, you're asking her out and you're becoming involved. Without three months of tourist pressure, you'd have never noticed her."

"Ranger McIntyre," Vi said, "I don't know whether you've made me feel better, or worse. In any case, I think I like you."

"I think I like you, too," McIntyre said with a smile. "But look who's waiting for us!"

They had reached the outskirts of Longmont. There was little to see of the place and even less to recommend it: a dusty grain elevator rose on one side of the road, surrounded by the summer's crop of weeds, and on the other side of the road a square two-story brick building overlooked an acre of scrap metal and a railroad siding. The one lonely freight car sitting on the siding looked almost resentful at having been left there.

The sign on the brick building announced that it was the jail, which was redundant information given the fact that every window featured heavy steel bars and two police cars were parked at the hitching rail. Agent Canilly was sitting on the fender of his own car, smoking his pipe and watching McIntyre's little pickup as it pulled into the parking area and stopped.

"Small Delights?" he said, smiling while he opened the pickup door for Vi to alight. "Are you bragging, Ranger, or just advertising?"

"You know something, Agent Canilly?" McIntyre replied as he climbed out of the truck. "You need to cure your habit of always assuming I'm in a good mood and won't mind being joshed. One of these days I might not be."

"Any man who can spend time with Miss Coteau and not be in a good mood probably needs his head examined."

"I'll put it on my list of things to do," the ranger said.

The three of them lingered long enough to exchange information and ideas about the two murders. There seemed to be no doubt but that they were done by the same killer. Or killers. The FBI agent repeated several times that Mr. Leup was making life miserable with constant phone calls and offers of help, including hiring private detectives. One benefit of being wealthy and influential, apparently, was that he could manage to hold off the newspapers. Thus far, no reporter had turned the two killings into a sensational fright story. McIntyre assured Canilly that he was still following the trail.

"Don't care much for working in the city," the ranger said, "but I'll drive over to talk to the librarian and see whether I can find any fraternity friends of the two boys. Might help me see the whole picture better."

When it was time for them to go, Vi Coteau wordlessly held out her gloved hand for the keys to the FBI sedan. The way Agent Canilly surrendered them suggested that it was she who generally did the driving. McIntyre didn't envy the agent: he had ridden in Vi's overpowered six-cylinder Marmon coupe and while she was an excellent driver, the lady had a very heavy foot. McIntyre said goodbye and closed her door for her, cutting off his view of her perfectly proportioned ankle and calf, and with a final smile and wave of her hand she was away again and he was again alone.

Walking back to his pickup, Ranger McIntyre looked at the scrap metal yard behind the jail building and had an inspired idea. A logical idea. An idea good enough to almost erase the sight of that ankle and silk stocking from his mind.

He drove through the gate and stopped at a corrugated tin shack where a hand-lettered sign saying "OFFICE" seemed not only overly grandiose but overly optimistic as well. The ranger mentally braced himself for another of those monosyllabic conversations with a grumpy individual, the kind who usually took the salutation "how are you?" as a rude invasion of privacy. McIntyre knew these people. He worked with them nearly every day, laborers who may have seen a poacher, loggers who just drove trucks and minded their own business, merchants who apparently didn't want to sell anything. It would probably take over an hour of careful talking before the junk dealer would open up and tell him anything useful.

This particular junk dealer, however, came as a surprise. Overalls, as expected. A hat older than its owner and looking as though it had been much abused through its long life. Nothing unusual about the overalls or hat. However, the hair escaping from under that oil-stained relic was bright red and curly and the eyes that looked out from under the hat brim were the blue of Irish forget-me-nots. Tiny light brown freckles speckled her nose and cheeks. When she spoke, her voice had the soft accents of the British Isles.

"Good afternoon, sir," she said. "And how is it with you this nice day?"

She leaned to look around the ranger at his parked truck outside, then looked back at him with a quizzical expression. As for McIntyre, he was still trying to find his voice, or any voice, for the occasion.

"Looking to sell scrap, are you?" she went on. "Or perhaps you're in need of a particular item, a bit of angle iron or a steel post for your gate?"

McIntyre read a great many cheap novels during his long winter nights at the cabin. In more than one story there was a poor soul who had been captured by the enemy and was being injected with truth serum to make him reveal secret information. Those bright blue eyes were having the same effect on him. Where he had prepared a number of reasons to be asking after the scavenger of Big Horse Park, he now heard himself blurting out the truth. His fingers finally found one of his cards in his coat pocket and he handed it to her.

"National Park Service," he said.

"I see," she said sweetly, reading the card. "Ranger T. G. Mc-Intyre, it says. How may I help you?"

"I was just passing by . . . that is, I was driving a lady to meet a gentleman . . . anyway, I happened to notice your establishment."

"Rather hard not to!" she said with a laugh.

"Yes. As I said, I wondered whether a certain person had sold you metal scrap recently, probably bits of old iron from mining operations."

McIntyre went on to describe the man, including his prominent hawklike nose and gruff demeanor.

"Of course!" she said. "I remember him well. He had eighty or ninety pounds of metal of various description. But you know what? Just between you and me, I think his growly mean attitude was a bunch of guff. I think he was putting it on."

"What sort of metal?" McIntyre asked. "Maybe a very thick rod from a hammer mill?"

"I really couldn't say, Ranger. We do pay a little extra money for usable pieces such as steel fence posts and girders and angle iron, provided they are not bent or rusty. Otherwise a seller drives onto our scale behind the shed and then drives to the railroad siding where he dumps his load into the railcar. Then we weigh the empty vehicle and pay the driver accordingly."

"He had a vehicle?"

"Yes, of course. An automobile. A coupe with rumble seat. Older looking, but not all that old. What I remember is that he had apparently removed the seat cushions from the rumble seat and carried his scrap there."

"Odd," McIntyre mused.

"That's what I thought," she agreed.

"No, it's not odd that he hauled junk in a coupe. It's that he offered to buy my truck. Almost insisted on it. Not many days ago. If he had a car, why would he want my pickup?"

"Perhaps he liked the sign on your door. What's 'Small Delights' in reference to, anyway?"

"A long story," McIntyre said. "I wonder if he was bluffing? Maybe he did have a car but wanted me to think he didn't, wanted me to think he needed one. Now I'm wishing I had pressured him about it."

"One moment," she said. She slid a window open and called out the name "Joe." Within the space of two minutes, Joe was standing face to face with the ranger. He looked exactly like the man McIntyre had expected to see when he first walked in.

"Joe," she said, "didn't that fellow with the long sharp nose tell you about his car? You remember. He was here less than a week ago, I think."

"Yeah," Joe replied. "Tore out the back seat, he did. To haul junk."

Joe kept a suspicious eye on McIntyre as if he expected the stranger to ask him personal questions, such as "how are you?" or "nice day, isn't it?"

"He didn't happen to say where he got this car?" McIntyre asked.

"Lemme think. Yeah, manner of fact, he did. I ast did he have it long and he tol' me yeah not long and I said did you get a good deal on it. You know, jus' makin' conversation?"

"And?"

"And he says he got it off'n a college kid. Says there was this kid lookin' to sell his car and wanted sixty bucks for it but the guy with the nose, he talks him down to forty bucks an' a jug of good 'shine."

"Moonshine," McIntyre suggested.

"Didn't hear it from me," Joe said.

"Just barely," McIntyre agreed.

Ranger McIntyre was smiling as he drove back along the highway that would return him to the mountains. A while ago he had been ready to drop the entire matter. Vi Coteau was right in thinking that his memories of she who had died would always keep the two of them from a more serious involvement, and the realization had depressed him to the point that he didn't want to see Vi again, not for a little while at least. All the various scattered puzzle pieces about the murders had taken on a trivial feeling, too. But Mumbling Joe and the girl with the sparkle in her Irish blue eyes had acted like a good shot of Scotch whiskey on his brain.

Here was where a couple of puzzle pieces did snap into place, maybe. Charles Monde receives a message that he should drive to the Big Horse Mine site. He parks his car at the end of the Lantern Creek road. He walks up to the mine and whoever is waiting for him knocks him out, puts him under the hammer mill, and lowers the heavy rod to crush his chest. Later on, the scrap collector with the noticeable nose finds Charles Monde's car and makes off with it and that's why nobody found out how Charles got to the Big Horse.

McIntyre knew his next step. On the following day he would phone the sheriff and find out if Charles Monde had forty dollars in his pocket when he died. Also, if he had told anyone he wanted to sell his car. If the sheriff didn't have the answers, they might be found at the fraternity house. The ranger might soon be going back to college.

CHAPTER EIGHT:
McINTYRE ON CAMPUS

Slowly softening and losing its shape, pale yellow, the pat of butter melted. For a minute more McIntyre only watched as it slumped and began to spread; then, unable to deny his hunger any longer, he lifted the edge of the top pancake and used his table knife to distribute the butter to the rest of the stack. He would need to pour the warm syrup carefully to keep it away from the bacon strips, although he wouldn't mind if a little syrup were to flow onto the crispy edges of the fried eggs.

"Everything right?" Charlene asked.

"Perfect," he replied. "Thanks again. For everything." He had already thanked Charlene, multiple times, for engineering the miraculous transformation of his cabin.

He cut a little wedge of pancake and forked it into his mouth and marveled again at how the cabin renovation happened. He had only shared a concern with her, a simple small problem, and it was enough to prompt three ladies—three friends—to spend two days dusting and scrubbing and organizing his quarters. He couldn't get over the fact that they had done it. Their gesture stayed so much on his mind that it even entered into his preoccupation with the murder case. Maybe there was a similarity in what happened. Why not? Perhaps a small comment, a casual mention of the Dunraven Hoard legend prompted both boys to visit the mines where they met with death? It could have been as simple as a dropped hint. Maybe more than a hint. Maybe each victim was told if he went to the mine, alone, he would find something that would be a surprise to the other boys. An offhand remark, then death.

When Mari came to his table with more coffee, she had a fluffy-looking imitation insect in her hand.

"What do you think?" Mari said as she filled his coffee mug. "I'm learning to tie flies. Pretty good, huh?"

McIntyre picked it up and examined it. He couldn't tell exactly what kind of pattern it was supposed to be, but with a bit of trimming it might catch a trout.

"Not bad," he said. "You have an eye for it, I can see that. Now, if it was me . . ."

"Yes?"

"I'd take my scissors and shape the wings a little. Insect wings tend to be rounded smooth at the ends. While I was at it, I think I'd trim the tail. Leave about half as many barbs sticking out."

Mari agreed, and thanked him, and carefully tucked her creation into the pocket of her pinafore.

A dry fly. A few tiny feathers lashed around a steel hook. McIntyre's mind escaped from the inn, soaring out beyond the village and up a certain valley where it came to rest beside a familiar and quiet stretch of river. It was a stretch of water where the pan-sized brook trout rose to catch insects all the day long and where heavy, muscular rainbow trout could be enticed out of the shady depths. How odd the mind is, he thought, that the sight of a tiny hook wrapped with thread and feather can send it traveling. Like that darn Irish penny. Maybe to a treasure hunter a single glance at an antique coin like that would be enough to send him searching for more. Like a prospector catching "gold fever" from a single nugget.

When he went to the desk to pay his bill, Charlene asked what he had planned for the day.

"Not much," he replied. He was still thinking about fishing.

"I guess I'll drive down to Boulder and see if I can find the frat house where those two boys lived. I want to know about Monde's car."

"You can't ask his family?"

"Mr. Leup wants me to wait. He says the Mondes are in shell shock over how it happened. Anyway, I want to stop in at the college library and see if maybe the boys had asked for any particular books lately. I don't know what made them want to poke around those old mines, but it might have been a book. Maybe a local history or a journal, with a map or photograph. A clue to the location of the Dunraven Hoard."

"And you wouldn't mind finding that hoard yourself, right? You could be rich and handsome and single?" Charlene said, smiling deliberately at him over her shoulder like a flirty showgirl.

"Don't tell anybody I said anything," McIntyre said, "but I think maybe I already know where it is. But I don't think it's gold or cash. I'm not sure what it could be."

The ranger parked his truck on a side street where it would be less conspicuous and began strolling along Fraternity Row, trying his best to look nonchalant while feigning a visitor's interest in the various examples of exaggerated architecture. Each fraternity house seemed to be an oversized copy of this or that. Two of them were supposed to resemble the Greek Parthenon, if the Parthenon had been fitted out with bedroom windows and patio furniture. Two other houses were evidently supposed to look like English castles with recessed doorways that suggested drawbridges. The tall turrets seemed to have no particular function at all.

Halfway down the second block, he found the one he was looking for. This fraternity house was smaller, less ostentatious, but not by much. The architect had taken an English country cottage as his model, enlarging it beyond all reason. Some landscaper had taken pity on the house and encouraged draperies of ivy to cover the artificial leaded windows and the nonfunctional shutters. What informed McIntyre that this was the right place was the heavy black crepe framing the front door and the black wreath hanging from the knocker.

The young man who answered the door was evidently an inferior member, a plebe of such low standing that, while he was empowered to open the door to visitors, he was not allowed to answer any questions. Instead he left McIntyre standing in the foyer and hurried to find "an upperclassman" for him. McIntyre waited, bracing himself for a meeting with a typical glib, spoiled, self-important college boy who would probably dismiss his questions with haughty condescension.

The fraternity brother who actually came along the hallway to offer McIntyre a handshake was none of that. "Bruce Jones," he said. He was older than most college boys. His clean haircut and general posture, not to mention a certain look of age in the eyes, told McIntyre that he was in the presence of a fellow veteran, probably one of the many young men who came back from the war to enroll in college.

"Tim McIntyre," the ranger said, "formerly of the Second Aero Squadron."

"Fifteenth Field Artillery," Jones replied. "Officer?"

"Captain," McIntyre replied. "You?"

"Sergeant. What can I do for you?"

Jones led McIntyre to an oversized lounge where a number of oversized couches and club chairs were arranged in oversized groups as if fraternity members were expected to march into the room after supper and sit in mature conversation. He and the ranger took the nearest chairs.

"Now then," Jones said.

"It's about the two boys who died. Winston Dole and Charles

Monde? I've been asked to find out what I can about the two incidents."

"As a reporter? Private eye?"

"No. Just a park ranger with vacation time. Rocky Mountain National Park. A friend of a friend introduced me to Mr. William Leup, who thought I could be helpful in figuring out exactly what happened."

"Lots of the boys would like to know that," Jones said. "However, I'm surprised Mr. Leup would care. Richard's father had little use for either Winston or Charles. As a matter of fact, at the end of the last school year, he offered to make a sizable donation to the house if I could manage to separate the two of them from his son. Apparently, he didn't think they came from the right families. But I guess that's neither here nor there. What did you need to know?"

"I'll start with my easiest question first," McIntyre said. "Did Charles Monde own a car?"

"Yes. A Franklin coupe. I think he was looking to sell it, though. Couldn't afford to keep it. He and Winston both were just barely scraping by, you know. Personally, I think maybe young Richard Leup was helping them out with money from time to time. Richard's father would not have liked that. At all."

"Okay," McIntyre said. "Now a tougher question. Have you heard any of the boys say what Charles and Winston were doing up there at the abandoned mine sites? It looks like they skipped class to do it."

"No surprise there. These young kids, they don't care about attendance. They're here to meet girls and have fun and if they squeak by with average grades, fine. From what I gather, talking to the other boys, the three of them received a message from the Denver library and decided to go down there. A phone message. The next day—like you said, it was a day they were supposed to be in class—they took off for the mountains. And that's when Richard and Charles lost track of Winston, the poor kid. He was found dead. Stuck in an abandoned mining bucket."

"Any mention of treasure hunting?"

"You mean the Dunraven Hoard. Sure. They talked to several boys about it that evening when they came back from Denver. Even after Winston died, Richard and Charles were still bent on locating it. Lots of chatter about 'finding it for Winston's family' and 'finish what Winston started' and all that kind of stuff. They sounded like one of those phony war movies where the Yank charges into a Hun position to avenge his buddy."

It seemed to McIntyre that the edges of these new pieces were matching up into a picture that he didn't like. After some careful consideration to decide whether it was the right thing to do, he shared his concern with Jones.

"I had the same thought," the fraternity secretary agreed. "Each kid's family thinks he met with a fatal accident while hunting for treasure. But when you assemble the details it almost looks deliberate. As if they were lured into the mountains to be killed. Or to have the hell frightened out of them, at least."

"Who do you think would do that?" McIntyre asked. "And why?"

"No idea. Mind you, Charles and Winston—and Richard— were not universally liked. No sir. They enjoyed playing the bully too much. From what I understand, it began in high school. There was another boy, no longer at college, who lived here and actually lived in physical dread of those three. He'd been in secondary school with them and said they were a three-boy gang who bullied everyone. You probably know the kind of thing? Stealing lunch buckets, punching skinny kids on the arm, knocking their books to the floor, catching them in the boy's restroom and stealing their pants, maybe locking them in a closet or a locker. It didn't stop after high school, either. After becoming college upperclassmen, they got their jollies by tormenting the new pledges. Nobody stopped them. Not even the new pledges, because that's what new pledges expect. Part of the rite of passage, etcetera."

"This boy," McIntyre said. "Any idea what happened to him? You say he dropped out?"

"That's what I heard. Sophomore year. He was a pledge candidate. Several houses had him on their list of possible members. I think he found out, though, that Richard and Charles and Winston were members and he withdrew his application. If you ask me? I think he was just plain terrified of them. I don't really know who he was. I wasn't secretary at the time, see? I think I heard one boy—maybe it was Winston—refer to him as 'Beeky' or 'Becky' or something like that. A nickname."

"Part of his name, maybe?"

"Maybe. Or maybe because he looked kind of birdlike. I remember him as having a skinny face and kind of a hooked nose. Bad complexion. You had to feel sorry for him."

"But there's no way to find out his name?" McIntyre asked.

"I don't know what it would be. Unless a clerk at the registrar's office or maybe the college library would remember him. You know, a person who'd have a reason to write his name down. We probably put his name on a list of potential pledges here at the house, but we wouldn't have kept the list. Usually when we talked about applicants or 'possibles' we just called them 'that kid with the yellow necktie' or 'the one with thick glasses' or 'the mustache.' Things like that. I think we called him 'the skinny one' or 'beanpole.' I seem to remember Winston or Charles, or maybe both of them, calling him 'Beeky' or 'Becky.'"

Ranger McIntyre loitered near the front desk of the university library, trying to look as though he was waiting for a friend to meet him. In actuality, he was watching the library staff as they came and went, waiting for the right one to show up. Before long his vigil was rewarded. The librarian who came to relieve the young lady beneath the INFORMATION sign was a man of mature years who had a sparkle in his eyes and a bit of a smile to his mouth. Once behind the information desk he rearranged the ink stand, the pen holders, the brochures, and the books to suit himself and then looked around brightly as if to say "who can I help?"

A methodical man, a person interested in details. A man interested in people.

McIntyre walked up to the desk and came directly to the point. He had been assigned to investigate the two deaths. The librarian had read the sad news; he agreed with the ranger that someone needed to look into the matter.

McIntyre had two questions. First, did the librarian remember a thin, nervous student nicknamed "Beeky," and second, had the unfortunate deceased boys—or a student named Richard Leup—ever asked about books or reference materials related to the legend of Dunraven's Hoard. He took out one of his calling cards and handed it to the librarian, who accepted it, carefully wrote the date on it, and put it into his coat pocket.

"We don't usually disclose what other patrons have come to the library for," he said. "Especially at a university where a researcher or professor might be working on a project that could be compromised by publicity. Seeing that you mentioned young Mr. Leup, however, I'll help you in rather general terms. There is another boy at the school. He and I have become acquainted since he comes to me for assistance on a weekly basis. An excellent, inquisitive mind, you see. He was enrolled in the same history class as Richard. Unlike Richard, this young man worked hard, did his work on time, earned good grades. Richard Leup evidently saw him as a rival in the history class. Richard learned that—this other boy—was preparing a paper concerning Machiavelli. And what did Richard do? He came in and checked out all the most important books about Machiavelli. The other boy missed the deadline for handing in his paper. A dirty trick."

"In view of the fact that these two boys are dead . . ." McIntyre suggested.

"Yes. I understand. Your second question. I can tell you that those two unfortunate young men did appear to have taken an interest in local history books and asked if I knew of any books that mentioned the English Hotel in particular. I referred them to the Special Collections area where I am told that they examined various handwritten journals and diaries. You might ask the Special Collections librarian, but I doubt whether he will be willing to disclose what you want to know. The hours are nine o'clock to noon daily. I do happen to know that most of the primary research material concerning Lord Dunraven and the English Hotel is to be found at the Denver Public Library."

McIntyre looked at his watch. He had missed the Special Collection hours and now he was in imminent danger of missing lunch.

"Interesting you would mention Beeky," the librarian continued. "Interesting, I mean, in light of the fact that he was another victim of bullying by the aforementioned deceased students and Richard Leup."

"And how do you know this?" McIntyre asked.

"He worked here, until he dropped out of the university. He had a student assistant job, shelving books, preparing index cards, copying checkout records, the usual clerking chores. He often seemed sad or moody. A couple of times he spoke to me about his problems."

"Can you tell me . . . about his problems?" McIntyre said.

"Oh, I suppose it would be all right. An old, old story, really. His father wanted him to become an engineer. Well, fully half our students are here to become engineers of one sort or another. His father wanted him to be an engineer and join a fraternity and try out for one of the athletic teams. Become a 'real collegiate' in other words. Unfortunately, Beeky is a small-ish lad, quite thin. I believe he was sickly as well. I seem to remember that he was excused from physical education class. He was extremely shy and therefore a tempting target for bullies. He couldn't find the courage to try out for any kind of sport and when he signed up to pledge a fraternity he was razzed and abused to the point of tears. It was awful. Just awful."

"That's too bad," McIntyre said.

"Very bad," the librarian agreed. "However, he did realize a certain amount of happiness in working for the library. He began to read books about librarianship. He read Miss Kroeger's guide to reference books, cover to cover. When last I saw Beeky, he had secured a job with the Denver Public Library. I only heard of him once more, and that was the day when his father came to campus in a high dudgeon indeed. A rage, one might say. The father came here and ranted at myself and the head librarian for 'corrupting' his boy. He visited the dean of the Engineering College and accused him of not doing enough to encourage Beeky to stay with engineering. He went as far as to threaten the president of the Greek fraternity coalition. Between you and me, I sympathized with him. The bullying was extreme and should not have been allowed to happen. To anyone. Oh, I tell you, it was a very awkward time for us all."

"Can you tell me his name? The one you call 'Beeky' I mean."

"Let me think. Odd, isn't it? I can tell you the name of virtually any author of any book in our stacks, yet at times I can't remember the name of my own butcher. It had to do with his nickname. Beekman? What's the name of that chewing gum that starts with the letter B?"

"Black Jack?" McIntyre suggested. "Bazooka?"

"Beemans!" the librarian said triumphantly. He immediately glanced around to see if his outburst had disturbed any patrons. "Beeky Beeman," he repeated in a whisper. "Sounded like that. I do recall associating it with that chewing gum."

McIntyre thanked him and left the library building in search of lunch. The problem with lunching on a university campus is that it's difficult to find a place where eating is considered relaxing. With textbooks propped up against napkin dispensers and students eyeing their wristwatches between each mouthful of food, your typical campus lunchroom was a living example of the difference between "dining" and "feeding." The other problem with a campus is that there's no trout stream where a man could engage in productive thinking.

It was nearly two o'clock when McIntyre wiped his lips with the paper napkin, swallowed the last of his root beer, wadded up the waxed paper from his ham sandwich, and then carried his tin tray to the dishwashing window. There wasn't time to drive all the way to Denver. He might as well climb into his truck and go home. Maybe there would be enough daylight left to do a few minutes of fly fishing, even if fishing season had closed. A man had his needs, after all.

Bullying Beeky Beeman, he thought as he drove along the Foothills Road. *So we can add one more motive for murder to our list. Thus far we've got greed and jealousy, a hermit protecting his territory—or protecting something we don't know about—simple homicidal insanity, rivalry between people looking for Dunraven's Hoard, and now the idea of taking revenge on bullies. Seems like the only missing motive is sex.*

CHAPTER NINE:
ONE MORE GOLD MINE

"No, no! No!"

Richard Leup's outburst made McIntyre hold the telephone earpiece at arm's length. The ranger had thought that phoning young Leup might tell him something, something he could mull over in his mind while dropping off to sleep. Now he was thinking that the phone call would only leave him with an earache.

"I've told everybody, my father, you, that sheriff, that FBI woman!" Richard shouted. "I don't know who is after me! I don't know! All I know is that two of my friends are dead, dead! You hear me?"

Hard not to, McIntyre thought. The whole forest probably heard him.

"I was just thinking . . ." he began.

"I don't know!" Richard shouted again. "I only know that I'm afraid. I'm keeping a gun with me all the time now."

"Richard, listen to me," McIntyre persisted. "This attacker, whoever killed your friends, could it be a boy you and Winston and Charles might have bullied in school? Your dad wants this solved and that's one of my theories. Maybe a kid you picked on has gone crazy and is getting even with you and your friends. It's darn macabre, if that's the case, but I've got to ask."

"Look, Ranger," Richard said loudly, and with the tone of an adult explaining to a three-year-old, "what about the gruesome details? Dole being found in that old iron bucket and poor Charlie under that rock crusher thing? I don't like to think about it but it obviously took a man who was pretty darn strong and fit to do that to them, yeah? Sure, we picked on lots of boys, but all of them skinny little wimps. That's the fun of it. The kind who take it and don't fight back, 'cause they don't want to make trouble. And where's the harm in de-pantsing a sissy in the boy's restroom or maybe canning him once in a while for fun? No, it can't be revenge. I tell you what, and you'd better keep it secret if you know what's good for you: the three of us found proof that there's a hidden treasure in one of those mines up there. My friends went to check the clues we found. See? And that maniac caught them and tortured them to make them tell what they knew. Except Charlie and Winston didn't spill the beans, see, or else whoever it was would've dug up the treasure by now."

McIntyre looked at his watch. These long-distance minutes were adding up, even at night rates.

"How do you know?" he asked. "I mean, maybe it is gone and you don't know it."

There was a long silence as the logic of it sunk in. McIntyre changed the subject.

"One more question before I hang up. Did your friend sell his car to that hermit up there, the guy who collects scrap metal?"

"I don't know. Maybe. I know he wanted to sell it. Needed tuition money. But I hadn't talked to him, didn't even know he was driving back up there to check out a clue."

"And what clue would that be?"

"I told my father, and I'll tell you. My friends are dead because of that treasure, and I'm going to find it and give it to their families, and I'm not telling anyone any more information about it. If that's all, I'm going to bed. Good night."

"Thanks," McIntyre said. "Good night."

★ ★ ★ ★ ★

McIntyre woke the next morning to the sound of snow plop-
ping on the roof of his cabin. He could tell that it was the wet
and heavy kind of snow, the kind that piled up on the limbs of
the spruce tree and slid off in soggy globs onto the roof. Thump.
Thump. It was okay with him: he had known a snowstorm was
coming and had his truck ready for it. The little pickup was in
under the woodshed. The radiator was full of new antifreeze.
There was a full tank of gas and the new tire chains were hanging right there on the shed wall. Good boy, he said to himself.

Bravely he threw back the quilts and dashed barefoot across
the icy floor to light the stove and put a match to the kerosene
burner under the coffee pot. The kindling in the stove began
crackling and popping to life while McIntyre went into a comi-
cal dance around the cabin, trying to stay warm while pulling
on his cold pants, cold shirt, and even colder socks. He had just
wrapped a blanket around his shoulders and had stuck a larger
chunk of wood in the stove when the phone rang.

"Fall River Station," he answered, shivering. "Ranger Mc-
Intyre speaking."

"I was trying to contact the Arctic Circle ranger station."

"You got it," McIntyre replied. "Is that you, sir?"

Supervisor Nicholson's gruff-sounding voice was easy to recognize.

" 'Sir'? It's 'sir' you call me when you're on furlough and
'Nick' when you're on duty? I only wanted to know if you're
okay up there. We got a pretty good snow down here in the village. I'd say we got six, maybe eight inches. Not too cold,
though."

"It's about the same here," McIntyre said. "It's a wet snow."

"Listen," Supervisor Nicholson said, "if you're not doing
anything else this morning, why don't you stop on down to the
S.O., say about eleven. Sheriff Crowell's coming up here to see

about another matter. He'd like to have a meeting while he's here. That's if the roads aren't too bad. He might not be able to make it."

McIntyre consulted the alarm clock, which he kept on his rolltop desk rather than beside the bed where it would be too easy to shut off.

"Sure," he said. "I'll fix my breakfast, feed the horse, and head for town."

"Good," Nicholson said. "See you then."

McIntyre lit the second burner on his kerosene stove and put on a pan of water for oatmeal. Like Vi Coteau sometimes craved nonpareils, once in a while McIntyre got an irresistible craving for oatmeal. It had to be cooked right, not too mushy, not too soft, and there had to be a layer of raisins in the bottom of the bowl and a crust of brown sugar on top. And cream. Milk would suffice, but cream was the thing to have on oatmeal.

The cabin warmed quickly. He was sitting at the table enjoying his porridge and toast, with a mug of coffee, when he saw a dark green pickup truck come chugging up the Fall River road. The pickup didn't turn in at the ranger station: the driver honked his horn and waved and kept straight ahead. Jamie Ogg, the dependable assistant ranger, on his morning patrol. Good man, making an early start from the ranger barracks.

The meeting was more formal than McIntyre had expected. Supervisor Nicholson sat behind his desk in park uniform complete with necktie; Sheriff Abe Crowell sat in the heavy wooden chair facing the desk, while Dottie sat next to the desk with her steno pad at the ready. Ranger McIntyre took the other wooden chair.

"To knuckle right down to business, Tim," Nicholson said, "Abe here, he'd like for you to fill him in on this double murder thing. His own deputy examined the scenes as well as the two bodies and he turned in a detailed report, but I told him you wouldn't mind sharing what you found out."

"Sure," McIntyre said.

He took the Irish penny from his pocket and explained how he had found it, not forgetting to mention that Mr. Leup owned a collection of old coins. The ranger went through the whole series of events in detail, fitting pieces to the picture whenever possible, and ending up with his visit to the fraternity house.

"This iron scavenger," Abe said after McIntyre had finished, "he sounds fishy to me. Maybe you ought to show me on a map where you think he lives, and maybe I can send a deputy up there to talk to him. There's another thing I don't like about this deal, and it's Mr. William Leup's connection. He seems almost—I don't know—almost overly interested. They weren't his kids, is what I mean."

"I know," Supervisor Nicholson said. "I'd feel better about Mr. Leup if we knew more about why he wants to stay involved in the investigation. I'd like to find out, for instance, how well does he know the families of the victims? Is he doing all this stuff just for them? Or what else could he be up to?"

"I thought the same thing," McIntyre agreed. "He's a hard man to talk to. He likes to do all the talking. Questions seem to slide off of him."

"You think his son, Richard, might have done the killings?" Abe Crowell asked. It was a blunt question. Then again, the sheriff had never been renowned for his subtlety.

"I don't know what to think about that possibility," McIntyre confessed. "If it weren't for the idea of a treasure, and if it weren't for the fact that he seems frightened of being next on the attacker's list, I wouldn't even suspect Richard. But he seems to be overdoing it. He and his buddies 'found' this new clue and start thinking it's a huge treasure that people will kill for. He read a journal or came across a map that he won't talk about. Then he hints that 'somebody' would torture him to make him tell about it. When I spoke to him, I suggested there might be a simpler motive, that somebody with an old grudge was trying to scare him. He and his two pals were apparently quite the terrible bullies all through high school. They did the same at the frat house as soon as they became upperclassmen. I told Richard maybe he had an enemy he hadn't even thought of. But Richard sticks to his idea that the killer is after this treasure trove. Richard doesn't know how to find it, but the killer thinks he does know."

"Maybe our best course of action would be to try and find it ourselves?" Nicholson asked. "Whatever it is. Turn it over to the state and let Mr. Leup hire detectives to find the killer. Seems to me that finding it would uncomplicate matters."

"Just between you and me and the door post," McIntyre replied, "I've come up with a theory about where it is. But I don't think the hoard is the key to the puzzle. I think the key is Richard Leup and what he knows. Or thinks he knows."

Sheriff Crowell looked at McIntyre for a long moment, then at Supervisor Nicholson, then looked back at McIntyre.

"Treasure hunts and theories," Crowell said. "Dammit, my office doesn't have the budget for that kind of stuff. I've got another suggestion. That is, if you boys in green really want to keep trying to clear up this whole business. Everything is starting to point back to old documents or maps or whatever, down in the Denver library. Somebody needs to go there, talk to the librarian, find out what started those three boys off. In other words, you need to go back to where it began and follow the trail up to where it happened. I sure ain't got the time to do it, and neither do my deputies."

"But I . . ." McIntyre started to protest.

"Tim, I'm going to agree with Abe," Nicholson said. "You're the one who has the most free time. And William Leup gave you an expense account. Plus, you're the one who knows the most about the whole thing. You're the logical choice to go to the Denver library."

McIntyre protested.

"But the stuff in the library is probably all about the Dunraven Hoard," he said "Even if it's not a legend, even if it actually existed, I don't think it has a darn thing to do with the murders. I don't think it could be the motive. Like I said, I've got a theory about where it is, but why waste time looking for it? Especially in the library? It doesn't matter what the boys found out. The killer reconnoitered the May Day Mine and the Big Horse Mine, arranged the ore bucket and rigged the stamping mill, then persuaded Charles and Winston to go there. I think we need to start with the murder scenes. It's like finding a rogue bear, or even a poacher; you start at the kill site and you search around until you find the killer's trail. No, I vote for going back to the mine sites."

"Heck of a speech," Supervisor Nicholson said, smiling indulgently like a professional boxer getting ready to punch a street mugger. "I tell you what, Tim. We'll compromise. As soon as the roads are clear of snow, you go to Denver."

Abe Crowell looked surprised. "That's a compromise? What does McIntyre get in return?"

"Better not to ask," McIntyre said through clenched teeth.

And thus the matter was settled.

As Nicholson ushered them out of his office, he put his arm around McIntyre's shoulder.

"Don't feel too bad, Tim," he said. "Now that fishing season is closed for the winter, what else do you have to do?"

Nick was right: there wasn't much for a ranger on furlough to do. From the S.O., McIntyre headed to the post office where there was no mail for him and then over to Kitty's Café

("Usually Open") for a cup of coffee. Three locals were keeping three stools warm as they polished the counter with their elbows. The conversation consisted of "think it will snow again later on?" "how much did you get up your way?" "been purty dry, we can sure use the moisture," "at least it ain't that cold," and "probably be a lot of mud once this all melts." McIntyre contributed the information that the snow might drive the deer down to the lower elevations in time for hunting season, and then he, too, was out of things to talk about.

He took his time driving back to Fall River Station, half-hoping he might come upon a stranded motorist who needed help. But he was alone on the road and with the forest muffled in snow it seemed as though he was all alone in the entire valley. Once he had backed the pickup under the woodshed roof and turned off the motor, a deep clean silence took hold. The cabin was silent; the road and the meadow across the road were blanketed with snow; and they, too, were silent. Even the rippling and burbling of the stream was hushed by snow. The very thought of being inside his cabin all alone made his soul wince, so as soon as he had parked the pickup near the shed, McIntyre addressed himself to outdoor chores.

With Brownie looking on, offering neither encouragement nor criticism, he split a week's worth of firewood and kindling and carried it in armloads to the covered porch where it would be dry and handy. He took his government-issued square spade, probably a relic of the trenches of the war, and he shoveled paths in the snow. Performing his tasks gave no respite to the silence, except for his breathing as he hoisted spadeful after spadeful of snow, but there was a kind of renewal of energy in the effort, a pleasant sensation of the muscles doing work. He cleared a trail to the outhouse, another to the edge of the road, and another leading to the spring on the side of the mountain where his water came from. If the pipe froze, the pipe that brought spring water to the cabin, he would need to walk up there with a pail each day.

Having run out of places to make paths, McIntyre put a bridle on Brownie and rode bareback for an hour to let her stretch her legs. And then, except for cooking supper and laying out the pieces of a new jigsaw puzzle, he was all out of things to do. While building up the fire in the stove, he swore an oath that tomorrow, by cracky, he would not spend his entire day at the cabin. If the road to Denver was still slick and icy, he would put chains on the truck and see if he could make it all the way to the Big Horse Mine. He didn't quite know why he wanted to go there, but he couldn't shake the feeling that he hadn't finished with the place.

On the phone the next morning Dottie told him that the road to Denver was still snow-packed and icy, that several cars had been reported in the ditch. True to his oath, therefore, McIntyre put tire chains, shovel, axe, crowbar, and sandbags into the bed of the pickup and headed for the Big Horse. The "new road" leading south out of the village was icy and packed with snow: before he was halfway to Lantern Creek, McIntyre was forced to pull over and put the chains on.

When he turned off onto the Lantern Creek road, he was surprised to find recent tire tracks. Evidently a car or pickup had driven it since the snowfall—more than one vehicle, in fact. The tracks were packed down pretty good. He was even more puzzled when he got to the turnaround at the end of the road. It was where hikers parked for the trail up to Fawn Lake. The tracks of the other vehicle didn't end at the turnaround: they left the established road and headed up a fairly steep hill in the direction of a third abandoned mine, the old Betsy Mine. McIntyre was certainly not going to risk having his Small Delights pickup slide off into the trees trying to follow that other car's trail, but he was very curious about it. Might have been the metal scavenger, or that mine inspector. Or a local looking for firewood, maybe a hunter making an early start on deer season. McIntyre parked at the turnaround and hiked over the hill to the Big Horse Mine. And again, he discovered that he wasn't the first one to arrive since the snow. A man wearing heavy boots had walked around the timber frame of the rock crusher at least twice, had stopped at the tree with the arrow carved on it, and had gone into and out of the mine tunnel. McIntyre cussed himself that he hadn't thought to bring the flashlight from the cabin. The one in the glove box had a dead battery. He stomped around through the trees until he found a pitch pine stump, which he managed to kick apart. One thick piece would make an adequate torch.

The torch threw enough light on the mine supports to show fresh gouges and scars like a geologist's pick or maybe a hatchet would make. Smoke from the burning pitch made McIntyre's eyes water until he couldn't be absolutely certain, but it looked as if whoever had been there was not trying to knock the supports down or cut them or split them. It looked like somebody had hammered on them trying to find out if they were hollow.

McIntyre stayed long enough to assure himself that the water seeping through the mine tunnel really was vanishing before it reached the mouth of the mine, then hurried out into the fresh air. He walked through the snow to the edge of the tailing pile, took a long look at the thicket of chokecherry and the stand of aspen growing just over the edge, and started back down toward Lantern Creek. Those trees and bushes were getting underground water from somewhere.

He returned to his truck to eat his lunch, glad that his sandwich hadn't frozen solid. Then he decided to make the hike up to the Betsy Mine after all. Those tire tracks in the snow had him curious.

Tiny Brown stood behind the counter of his Beaver Point Store stirring a saucepan over an electric hot plate. At least that's what it looked like he was probably doing. His three-hundred-pound body tended to hide his movements, not to mention half of the merchandise shelf behind him. The stirring spoon was barely visible in his big fist.

"Cowboy chili," Tiny explained over his shoulder. "Here lately I've been getting a few of the construction guys from that Bear Lake road project. They stop in after work to eat chili and have a sandwich for the long drive home. Want a bowl?"

"Sure," McIntyre said. "That'd be just the ticket. I've been out in the cold all day, up the Lantern Creek road."

"Much snow up there?" Tiny asked.

"About the same as here. Wet, but not too deep. My truck made it to the turnaround okay. Somebody had been there ahead of me, though, and their tracks went all the way up to the Betsy Mine. In fact, that's why I stopped to see you. What do you know about that place? The history of it, I mean."

"Betsy Mine? Well, let me think. Here's your chili. Want oyster crackers with?"

"Sure."

"Betsy Mine," Tiny mused. "It goes back before the war. I think it was opened in 1902 or thereabouts and operated for maybe five years? The owner was named something like Heckendorm. In my back room, I've probably still got the newspaper article about the cave-in."

"What happened?"

"Heckendorm or Heckerdorn, he and his brother and his wife, Betsy, they worked that mine all alone. Never built a mill, according to the newspaper, but they brought out the chunks of ore and crushed them with sledgehammers, and tried to smelt it themselves. On an iron stove in the bunker, that square concrete building up there by the mine tunnel? They probably spent more money and time building that concrete bunker than they did digging for ore. But I'll say this for them, they built it strong. It's like a little fortress. Anyway, one day in 1904—March, I think it was—there was a cave-in and Betsy was killed in it. The husband moved into the bunker and people said he'd gone crazy, turned into a hermit almost overnight. I don't know whatever happened to the brother."

"This guy lived in that bunker?" McIntyre said. "My god. There's no windows, just the one door. It's a regular blockhouse, all concrete and stone, even the roof is concrete. I figured they used it for storing blasting powder."

"All I know is what Abner told me. He used to own that property but never did anything with it. There was a cabin up

Blockhouse

123

the hill, a pretty good one apparently. But Abner said Betsy's husband burned down the cabin and moved into that concrete bunker. He'd barricade himself inside at night. According to Abner, Heckendorn only had that iron stove for heat. Can you imagine trying to smelt gold on a stove? They didn't really know what they were doing."

"There's no stove in that bunker now," McIntyre said. "There's nothing in there except a busted chair and scraps of wood and a couple of dynamite boxes. Come to think of it, there is a stovepipe sticking down through the roof."

"I guess a scavenger or somebody took that iron stove away," Tiny said.

"Probably," McIntyre replied. "It's still a weird building, though. Looks to be perfectly square, all concrete and stone, no windows, and there's a pair of heavy bars that drop across the door from the inside. You could lock yourself in there and it would take a cannon to blast you out again."

Tiny watched with satisfaction as McIntyre scraped the bottom of his chili bowl and licked the spoon. It was a real pleasure to watch how the ranger's eyes seemed to be smiling with every bite he took, whether it was a bowl of soup or one of Tiny's famous sandwiches. Speaking of which, Tiny told McIntyre, it was a pleasure to have the ranger's lady friend from Denver in his store. She seemed to be a true connoisseur of egg salad sandwiches.

"So, you say somebody else drove up to the Betsy in the snow?" Tiny asked.

"Yeah. Easy to read his tracks. He drove up there, walked around the bunker, went inside it, then walked to the opening of the tunnel, took a pee in the snow, and drove back down the hill. I figure it was either that scrap metal scavenger or else the mine inspector."

"Suppose he was looking for Dunraven's famous hoard?" Tiny said.

"Maybe, sure. But according to you, that mine wasn't even there until years after Dunraven's bunch left the valley. So, it follows that the hoard couldn't be hidden there. Then again, if it was a treasure hunter, he might not know that."

The ranger paid for his chili, wished Tiny a nice evening, and drove back toward his cabin thinking that, except for that bowl of Tiny's cowboy chili, his day had pretty much been a waste of time.

CHAPTER TEN:
PERFUME, BULLIES, AND REPORTERS

The highway out to Denver was clear and dry again, although snow still lay on the farm fields like a rumpled white blanket. Traffic was sparse and McIntyre was making good time. At least the speed indicator and his wristwatch told him he was making good time; in his eagerness to see Vi Coteau again, the miles seemed to crawl. He thought he'd never top that final hill and see the skyline of the city.

He told himself—several times—that when he arrived in Denver he'd go straight to the library. He still wasn't convinced that the Dunraven Hoard had anything to do with the two murders, but both Nick Nicholson and Mister Leup had made it clear that they expected an investigation in that direction, and thus to the library he would go. And he supposed he should try to find this "Beeky" character. He didn't know why, but it seemed like he ought to do it.

What he really wanted, he confessed to himself as he drove past the city limit sign, was to find Vi Coteau in the FBI office. At Sixteenth Street the pickup's steering wheel began to twist in his hands of its own accord, like a water diviner's forked wand, and Small Delights headed for Vi's building.

"I figured it wouldn't hurt to stop here first," he explained to her. "Maybe the library doesn't open until ten, anyway. And besides that, you'll probably be busier later on in the day."

Vi Coteau rearranged the three items on her otherwise empty

desktop. Agent Canilly hadn't yet come in and they had the office to themselves. After hanging up his coat, Ranger McIntyre took the chair opposite the desk. Vi pointed to the coat tree.

"I thought you said you didn't own an overcoat," she said.

"That?" he said. "That's the one they let me keep when I got out of the army. It wears like canvas. And the sheepskin lining is just the ticket for driving on a cold winter morning. It's a really nice overcoat."

She gave him a patient smile, rather like a mother smiling at a toddler who has put his own pants on backward.

"Nice?" she said. "No, it isn't. Whoever dubbed that particular color 'olive drab' certainly knew what they were talking about. However, enough with the fashion news. When are you going to take me on another picnic?"

"It would have to be in the snow," he said.

"I don't mind. In fact, it might be fun."

"You'd have to drive up to the park."

"I don't mind. The Marmon loves to open up and race along that highway."

"Okay," he said. "I can manage to tear myself free almost any time. Maybe you could phone me when you can make it and if it looks like sunny weather, we'll just go have a snow picnic."

Before Vi could say anything further the office door opened and Agent Canilly walked in.

"So!" he said, a twinkle in his eye, "all this crime in the streets and here you two are, lollygagging and making goo-goo eyes at one another."

"That's a funny word," Vi said. " 'Lollygagging.' Sounds like choking with one of those Dum-Dums on a stick stuck in the throat. You know, gagging on a lollipop. I wonder what lollygagging means? Maybe Tim can look it up when he goes to the library."

"Oh?" Canilly said. "Going to our library? They don't have

any books in your village?"

"I'm still following the murder trail. For Mr. Leup. Don't much want to, but I said I would, so I will. Those kids who died, they showed serious interest in that collection. Maybe I can find out why. Maybe it could help explain why they were up at the mines. Plus, there's a young man who works there at the library and he knew them."

"I see," Canilly said.

"What are you two working on these days?" McIntyre asked. "Vi told me she hasn't had time to shop for hats and shoes in almost a month."

"Tragic, that's what it is," Canilly said. "Pure slavery. Mark my words, Ranger, one of these fine days, the working women of the world are going to rise up as one, throw down their steno pads, cover up their typewriters, and march through town looking at every hat in the city. As for what we're working on, well, I guess we can trust you not to spill any beans. It's smuggling. There's been a lot of smuggling activity lately, involving very high-quality liquor and airplanes."

"Airplanes?"

"That's what I said. And just to let you know, the name William Leup has come up more than once. We think he's receiving the stuff, or is in on it, but we don't have any evidence for a search. French champagne, European brandy, absinthe, that kind of thing."

"By air?"

"It's possible. It seems like Colorado's flat prairies mean a plane can land just about anywhere. That, and we're located halfway between Mexico and Canada, so it's a natural place to fly booze in from either border. And there seems to be no shortage of veteran pilots such as yourself who are looking to earn a few bucks."

Vi stood up and walked to the window. Watching Vi walk in

her snug-fitting tailored skirt and patent leather heels was enough to make a man wish he were single. And wish that he was more interesting. She cautiously bent one of the slats in the window blind and peeked out.

"Still there," she said. "Those two characters with the matching fedoras. Did you see them when you came in?"

"Sure," Canilly said. "They think they're too sly for anybody to notice, but they're about as unnoticeable as an elephant perched on a fire hydrant."

"Who are we talking about?" Ranger McIntyre asked.

He left his chair and crossed to the window. With one perfectly manicured finger Vi held the window blind for him. As he bent to look outside, he caught the scent of her gentle perfume. With that slight, nearly imperceptible suggestion of feminine fragrance, the men on the street were forgotten and for some reason McIntyre's brain filled instead with a vision of Paris, of Paris on a warm evening, a warm evening when a pretty young mademoiselle selling sprigs of lavender had pinned one to the lapel of his uniform. McIntyre shook his head as if he had been softly slapped on the ear.

"Problem?" Vi asked.

"Uh," McIntyre said. "You mean those two guys?"

"Do you see any other two?" she said.

The two were wearing matching fedoras. They were smoking cigarettes and had their hands shoved into the pockets of their overcoats while they seemed to watch the street, like men waiting for a bus or a cab to come along.

"You got a gun?" Canilly asked.

"Oh, sure," McIntyre replied. "A beauty. It's just a standard Colt .45 service revolver, but I like it."

"I mean with you," Canilly said.

"No. It's back at my cabin."

"The agent is just having fun with you, Tim," Vi said. "Those two aren't dangerous."

"That's good," he said, "because neither am I."

"What?"

"Dangerous."

She laughed and her laughter made it even harder for him to take his leave. Under all the joshing and grinning he was coming apart and needed to be out of that office. Now that he had caught it, the light hint of her perfume seemed to permeate the very air, and now that he had once again heard her lilting spontaneous laughter, he wanted to go on trying to entertain her. But he knew better. Any attempt to do so and he'd end up making himself sound stupid.

"Okay," he said, "I'll be off to the library. If I happen to meet with Mr. Leup and he's guzzling Armagnac, I'll let you know right away."

Vi looked at him with one of her perfect eyebrows raised.

"You know Armagnac?" she asked.

"And I like it, too," he said. "If I ever started lollygagging, I would hope it would be on Armagnac."

She laughed that laugh again, he said goodbye again, and this time he actually took his olive drab overcoat and headed for the door.

The two men were no longer on the street when McIntyre exited the building. As he started up his pickup truck and pulled away from the curb, however, a coupe began to follow him. It kept its distance, but after he turned toward the Civic Center and then turned another corner it was still following. When he drove into the parking area behind the Carnegie building, the coupe went on by, but he saw its brake light come on.

The young library employee dubbed "Beeky" was approximately the same age as Richard Leup, but that's where the resemblance between the two young men came to a whining halt. Beeky was thin with gangly long arms. His wrists hung out several inches from his sleeves. He wore a nondescript cotton lab coat, a long garment of dusty gray, the top button of which he kept nervously undoing and doing up again as he talked to McIntyre.

He read the calling card McIntyre had given him. He extended his hand, looking away at a spot on the floor as they shook hands. He mumbled his full name and McIntyre didn't want to further embarrass "Beeky" by asking him to repeat it. He decided to ask one of the other librarians before he left.

"I guess you're here about that English Hotel journal, huh?" Beeky asked.

"I'm interested in finding out what three college boys found out about the English Hotel, and the Dunraven Hoard. Or might have found out. Or thought they might have found out. We think something about this library made them go poking around those old mines. They were Richard Leup, Winston Dole, Charles Monde."

"I knew them."

"I guess they all belonged to the same fraternity?" McIntyre said.

"Yeah."

"And you say it might be a journal that they found?"

"Follow me," Beeky mumbled.

Beeky led McIntyre through a corridor, up a flight of stairs, and along another hallway until they came to a door marked "Special Collections." He pulled a fist-sized wad of keys from beneath his lab coat and opened the door.

The room smelled of ages-old dust mingled with the scent of damp glue. There was also, and everywhere, the antique odor of leather bindings that began drying a century ago. Shelf after shelf supported rows of venerable leather books and books in faded cloth bindings that looked as if they might turn to ash if they were touched.

Beeky vanished into the gloom of the stacks and reappeared with a quarto-sized leather journal. He took it to a table and set it down with reverential care.

"It's okay to touch it," he said. "But I gotta stay and keep an eye on it. Library rules."

"Does that mean you watched the three boys when they looked through it?"

"Mostly. But they got to picking on me, making fun of me again. I had to go out for a while. It was all right. They didn't do any damage to the journal. It's just that they always keep making fun of me whenever I'm around. They think it's funny that I ended up working here."

"Sorry," McIntyre said. "What is it we're looking at here?"

"This is a journal by one of Lord Dunraven's foremen, a man named White. If you read the first page, he intended it for his fiancée back in Ireland. He writes that the journal is for her amusement and will someday be a record of what he calls the 'American enterprise.' "

"What's it doing here?" McIntyre asked.

"When the English Hotel burned, a whole crate full of ledgers, journals, and letters was saved. Eventually it ended up here for safekeeping. I guess Dunraven's heirs back in Ireland never found out that it survived. Or else they didn't care."

Using a trick he had learned in college, McIntyre balanced the journal on its spine and slowly let the front and back covers fall open. Sure enough, the journal pages separated at a couple of places where the previous person had probably kept it open for a period of time. The librarian who had showed him this trick called it "manuscript's memory." He began reading. The handwriting in the journal was clear and precise, obviously the work of a writer thoroughly schooled in penmanship. It took only a moment for McIntyre to find the passage that had caught the attention of the college boys.

"September the Eighteenth," White wrote, "time we commenced the long journey first to New York and then, ah! Ireland. If the damned snows of these Rocky Mountains do not arrive to hamper it, hah hah, we shall make a final cartload up to the cavern tomorrow. Such a risky business but so necessary. (If I may be permitted, I should like to insert here an aside to any person who might out of curiosity happen to be perusing these pages. Be warned that our cache may not be worth the effort to discover and indeed might prove hazardous to their well-being should they succeed in finding it.) Had we not deemed it necessary to construct such heavy crates to hold the hotel treasure we might have completed the task in one fewer trip at least. Nonetheless, it will be a satisfying feeling to look back from the hotel porch on the morrow eve and reflect that all will be safe and secure until our seasonal return. Did I mention with a strong telescope, we can see the hiding location from the porch, hah hah."

"How did the frat boys happen to find this journal?" McIntyre asked.

Beeky looked down at his shoes, then looked out the window at a bird on a tree branch, then wiped an imaginary fleck of dust from the table.

"My fault," he muttered. "I'm the one who found it. I'm reading stuff in here all the time. I read right through my lunch break, even while I'm eating. I told my dad about this journal and he said 'it's that old story of the Dunraven treasure' and he said 'I bet if you found a treasure chest, then those hotshots at the university would show you a lot more respect' and stupid me, I went and blabbed to them. Well, I blabbed it to Richard one day when he came in the library looking for girls. He did that when he wasn't in school. He likes the smart-looking type of girl."

"He came all the way to Denver?" McIntyre asked.

"Richard said a girl who lives on campus is a royal pain. Always hanging around expecting to be entertained. Always keeping track of a guy. I wouldn't know."

"So what happened?"

"He was picking on me as usual and bossing me around. I wanted him to shut up so I told him that me and my dad were going to go find this Dunraven treasure. So there, I said. Our story will be in all the papers and I'll tell reporters what a crummy frat house you got. The next weekend him and Winston and Charles show up at the library and bent my arm up behind my back and made me show them that journal you're looking at. After that, they got all excited and kept rummaging through all the books and papers about Dunraven and the English Hotel. I couldn't stop them. After they left, it took me hours to put it all back again. Maybe you don't know what treasure hunters are like. It gives them a sickness. That's why they go off into the jungles and canyons and deserts and dig holes and kill themselves in all kinds of ways."

"Gold fever," McIntyre said. "Makes you wonder how many men have died looking for the Lost Dutchman, or Cibola. I'm sure sorry to hear about the bullying. I hate bullies. Your problem with those three goes clear back to grade school, or high school?"

"Yeah," Beeky said. "High school, mainly. It was their sick way of showing off. Not just showing off for girls, either, for other guys. Even back in grade school, though, they were the ones who'd talk me into sitting on one end of the teeter-totter, then when my end was 'way up in the air, they'd jump off and I'd come crashing down and bruise my butt. Or on the swings. On the swings they'd pretend to be all friendly and everything and push me, then when I got going, they'd grab the swing and make it stop so I'd fly off and land facedown in the dirt. One day I was bent over taking a drink from the fountain, the one for little kids, the one closer to the floor, when Winston came along. I thought he was going to push my face down on the spout like usual but instead he opened his fly and pissed in the basin right in front of my nose."

"Cripes," McIntyre said. "Teachers didn't put a stop to that kind of stuff?"

"Nah, why should they? I told Dad, he made a couple of complaints to the principal, and that was it."

"And it got worse in high school," McIntyre suggested.

"Yeah. Well, it got more physical. Like pulling my pants down in the hallway between classes. De-pantsing, they called it. Or the Indian burn. Ever had a boy put the Indian burn on your arm?"

"Just once," McIntyre said. "The kid who did it to me went home with two of his own teeth in his pocket."

"See, I wasn't heavy enough to do anything. Dad would get furious when I came home all bruised up. Then there was the knuckling, they called it. Two or three would hold me down and then one of them, usually Charles, would take his knuckles and grind them into my sternum as hard as he could. It'd leave a huge bruise there for weeks. Or they liked to can me."

"Can you?"

"You know, two husky guys pick up a little guy and shove him headfirst down into a trash can and leave him there? You have to kick hard enough to tip the whole thing over, so you can wiggle out backwards."

"Was that the worst thing?"

"Was that the very worst? Nah. Not even when there was old garbage and banana peels in the can. The worst was the dark place when they locked me in it. I never dared tell anybody outside the family, but I'm sorta claustrophobic. And afraid of the dark, sorta. Winston and Charles and Richard never knew that, but they got the idea of using an old empty coal cellar left over from when the school converted to fuel oil. Totally black walls from the coal. No windows. Door was thick and sheathed with tin. When they locked me in there it was like I couldn't breathe. I don't know how long I kept kicking at the door until the janitor heard me and let me out, choking on dust. Filthy place."

Beeky fell silent and McIntyre went back to reading the journal. As Beeky said, the first page showed that the journal had been the property of Lord Dunraven's ranch foreman and estate manager and was intended for his fiancée back home. The foreman owned an interest in the English Hotel, apparently, and devoted his time to managing hotel affairs.

"Barring any unforeseen event such as cave-in or landslide," White wrote, "we expect the 'goods' to remain undisturbed until our return next spring. Three of the worker lads and myself only know the hidden location and no one else can be imagined to discover it, even should they stumble across the cache, I say stumble hah hah. Riley intends to remain in Ireland next season so perhaps only one or two will be able to find the cache again besides myself. They can be trusted I am assured and am further assured by the assumption that they would have no particular use for our 'goods' other than to sell, and who in this barbaric land would have the money to pay them a sufficient price? My Lord Dunraven continues to hint that he might not leave his Adare estate next season to make the long trip into the American West, in which case, ownership defaults to the English Hotel and principally to myself. Naturally, the Lord would like to have it all back at Adare to be enjoyed but costs of shipping across the Atlantic would be more than it's worth."

That's odd, McIntyre thought. This foreman never comes

anywhere near saying that the hoard consists of cash, coin, or even gold. If it was, would he talk about "selling" it? If he thought a stranger might "stumble" across it, hah hah, did he mean literally stumble? And why wouldn't they know what it was really worth if they did stumble across it?

When he felt that he had seen all there was to see, McIntyre turned back to Beeky. Beeky looked like he had been napping. Or daydreaming, at least.

"That's all there is about a hoard, then?" McIntyre asked.

"Ten or twelve pages earlier he writes that him and his men had cut beams or timbers for a cache. I don't know what cache he was talking about. Maybe a meat cache near the hotel, maybe a powder cache where they could keep their ammunition. They shot a lot of animals up there so they must have used lots of powder."

"Timbers?" McIntyre said. "Like mine timbers? That could be a clue to think about. I might come back later and have another look, but thanks a lot. You've been a lot of help. Really. Thanks to you I think I'm starting to understand why those boys went up there to the old deserted mines. I think I'll head for home."

McIntyre thanked Beeky again and left him to reshelve the journal. He went back along the hallway and down the stairs but before he could reach the front doors of the library, he felt a hand grab his arm. The two fedora boys had been waiting for him.

"You're FBI, right?" one of them whispered loudly.

"Got a minute?" said the other one, who was holding McIntyre's arm.

"Where'd you find the truck?" the first one asked.

That settles it, McIntyre thought. *I don't often need a gun when I'm in the wilderness, but I'm going to start carrying one when I come to the city.*

They ushered him outside and around the corner of the building to a spot where the winter sun warmed the wall. The litter of cigarette butts and cigar ends showed that it was a popular spot for enjoying Denver's fresh air without freezing to death. McIntyre shook loose of their grip and turned on them.

"Want to tell me who the hell you are?" he said.

The first one reached into his coat, took out a pack of cigarettes, selected one, and stuck it between his lips.

"I'm the *Denver Record,*" he said. "That there is the *Rocky Mountain Tribune.* And you're FBI, right?"

"Newspaper reporters?" McIntyre said. "What's the idea of following me around?"

"Oughta be obvious," said the second one. "We're after the bootlegger story. What's with the Small Delights truck? Small Delights is that place where those Chicago mobsters wanted to set up their so-called mountain resort with gambling hall and speakeasy. What are you doing, posing as a mobster from Small Delights looking for a supplier? I'll tell you a fact for free, no charge: you don't look a damn thing like a mobster. You don't even look like you ever saw Chicago, let alone come from there. What's with the truck? And don't say it ain't yours because we saw you drive away in it."

"Yeah," the other one put in, "and don't say you're not FBI because we saw you go in and then that Agent Canilly went in and then you came out right quick. Like he gave you your orders and sent you on your way. What's the story, anyway?"

"Hey, Harry!" the *Record* reporter said. "I just now got it! Small Delights! I think I recognize this guy. He's outa uniform is all. This is that forest ranger, the one what shot the two gangsters at that Small Delights lodge up in the mountains! Sure, that's who he is. I wouldn't have figured it out without seein' the truck with the sign on it. What'd they do, give you the truck as a reward for killin' the gangsters? I didn't think you were FBI, that was all Harry's idea. What's the poop, Ranger? What're you doing in the Denver library? Care for a cigarette?"

McIntyre sized up the two fedora characters. He had an impulse to simply deck the both of them and walk away. But as satisfying as it might be to punch the twerps, it would probably lead to trouble. Or publicity, which, in McIntyre's book, amounted to the same thing. He could imagine the headlines: "National Park Ranger Brawls With Reporters."

"I'll make you a deal," he said. "I'll tell you what I'm doing here, and there's nothing newsworthy about it, and then you'll shut up and go away."

"Deal," said the *Tribune* man.

"Okay. Plain facts. Tourist season is over and I'm on my vacation. Two college boys got killed pretty near the park and I've been asked to take my free time and find all the facts for the families. I'm at the library talking to . . ." McIntyre stopped himself. No need to explain about Beeky ". . . a reference librarian. I want to know who owns the old mines where the boys died. But I'm in the wrong building. I need the county records office. That's it, that's all, and it's no news."

"Harry!" the *Record* man exclaimed. "The dead boys in the mountains! It's the story that guy from the *Post* is on! That rich guy, what's his name, Leup! He's involved. His son, he's in a fraternity with the dead kids. Tell us, Ranger, what was it? Gangsters killed those two boys, that the angle? What's the connection? We heard it was a couple of accidents, but you're saying there's a Chicago connection with the Small Delights caper, right? How are those two deaths connected, anyway? You going to tell us or not?"

"I'll tell you who you need to talk to," McIntyre said.

"Who?"

"You go up the Lantern Creek road and walk around until you run into a mine inspector. He knows all about dangerous places. He can describe the old mining equipment and how it can kill people if they're not careful. But you be careful, too. There's a foot of snow up there and a man could step into a hole or slip into a shaft, or maybe an old piece of mining machinery could fall on him. But you go up there and find that mine inspector; he's the man you want."

"Harry, I think the ranger is funnin' us," said the man from the *Record*.

"Yeah," said the other, "I'll bet a dime against a doughnut those death cases are some way connected. That's where the story is, right, Ranger? Ain't that right?"

"Okay," McIntyre said. "Enough's enough. You said you'd shut up and go away if I told you what I was doing."

"Yeah?"

"I told you. So shut up."

McIntyre turned his back on them and stalked away, daring them to come after him. They remained where they were, however, exchanging notes and excitedly making up a whole new drama of college murder and Chicago gangsters. The last thing he heard was one of them saying "Hey! A connection with that Small Delights lodge mob! That's it!"

Reporters usually made McIntyre think of those little German sausage dogs determined to dig a mouse out of its hole, totally intent on what they're doing right up until they hear the icebox door opening. He got into his truck and started it up, his first impulse being to go back to the FBI office to see Vi Coteau. By the time he reached the street, however, he thought better of it. It would be just like those fedora sports to follow him right into the FBI office where no doubt Vi Coteau would pick up her personal Thompson submachine gun and perforate their pocket notebooks. Better not bother her. Instead, he would hunt up a diner, have a bite to eat, and make the long drive back home.

"Damn!" said the ranger, remembering that he had wanted to ask one of the librarians for "Beeky's" full name. The name that sounded like a brand of chewing gum.

CHAPTER ELEVEN:
LOST AND FOUND

Vi Coteau's family heritage was French, but whenever she felt mischievous, there came an Irish lilt to her voice. Even over a long-distance telephone line it could be heard.

"The sun is up," she announced merrily. "Time for all good rangers to come to the aid of their chipmunks."

She hoped, being in a naughty mood, that her early morning phone call had caught Ranger McIntyre sleeping. In fact, he had already been up and outside to give Brownie her grain and let her out into the pasture for the day.

"Hold the phone a second, Miss Early Bird," he said.

He put down the earpiece long enough to take off his gloves and coat and pour a mug of coffee.

"There we go," he said, sitting down at the desk and picking up the earpiece again. "How's everything at the crack of dawn down in Denver?"

"My, my," she said. "Not only are you awake, you're alliterative. But since you asked, I'm glad the week's over with. Although we might have a new problem. Now Mr. William Leup has gone missing. His wife is very concerned, especially in view of the fact that she hasn't been able to reach Richard, either. Richard hasn't phoned home and he doesn't seem to be at college."

"Oh, oh," McIntyre said.

"That was my reaction, too. Both men missing. I tried to persuade Mrs. Leup to calm herself, then I asked her to put their butler on the phone. He told me that Mr. Leup had dressed in heavy clothes early yesterday morning, a full winter outfit, took a rucksack with food and blanket. And a gun."

"Didn't say where he was going? What kind of gun?"

"One of the pistols from his collection. The butler asked where he was going, but he didn't understand Leup's reply. The butler thinks it had to do with Mr. Leup going to a meeting or a showdown, maybe a type of confrontation. Agent Canilly's theory is that Leup drove out into the plains somewhere to rendezvous with bootleggers."

McIntyre's mind shifted into high gear and started sorting puzzle pieces. Leup had been kept up to date on the two murder cases, knew almost everything McIntyre knew. He took food, blanket, winter clothes . . . it sounded like a man who was going hunting.

"A pistol?" McIntyre asked.

"So the butler says."

Then he's not hunting deer, McIntyre thought. A pistol probably means that he's either hunting men or that he's afraid of being hunted himself. First there was Winston, then Charles, and now Richard's missing. Leup's gone to look for him. And judging from the gun and rucksack, he seems to think he's figured out who the killer is. He's just not sure where he'll find him.

"But I think I know," he found himself saying aloud.

"Know what?" Vi asked.

"Never mind. Listen, I ought to go up to the old mines again and look around some more. I've got what you might call a hunch. Anyway, I'm going up there today. Would you want to come along? Make it a kind of cold weather picnic?"

"Sure I would. Where do you want to meet?"

"You would? Oh. Well, let me think. If you can come to the Pioneer Inn . . . no, wait. It might be quicker if you drove up and met me where the Lantern Creek road takes off from the highway to Denver. Remember where that is?"

"You bet! I'll dash home, slip into my long johns and wool pants and see you there."

"I'll collect the lunch," McIntyre said.

Brownie eyed McIntyre suspiciously when he poured an extra measure of grain into her tray and propped the pasture gate open with a rock. He's doing it again, she thought. He's going to drive away in that smelly truck and leaving the loyal ranger horse all alone. But considering that there would be snow covering the wild grass and that there would be ice on watering holes in the streams, she was content to remain home with her warm stall and soft bedding.

A quick phone call to Beaver Point and Tiny flew into action packing a box with everything McIntyre would need for his winter picnic. Assuming—correctly—that the gorgeous woman who appreciated his artful egg salad would be the other person on the picnic, Tiny included extra sandwiches and extra pickles. By the time McIntyre's Small Delights pickup slid to a stop outside the store, the box was wrapped with string and ready to go. When McIntyre put his gloves on the counter and opened his overcoat for his wallet, Tiny noticed the holster strapped to the ranger's belt.

"Packing your .45 this morning," Tiny observed. "Gonna shoot rabbits?"

"I don't think so. But I might run into a scavenger before the day's over with."

"Well, don't let that lunch box freeze. There's a couple of bottles of root beer in it."

Since most of the snow had melted from the road, except in the

shaded places where it was packed hard and slick, Ranger Mc-
Intyre made good time on his way to Lantern Creek. The storm
had left a half a foot of snow, making white pillows lying along
the spruce and fir branches and leaving an unbroken blanket
over forest and meadows. It was just about the right depth for
walking. Not that McIntyre would mind if he had to use
snowshoes or skis, but he would prefer not to. Hiking through
crunchy snow, especially on a day of clear sky and sunshine,
was one of the quiet pleasures of life.

The clear roads had also allowed Vi Coteau to make good
time and she took full advantage. To Ranger McIntyre it seemed
like her overpowered Marmon convertible coupe had only two
speeds: dead stop and full throttle. He teased her that she drove
faster than his army biplane at takeoff speed.

"See?" she had said, smiling sweetly, "you just confessed to
going fifty miles per hour and on only two wheels!"

"Sure," he countered, "but that was on an airstrip, not a
parking lot."

Thanks to the way sound carries through the clean air following a snowfall, McIntyre heard the feline purr of the Marmon engine long before she came into sight. He had finished
fastening the tire chains on his pickup and was putting the
lunch and car robe into his backpack when she arrived. Not for
the first time, she arched one eyebrow at the door of his truck
where it said "Small Delights" and shook her head.

Also, not for the first time, she made him feel drab by
comparison. He was dressed in brown: brown high boots, brown
riding pants, brown and black checkered flannel shirt, brown
leather jacket. His cap with the earflaps was dark red plaid, but
that was only because he didn't own a brown one. Coteau, in
contrast, flashed out of the coupe and stood there like one of
those Sun Valley skiing posters created by overly romantic
advertising artists. The knee-high boots were maroon leather,

maybe cordovan; the ski pants snug and white, the parka a pinkish pale tint and lined in golden fur. Her maroon cap matched the boots and was a larger version of those worn by city newsboys. And if her outfit hadn't already made McIntyre feel drab, her dark sunglasses and red lipstick certainly would have.

He made a deliberate show of appraising her outfit's winter suitability as she stood there like a poster girl.

"Those pants look pretty much too tight for warmth," he said. "I thought you said on the phone that you were going to wear long johns and wool pants."

"These are just as warm as wool," she replied. "And for your information, not that it's any of your business, I am wearing long johns. Silk ones. Very warm."

Seeing that the mention of her silk underwear had rendered the ranger immobile, his imagination suffering from temporary overload, she stepped around him and tossed her backpack and hiking stick into the back of the pickup alongside his.

An earlier car or truck had already broken trail through the snow on the Lantern Creek road; McIntyre hoped it wasn't merely a hunter or a hiker headed for the same place. If he was lucky, the tracks had been left by that iron scavenger or by Mr. Leup Senior. Could be anybody: this was national forest land, after all. Anyone could drive pretty much anywhere they wanted to. It looked like there had been two, possibly three snowfalls in the past couple of days. There might be more tracks hidden under the top layer.

"What a day!" Vi said with enthusiasm. "That sky! It seems to go on forever, doesn't it? And the snow lying in the forest, all the little bushes and the grass covered up. You know, Tim? Look. Look up there. See how the snow makes it look like there are trails leading all through the forest? Every direction you look, there seems to be an open corridor. Wonderful."

"Maybe one of these days we'll take skis and have an outing," McIntyre said. "Maybe ski up that road to the lake where we had our first picnic. Lake would be frozen over, of course, but it's a beautiful park and valley. But first we need to get this other stuff straightened out. Any news about William Leup? Did he show up before you left?"

"No," she said. "Where are you taking me, anyway?"

"I know you're going to razz me about this, but it's not really a picnic. I want to drive to the Betsy Mine and thought you'd like to come along."

"We're not searching for the Leups?"

"Not deliberately, no, but my guess is that we'll find at least one of them somewhere up here."

"Do you think there's been another murder? Richard?"

"I hope not. No, while I was driving home from Denver, the Betsy Mine started nagging at my mind. I was there a couple of seasons ago—it's right on the edge of the park boundary. The Dunraven foreman wrote in his journal that with a telescope you could see the cache from the English Hotel. According to my map, you could see three mines from the English Hotel, including the Betsy. So, I want to look around. Our chance of coming across some sign of the Leups is as good as anybody's. Assuming the police are looking. Besides, the Betsy Mine's got a fantastic view. It's even on the south side of the slope so we should be able to find a warm rock to sit against. Great place to picnic."

"Golly gee, Mr. Valentino, rocks and a mine dump, too? How can a girl resist? With you I bet she'd be safe on a mountain outing since your mind is on murders and old mine tunnels."

"Sorry," he said. Had he taken his eyes off the road, he would have seen her smiling at him. Indulgently again.

"Such a romantic," she said with that little Irish lilt to her voice. "But I'm teasing. Okay, let's talk shop a while. You saw the kid at the library, and what did he say?"

"He gave me an idea about motive. I think motive's going to be the key piece in this puzzle. Don't you? Having a good motive could turn out to give us a connection between the two victims. What he said was that ever since grade school Winston and Charles and Richard had been the school bullies. Other kids were afraid of them. The kind of bullies who would lure a boy onto the teeter-totter, then send him slamming into the ground, or who'd launch him from a playground swing to go flying through the air and land in the dirt. In high school, they'd catch a defenseless boy alone and de-pants him—rip his pants down in the hallway—or force him into the bathroom and shove him headfirst down into a trash can. They called it 'getting canned' and thought it was pretty funny. And there's more: one of their juvenile 'tricks' was to trip up a kid, hold him down on the floor, and grind their knuckles into his chest until he yelled 'Uncle!' Interesting, huh?"

McIntyre punched the clutch and downshifted, making the truck lurch.

"Sorry," he said. "We're coming to a steep section. The road goes up the hill here and makes a loop to avoid a swampy place. There's beaver ponds in there, good place to catch brookies. Anyway, you can see where I'm heading with this. Winston head-down in the ore bucket, it's like he got lured up there and got himself canned by somebody. I don't know if he was supposed to die or just feel really scared, but he did die. Then Charles, see, he's tricked or persuaded into going to the mine where the stamping mill is and ends up with his chest knuckled under a heavy steel ore-crushing rod. Maybe he was just supposed to be scared, too, but the rod slipped and he's killed."

"What you're implying," Vi said, "is that this 'Beeky' character, or some other boy that those three bullied, is getting even with them?"

148

"Haven't worked out the 'who' yet," McIntyre said. "Beeky's awful scrawny to have rigged up the bucket and the stamping mill. He doesn't look much like an outdoorsman, either, at least not the kind who could stay out here waiting for his victim to come along."

"And Richard Leup, what about him?"

"The way I see it, is that he's the only remaining bully. One bully left. This third deserted mine we're going to, the Betsy, it also has a line of sight to the place where the English Hotel once stood. It's a long, long ways, would be only a speck with a telescope, but it's there. Given the pattern so far, I'm thinking maybe our killer could talk Richard into looking at the Betsy for the hoard. Maybe he's planning to can him, like Winston, or knuckle him, or take his pants and leave him up here to freeze . . . say! Look! What's that?"

The dark object in the snow just off the road proved to be a car, an expensive coupe. McIntyre drove past it and up the slope until he came to a level place to stop, then he and Vi Coteau walked back. Evidently the coupe had slid off the road, come to rest against the bushes, and then sat there through the latest snowstorm. A couple of inches of fresh snow had covered the top and the hood. It had also obliterated any footprints.

"The driver could be anywhere," McIntyre said, trying the locked door. "Maybe he got a ride from somebody else who came up this road. Or maybe he walked out to the main road."

Vi dusted off the hood ornament and bent down to look at the automobile club medallions on the front bumper.

"I can't be sure," she said, "but I think this is Mr. Leup's car. Mr. William Leup, I mean."

"You think he was driving it? Or possibly Richard?" McIntyre asked.

"Richard could have borrowed his father's car to come up here. This road is the only one you'd take if you wanted to arrive at either one of the two mines, right? Or is there a third road?"

"There is. Not a very good road. More of a wagon track. It leads to where that scrap metal scavenger lives. There's an old mine and a couple of cabins there. But it's an awful long way around."

"What do you think?" Vi asked. "Was it Richard?"

"Maybe Richard did get lured up here just like Charles and Winston. Except the car slid off and got stuck. It's not far back to the main road, a little over a mile. The logical thing would be to hike out to the road and head toward the village hoping another car would come along to give him a lift. The Lantern Creek road turnaround is about two miles ahead. If he was determined to make it to one of the mines. The Big Horse isn't too far from the turnaround. Neither is the Betsy Mine. So, would he try to go ahead on foot, or would he go back to the main road? It probably started to snow. It might be that he stayed in the car all night and then in the morning, he hiked back to the main road."

"I hope so," Vi said. "I'd like to think he's warm and safe somewhere. In the village, maybe."

McIntyre was looking around, but not because he was admiring the mountain view. He was thinking of a man alone in all those hundreds of square miles of snowbound forest. Whoever the driver of the car was, he hadn't been here since the storm. Sadly, there would be no point in trying to find him. He either went up to the mine, or back down to the main road. There was nothing to be done except finish their own mission and report the stranded car when they got back to town.

"Let's go have our picnic lunch," he said.

The stranded coupe wasn't the only vehicle that had used Lantern Creek road recently. Leaving the turnaround to drive up to the mine higher on the mountain, McIntyre saw that he and Vi Coteau were following somebody's tire tracks and in places he could tell that the tracks also came down again.

"Here's the Betsy," he announced. "Looks like our other vehicle stopped here on top of the tailings dump, then turned around and went down the road again. Wonder who it was?"

"Maybe whoever it was picked up the driver from the other car. The one we found stuck in the snow," Vi suggested.

"Maybe. Well, let's find that warm rock to sit against."

As the ranger had promised, the open level spot on the side of the mountain afforded a panoramic view of the forests, the foothills, and the vast high plains beyond the foothills. There was blue sky everywhere, and postcard-like vistas in every direction.

They went to the edge of the tailings pile, where McIntyre pointed out the little towns in the distance and the far-off dark lines on the high plains beyond the mountains. The dark lines were trees lining the rivers, and he told her where all the rivers were going.

"Here," he said, taking her hand and lifting it to her eyes. "Put your hands above your nose, like this, until you can't see the ground. Only the distant horizon and the sky. Okay?"

She held her hands palm down, finger tips touching, just above her cheeks.

"That's what it's like to fly," he said. "You look out over your engine and the edge of your cockpit and you see the sky and the horizon and there's nothing else. You're free of the ground, free of everything. You feel like you could go on forever flying."

"You're right!" she said. "Can we see where this English Hotel place was?"

"Over there," he said, pointing toward a distant mountain.

He was enjoying himself, chatting with Vi and showing her his mountain world, but down deep in his heart, McIntyre was worried that this picnic might not be a good idea. He didn't like the fact that both Leups were missing. The empty car stuck in the snow haunted him. Equally haunting in view of the murders was a feeling that the killer might be lurking somewhere. And if not the killer, the scrap metal scavenger could be almost anywhere, watching them. Instead of larking about in the mountains trying to entertain Vi Coteau, he should be concentrating on the Leup problem.

Together they explored the rest of the mine site, watching out for a good place to spread the car robes. The blockhouse building offered a sunny, sheltering wall, but there was something stark and looming about the building. Vi Coteau touched the hasp on the heavy wooden door and the rusty spike holding it shut.

"Want to look inside?" Vi suggested.

"Done that," McIntyre said. "Last time I was up here. Nothing to see. Tin cans, bottles, a couple of broken chairs. And it smells pretty bad in there. But just for the heck of it . . ."

The ranger pulled the spike out of the hasp and pushed the door, but nothing budged. He pushed harder, and still the heavy door remained solidly shut against the doorframe.

"Must be jammed," he said. "Let's go on over to the tunnel and find a picnic spot."

Unlike the gloomy blockhouse, the mouth of the mine tunnel seemed welcoming and cheerful, probably because of the way the winter sun was warming it. A flat place near the entrance was protected by a roof-like overhanging ledge of granite and had no snow on it at all.

"This will do," McIntyre said.

"Good," Vi replied, shrugging off her rucksack and opening it to take out the car robe.

"Don't make yourself too comfortable," McIntyre growled. "We need a fire first. You can bring a few of those rocks over there and start making a fire circle. We'll put it up against the boulder here and the heat will be reflected out."

"Collect rocks?" she said. "These are new gloves! And they weren't cheap."

"Better take them off, then," he said.

He dropped his own backpack and hiked off in the direction of an aspen grove just over the edge of the tailings pile. When he came back, his arms loaded with dry branches, Vi had finished making the stone circle against the boulder.

"You've done that before," he said.

Indeed she had. She might be a city girl now, but had grown up with a father and brothers who spent many summer weekends car-camping. Her firepit was two rocks high and had a small opening for an air vent. She had arranged a niche of rocks so the coffee pot could sit over the fire.

"I broke a damn fingernail," she said.

"Did you say 'damn'?" he asked.

"Did I?" she challenged.

"If you did, I guess I never heard it."

They chuckled like schoolkids while they snapped small twigs and stacked them into a miniature log cabin in the fire circle. He broke larger limbs by stomping them under his boot and Vi arranged them around and over the kindling.

"Good," he said. "Okay, here comes the real test!"

He reached into his pocket and handed her a single kitchen match. She knelt there holding the match between her fingers and looked up at him. One match?

"You think I can't do it with just one match? Know what I think?" she said.

"What?"

"I think you're a very silly ranger."

She leaned in, put the match near the little cabin of twigs, pressed it to a rock, and in less time than it takes to tell, flames

153

from the kindling were snapping and licking at the thicker branches. The aspen would make less smoke than pine or spruce; after the fire was good and hot, McIntyre would add the chunks of dry juniper he had found.

It was as near perfect as a picnic campfire can be: the granite face of the rock not only reflected the heat, but drew air upward like a chimney, keeping the smoke going up instead of into their faces. The dry aspen and juniper burned hot and clean. Two car robes spread in front of the fire gave them a warm place to sit. And sit they did. They left the picnic box in the truck for the time being because neither of them wanted to be in a rush to eat lunch and leave. They sat close, making the smallest of small talk, taking turns feeding sticks into the fire, sharing life trivia— books they had read, favorite ice cream flavors, the strangest place they had been, how they got their jobs—letting the day just move along. Anyone seeing them there would never imagine that they also had missing men and grim murders on their minds.

She sat with her knees drawn up and her arms around them. He pointed at her foot and laughed.

"You were in a hurry this morning!" he said.

"What do you mean?"

"Your boot. When you laced it up you missed a hole. See? Right there. Third hole down from the top."

She extended her foot toward him. "Why don't you fix it, smarty."

As he leaned closer and untied her shoelace it was Vi's turn to tease.

"And you, Mister Perfect," she said, "you left home with a lopsided knot in your necktie. What's that supposed to be, anyway? A half-Windsor knot?"

He finished lacing her boot and her little finger beckoned him to come nearer. She removed his tie clip and stored it in his shirt pocket. As she undid the knot in his necktie the scent of Paris and lavender once again drew that gauzy curtain over his thoughts.

The voice that interrupted them was gruff and blunt.

"What in hell's going on?" the voice demanded. "Think this is a damn city park or somethin'? Private property. Get the hell out!"

McIntyre was on his feet in an instant, sizing up the metal scavenger. And the double-barrel shotgun he was holding.

"You again," McIntyre said. "You know something, mister? I've about had enough of you. What's your name, anyway?"

"None of your beeswax, but it's John, John Péguy."

"French name," McIntyre said. "And I'm Ranger T. G. McIntyre, National Park Service."

McIntyre took a step forward. John Péguy pointed the shotgun.

"Hell, I knowed you was a ranger," he said. "I might live alone, but I sure as hell don't live in no damn box."

McIntyre took another step, then another. The shotgun was only inches from his belly.

"Appreciate it if you'd stop swearing in front of the lady."

With a quick sweep of his hand he tore the shotgun away from the scavenger and pushed the man backward into the snow. Now it was his turn to aim the gun, only this time he cocked the hammers first.

"Extra shells," the ranger said calmly. "Which pocket? Let's have them."

Meekly the scavenger took shotgun shells from both of his coat pockets and handed them over. McIntyre briefly considered tossing them into the woods, but reconsidered and slid them into his own pocket. He pointed the shotgun skyward and discharged both barrels with a deafening roar. Vi Coteau was standing now. She had her hand in her jacket. *I've just got to find out where that lady carries her gun,* McIntyre thought. *Just got to.*

"Okay, Mister John Péguy," McIntyre said, "first off, we both know this isn't private property. It's national forest. Second, we know you're squatting up that canyon beyond the Big Horse Mine. You're living in a derelict cabin up there where some old prospector dug a hole in the mountain. You probably think it's a legal abandoned mining claim, but it isn't. You're the guy who cleared the long road to haul your metal scrap to Longmont. And I'm thinking you 'found' the college kid's automobile and appropriated it for yourself. Stole it, in other words."

"Ain't true!" Péguy said. "Bought it off him fair and square."

"Got a bill of sale? Did he sign it over to you? Was his signature notarized?"

Péguy looked at the ground and said nothing.

"That's what I thought," McIntyre said. "You can't prove you didn't steal it. You could spend a lot of time down at county jail explaining how you got it. But let's talk about your living arrangement instead."

Péguy's head snapped up.

"What do you mean? Ain't your business."

"Happens that it is," McIntyre said. "I'll tell you how I know your so-called 'abandoned mining claim' wasn't up for grabs. There's some little tin signs nailed to trees, unless you sold them for scrap. They mark the boundary of the national park. You're living inside the park, my friend, and for that you can be arrested and fined. By me. Trespass, illegal occupation, illegal road, possession of a loaded firearm inside the park, unregistered vehicle . . . and I expect I could even find evidence of poaching up at your camp, if I looked hard enough. Fresh deer hides, maybe a gut pile in the woods nearby?"

"Dammit," Péguy said.

As it happened, Ranger McIntyre was not actually certain where he intended to go with this conversation. He had been startled by the appearance of Péguy on his picnic. The surprise had made him angry, but now he had calmed down and was no longer sure what he wanted to do with the fellow. While he was thinking it over, however, his picnic with Vi Coteau was interrupted again. This time it would be for good. A large man in a heavy raccoon coat came up over the edge of the tailings pile, pointing a revolver in the general direction of John Péguy.

"You okay, Ranger?" the newcomer asked.

"Just fine," McIntyre replied. "But the people down in Denver are worried whether you are. Mister Leup."

"Can't help what other people worry about," William Leup said. "Slid off the road. Miles to a telephone. Luckily, I am not a man who gives up easily. Rather than walk out to the main road, as an ordinary man would do, I hiked on to my objective."

"Which was?" Vi asked.

"Hello, Miss Coteau. How nice to see you again. Enjoying a day off, I presume?"

"It's been entertaining. As for enjoyable, that would depend on your definition. But what brings you to the mountains?"

"Searching for Richard, of course. Bull by the horns, take the lead, set an example. I telephoned the School of Mines and spoke with that Beauchamp fellow, who told me Richard had contacted him about other old mining holes in this region. He had told Richard about various prospecting holes up along Big Horse Creek. Obviously, they needed to be investigated. I determined to do it myself this time."

"I take it you didn't find anything there?" McIntyre said.

"Not even a footprint. Built myself a night fire, stayed there looking all around, had enough bread and tea and dried beef with me. A man plans for these eventualities, you see. I was actually on my way back to my car when I smelled your campfire. And then heard two shots. Not the same two as before.

That would have been the day I got off the road. I was starting up Big Horse Creek when I heard those."

"Two more shots?" McIntyre said.

"Yes. A pistol, from the sound of it. 'Pop, pop' you know. One more faint than the other, and spaced apart by, oh, I don't know, perhaps five minutes? But tell me: is your prisoner our murder suspect? He looks to be in disguise. Surely that scraggly beard, that weathered skin makes him look much older than he is. Look at the eyes."

McIntyre had noticed the same thing, that John Péguy had the eyes—and the muscular posture—of a young man.

"Thus far," he said, "all I know is that he says his name is 'Peeky' or sounds like that, first name John, and he has a hermit shack inside the park. He picks over the mine sites and abandoned homesteads for metal he can sell. I'd like to have a private word with him, if you don't mind. Vi? Maybe you and Mr. Leup could dump a few handfuls of snow on the fire and pack up the car robes. When I'm through talking to Mr. Peeky here, we'll drive down and see about towing Mr. Leup's car back onto the road."

The ranger took the scavenger by the elbow and led him to the stone blockhouse where the others couldn't hear them.

"I don't like it, John," McIntyre said quietly.

"You don't seem to like anything," Péguy replied.

"Don't crack wise with me. I'm not in the mood. I don't like it that this door is barred from inside. From inside, get it? How can it be barred from inside? Now, you're the guy who scavenged the cookstove out of this building, right?"

"Sure. Ain't illegal."

"Maybe, maybe not. What do you know about the inside of this blockhouse that I don't know? Is there a hidden way out? Maybe it's been built over a mine tunnel? Hidden door in a wall or anything like that?"

"Don't know as I thought about it. Dark as a tomb in there. No windows. That wall, the back wall I guess you'd call it, she's built right into the mountain. I don't know. Might be a hole into the mountain there. Me, I wrestled the stove out and took a quick look 'round for anything else I could sell and got outa there. Place gives me the creeps."

McIntyre studied the door again. He made another attempt to push it open. It still didn't budge. He studied John Péguy's face, trying to decide if the man was anything more than a gloomy mountain bachelor who happened to be living near the deserted gold mines.

"All right, John," he said, replacing the spike in the hasp. "I figure I can let all that other stuff slide, as long as you agree to move out of the park, and do it in the next few weeks. And if you'll do a favor for me in return. Otherwise . . ."

"I know what you're sayin'," Péguy said. "I ain't no dumb bunny."

"I'm thinking you 'ain't' no hillbilly, neither," McIntyre said. "But that's none of my business. Not yet. What I want is for you to meet me—or us—back here tomorrow morning and bring along that heavy steel bar you took from the Big Horse Mine."

"How do you know I took it?"

"John. Let's not play games. Bring that steel bar and meet me here."

"And you'll give me time to vacate my camp."

"Yes."

"Might take me a month or more."

"Deal."

McIntyre, Vi Coteau, and Mr. Leup squeezed into the cab of McIntyre's pickup and drove down the road to Mr. William Leup's car. They talked about Richard most of the way. He had left the frat house abruptly, according to his father, and showed up at the mansion in Denver not too long afterward. The butler reported that Richard had changed into warm outdoor clothing and had taken a gun from the collection and food from the kitchen, and had left the mansion without a word of explanation.

"What kind of gun?" McIntyre asked. "In case we find it?"

"One of my Lugers. A nine-millimeter."

"You have more than one?" Vi asked.

"Several. I like to collect small caliber pistols. Such an interesting variety out there. Spanish, Russian, French manufacture. And probably a dozen in the American .32 caliber."

When they got to Leup's car, McIntyre got busy uncoiling the tow rope and tying it to the bumper, but his mind was studying the puzzle pieces, trying to make them match. This newest wrinkle was like a jigsaw puzzle with a picture within a picture in it. Here's some maniac running around the mountains killing men, and here's a college boy running around with a pistol. Nagging at his brain was the thought that Richard had figured out the connection between the deaths of Winston and Charles. Richard might have already figured out the identity of the killer. And maybe Richard had gone looking for him.

McIntyre backed his truck as close to the stranded car as he dared, then tied a bowline loop in the rope and dropped it over his trailer hitch. With Mr. Leup and Vi Coteau sitting side by side on the tailboard for added traction weight, he gently eased the clutch out. The tire chains bit into the packed snow, the engine gradually came up to speed, and the coupe was back on firm ground. The ranger unhitched the rope and coiled it up.

"Back to Denver, then," Mr. Leup said. "I'll probably be back tomorrow with a couple of men. You have no ideas concerning my boy? Where he is? It's important I find him before the newspapers get wind of the fact that he's missing.

This entire business has already put me in an awkward position."

"Honestly, I haven't a clue," McIntyre said. "You and I both think that he's hunting for the killer, don't we? If I can figure out who that is, I've got a chance of finding him. Miss Coteau and I are going to drive back up to the Betsy Mine and have another look around."

Watching Leup's car go out of sight, Vi Coteau spoke up.

"If you don't have any clues," she said, "then I'm wondering about your motives. Are we going back so you can examine the place with your magnifying glass, Mister Sherlock? Or could it be that you want to resume our picnic?"

"It could be," the ranger said, keeping his eyes on the road, "that I'm thinking about a late lunch. My stomach is growling so loud that my mind can't hear itself think."

Lunch, however, would once again have to wait.

Coming into sight of the gloomy old blockhouse at the Betsy Mine site, the first thing they saw was the figure of a man on the roof. Almost at the end of his patience, McIntyre drove up to the building and yanked the parking brake lever.

"John, what now?" he said. "What the hell are you doing up there?"

"Whoever made this roof," John replied, "used a cast-iron pipe to make a flue for the stovepipe to go through. Figured I'd claim it. You got a flashlight?"

"Yeah?"

"You'd better bring it and climb up here."

McIntyre gave Vi a look that seemed to say he would rather take a gun than a flashlight. He wanted to have a quiet lunch with her, not stare into some musty old dark building. But he took out his flashlight and flicked the switch to be sure the new batteries were still okay. He walked around to where the back of the blockhouse had been built into the mountain. It was easy to clamber up onto the flat roof.

"What is it?" he growled.

"Look down the pipe," John Péguy said, indicating the cast-iron tube.

At first the yellow beam from the flashlight showed nothing but dust mites floating in the air over the concrete floor. Then McIntyre saw the stain. It looked recent, and it looked dark. Next to the stain, barely visible, was a shape that was either an elbow or a knee.

"I think it's a guy's leg," John said. "Dropped a couple of matches down there but couldn't get a good look. Pipe's too long and narrow."

"Vi?" McIntyre called. "Do you have a compact with you? One with a mirror in it?"

She took her compact from her shoulder bag and tossed it up to him.

It was awkward trying to hold the mirror down inside the tube with one hand and shining the flashlight with the other, but he saw enough to know that there was a dead body inside the blockhouse. And while he couldn't be certain it was Richard Leup's body, he could be certain it was dead. The pool of blood leaking from the head and drying on the concrete was ample evidence of that.

"Got a body in here," he called to her. He closed her compact and put it in his pocket. "Can't identify him for certain, but he's showing a good-size wound in his head."

They took the spike out of the hasp and the men put their shoulders to the door; after lunging at it four or five times, however, they had to give it up. The wood didn't even wiggle.

"As I recall," John Péguy said, "this door's got two crossbars on the inside. One about knee level, t'other about as high's your chest. Couple inches thick. I seen 'em standing in the corner, those crossbars. Tried to salvage the steel brackets, see? Four

162

pieces of good heavy steel where the crossbars slide. But I didn't have no tools and couldn't pry 'em free of the wall."

"Okay, John. Here's what's going to happen. You leave everything here just as it is, and I mean everything. Even if it's a tin can, don't pick it up. You go on home and thank your stars that I'm going to be too busy to come evict you from park property. Bright and early tomorrow morning I want you back here again, with that heavy steel rod from the stamping mill. We're going to use it to bash that door open. If we have to, we'll smash a hole in the wall. I know you're not going to run away. Are you?"

McIntyre and Vi Coteau watched John walking away through the snow.

"How do you know he's not going to vanish?" Vi asked.

"If he does, I know where he'll probably end up. I can tell you in two words. 'Blue eyes.' John Péguy isn't as old as he likes to look. He's not as sincere a hermit as he wants us to believe, either. And there's a blue-eyed pixie girl down in Longmont who pretends not to know him. No, if John bails out of the canyon, we'll find him hanging around a certain salvage yard."

Chapter Twelve:
"In Without Knocking"

"Did I hear a chuckle coming from the passenger's side?" McIntyre asked, shifting into second to descend the slippery hill. "Want to tell me what's funny?"

"Oh, nothing. I was just thinking about some girlfriends of mine, that's all. We meet regularly, every two weeks. Call ourselves The LAW. What if they could see me now?"

"All of you work in law enforcement? Or legal offices?"

"That's a good guess, but no. LAW stands for Lunch At Woolworth's. Last week the girls asked why in the world I would want to waste my days off by chasing around in the snow with a dreary park ranger. Now I can tell them. I'll also tell them that watching you collect puzzle pieces is more fascinating than watching a sheepdog rounding up sheep. Will you want the rest of this sandwich?"

"Would a chipmunk want a peanut?"

She had been feeding him by hand as he drove the truck down the snow-packed road. It was awful nice. She had set the picnic box against her door so she could sit right next to him. Even nicer was how she leaned on his shoulder as her slender fingers held a half a sandwich or a pickle to his lips. Awful nice way to eat.

The truck hit a bump and lurched. McIntyre reached for the shift lever again.

"That's my knee, mister," Vi said.

"Sorry," he said. "Had my eyes on the road."

"Want to try this root beer? It's only half frozen. Kind of a cold sludge."

Once they got down to the main road, he told her, where she had left her car, they would be able to make better time. And a good thing, too, for the first gloom of winter's early darkness was coming to close in around them. The air had taken on the unmistakable chill of winter; the tree shadows lying across the road became darker and longer.

"Here," she said, "take the last bite of this apple."

She held it to his mouth.

"Isn't that how Adam got in trouble, in the Garden of Eden?"

Vi opened her window far enough to toss the apple core out into the woods.

"For the squirrels," she said. She licked her fingers and put her gloves back on.

"Look," McIntyre said, "don't take this wrong or anything, but it's awful late for you to be driving all the way into Denver. Maybe you could stay at my cabin tonight and drive back tomorrow."

"Drive back to Denver? And miss the action?" she said. "Not hardly! I assume you and John Péguy are going to break into the stone building first thing tomorrow. I want to be there."

They had arrived at her car. McIntyre set the pickup's parking brake and turned to look at her.

"That's the plan," he said. "I'll phone the sheriff tonight so he can arrange for the county doctor and an ambulance to meet us there. Then I'll try to be there ahead of them. I'll need a couple of minutes to solve the mystery."

I hope she can't see how nervous I am, the ranger was thinking. *I think I'm starting to babble. She's damn beautiful.* His traitorous imagination was playing hell with his determination to act like a gentleman, bringing him all kinds of naughty pictures of the cozy little cabin in the forest. What would he do if she did end up spending the night? He wouldn't want it to change the way they were with one another; he had not experienced this kind of easygoing, intriguing, just plain "good" time with a woman since . . . since the car wreck. He was in no way sure that he was ready to go all the way with Vi. Not sure at all. He caught himself staring vacantly until he realized that she was studying his face.

"Well, Ranger," she finally said, "I sure don't want to make that drive tonight, and I sure do want to be there tomorrow when you take a look at the corpse and solve the case in under a minute, flat. Your moment of fame!"

They both laughed and the laughing helped bust up the tension.

"I guess we both know what would happen once you had me trapped in your comfy woodsy cabin, don't we?" she asked.

"Could happen more than once, would be my guess."

She laughed again, and he loved it.

"How about this instead," she said. "What if I stop at the Pioneer Inn and rent myself a room for the night. You meet me there for an early breakfast tomorrow morning. After which we'll go break down that door to the hut, then you can identify the body and solve the mystery. Okay? We can even take another five minutes and you can solve the two murders."

He laughed and smiled, but inside he felt like a condemned man who has been granted a reprieve. Actually, his inside feelings were all muddled up again. While he was smiling at her and simultaneously molding his eyebrows into what he hoped was a look of disappointment, inside his head a little man named Imagination was stomping around in circles like a schoolboy who has been told he can't have a piece of candy.

The first light of day coming through the cabin windows on the following morning found McIntyre struggling loose from a tangled-up dream, a kind of complicated fantasy. His pillow seemed to have a vise-like grip on his head, pulling him back down each time he tried to rouse himself. The cabin was gloomy and cold, the quilts and pillow warm and deep.

Finally, however, he made it to the floor, turned on the electric light, put a match to the kindling in the cookstove, and went outside in his long johns to feed Brownie and open the pasture gate for her. The mare watched with detached curiosity while the tall figure in red underwear danced and shivered in the light of a gas lantern as he pitched hay, dumped grain into the feed trough, and poured water. One difference between men and horses, Brownie seemed to be thinking, is that you never see a horse struggling out of warm bed in the dark to fix breakfast for a human.

He broke his own overnight fast with a thick slice of buttered bread and a mug of warmed-over coffee while he waited for the water tank on the side of the cookstove to heat. Once it was warm, he would be able to shave and then he could get dressed. He ran the polishing rag over his boots and Sam Browne belt and holster, checked his service revolver, took a stiff brush to the brim of his flat ranger hat, and gave his necktie a wipe with a damp cloth. If he was going to act like a lawman today, he might as well look like one. Too bad Jamie Ogg was using the official green pickup truck while McIntyre was on leave. Well, there was no help for it: he would just have to show up with Small Delights painted on his door.

Before leaving the cabin, he provided himself with fresh batteries for the truck flashlight and slipped his small mirror into his pocket. It was just barely possible that he'd be able to peer down the stovepipe hole and see some way to unbar the door and get into the blockhouse.

★ ★ ★ ★ ★

"Wowzy!"

Vi Coteau set down her teacup to admire the man coming through the dining room doorway.

"Don't you look snazzy!" she said. "That uniform fits you like a dream."

"Nice of you to notice," McIntyre replied, pulling out a chair and sitting down at the table. "It pays to have friends. Minnie March. She had such a good time tailoring Mike's tuxedo for me that she volunteered to do the same with my tunic and trousers. Pretty slick, huh."

"I'll say," Vi said. "I wish somebody would do some tailoring for my boss. Agent Canilly's jackets always look as though he's carrying bricks in both pockets."

McIntyre removed his flat brim hat and put it on an empty chair. There were plenty of chairs to choose from: no one else was up that early. In fact, the inn had only three guests including Vi Coteau. He would be having the set breakfast, since Charlene couldn't offer a full menu with only three guests, but he was looking forward to it.

"Stay awake all night solving the case?" Vi asked, offering him a piece of her toast as he waited for his own meal to arrive.

"Not really," he said. "I fell asleep thinking about suspects. And a name. And motives, you know. If it's a killer with a grudge who's out to avenge himself on a bunch of bullies, who the heck could it be? He'd have to be pretty strong and in good shape in order to arrange that ore bucket. And to fix up the stamping mill. He'd also be someone who knows the abandoned mines and the whole general area. And be unemployed—or on vacation."

"How so?"

"Obvious. He had time to reconnoiter the old mine sites and the roads and trails leading to them. He had time to talk the boys into going up there to search for Dunraven's treasure. Speaking of which, when we were looking at that tunnel, the one where you got mud on your shoes, did you see anything strange?"

"Strange? How?" she said.

"It was dark and all, but I thought I saw someone's shadow on the wall. It looked like a man in a floppy hat and old-fashioned deerskin hunting coat. He seemed to be pointing at the floor there where the mud was."

"I didn't see him," Vi said. "But you're right about it sounding strange. Maybe you were just hungry."

McIntyre's breakfast arrived—ham, eggs, a pancake the size of his hat—and Mari topped up his coffee.

"How come you aren't fat?" Vi asked, looking at his plate of food. "And what were you saying about a name?"

" 'Beeky' is what it sounded like. Remember? I should have made a note of who said it. They said something about 'Beeky' being the kid who was tormented by Charles and Winston and Richard. Obviously one of those nicknames kids give to other kids. What if 'Beeky' is a supposedly humorous version of 'Péguy'? Or, what if they called him 'Beeky' as in 'beak' because of his nose. You know, a bird beak?"

"It's a pretty thin clue, as clues go," she said.

"Yeah, I know. And I don't think it's 'Péguy' because I don't think our metal scavenger is the killer. He doesn't act like it."

"Aiming a shotgun at you isn't acting like it?" she said.

"Nah. That's all bluff, see? Your killer would have been all friendly-like, see? He wouldn't want us to believe he's a mean tough hombre who shoots people for trespassing. Besides, if he was the killer and wanted to shoot me—or the two of us—he would have done it from ambush."

"Good point. Maybe when you break open the blockhouse door everything will become crystal clear. Do you want to drive my Marmon up to the mine today"—she arched one eyebrow at him—"or are we going to share Small Delights?"

He had to love it. What man wouldn't love how Vi could say that while looking straight into his eyes?

"The truck, I guess."

They were the first to arrive. The sky was a blue crystal bowl arching over the mountains and although the sunlight on the snow was nearly blinding there was no warmth in it to speak of. While the ranger climbed onto the blockhouse roof with mirror and flashlight to peer through the stovepipe hole again, Vi took sticks and twigs and rebuilt the picnic fire. The sheriff and medical examiner might appreciate a bit of warmth when they got there.

"See anything else?" she called to McIntyre.

"Just a dead body," he replied. "Can't see his face! But John Péguy was right about that door. I can just barely see it. There's a couple of thick timbers across it, holding it closed. Looks awful sturdy, and it looks as if our corpse barricaded himself inside. It might be possible that somebody looped two ropes from this stovepipe hole to the door and dropped the planks into place that way. But it would be an awful tricky thing to do."

"Suicide, then," Vi said.

The ranger climbed down from the roof and walked around the blockhouse twice, looking for any sign of another way in. When Vi came around the building to join him, she found him holding his flashlight tight along the wall to make the beam show the shadow of every tiny bump and crack.

"What are you doing?" Vi asked.

"Haven't you ever done this to find a lost earring or a button on the floor? You lay a light down on the floor and the thing you're looking for throws a shadow, then you can find it. I hoped to find a loose rock in the wall, maybe a crack that might be a trapdoor. But the whole building is solid. I'd like to know what the miners used it for."

"Maybe we'll find out," she said. "Here comes your battering ram."

The metal scavenger was coming toward them out of the trees. A folded burlap bag made a pad on his shoulder where he carried the heavy steel bar. Apparently, McIntyre's threat to evict him had hit home, for he showed every sign of being ready to help break into the blockhouse.

John threw down his burden and hurried to the fire to warm his hands.

"Cold," he said. "Sunshine feels good. Back along in those woods I don't think the sun hits the ground until afternoon. Cold back there."

When his hands were warm again, John put his mittens back on and joined McIntyre, who was standing in front of the thick door holding one end of the steel bar.

"What's the plan?" John asked.

"I thought you and I might use this rod like a battering ram. Maybe we can create a gap and then use the bar to pry the door. I think our best chance would be to start near the top and see if we can hammer a bracket loose there first."

"Might work," John agreed.

They raised the bar to shoulder height and attacked the wood. With the first blow the bar merely bounced back. They put more muscle into the second blow and could feel the door absorbing it. A third blow, solid and strong. With the fourth attempt McIntyre's muscles were already starting to cramp up. Both men grunted with effort when they smashed the bar against the door for the fifth time; this time they were rewarded with a sound of wood cracking loose. A gap appeared along the edge of the door. They dropped the bar and rested with their backs against the wall.

"Too bad I didn't bring my Thompson," Vi Coteau said. She was staying near the warmth of the campfire. "I bet a few bursts would cut through."

John Péguy looked at McIntyre. "Is she kidding? She shoots a Tommy gun?"

"So I've been told," McIntyre said. "Probably silver plated with her initials engraved on it."

McIntyre noticed how Péguy seemed to have dropped his clipped speech and gruff attitude. It made the ranger suspicious. He had seen spruce grouse pretending to be wounded in order to lure a predator away from a nest, just as he had seen predators feigning indifference to a motionless rabbit even while slyly edging closer to it. Whenever he saw a human who seemed to be putting on an act, it caused him to raise his guard.

Having rested, the two men once again raised the bar to shoulder level and made a savage assault on the door. The second attempt yielded a fist-sized gap between door and jamb, enough to insert the end of the bar. Although they pried with sufficient strength to bend the bar, the only thing they accomplished was another slight cracking noise.

They rested again.

"Too bad the doorway isn't about a foot wider," Vi Coteau suggested. "You could bring your pickup and use the front bumper to push the door open."

"I'd rather not," McIntyre said. "A guy can do a lot of damage to his vehicle doing stunts like that. My assistant ranger, Jamie Ogg, he yanked a rear axle loose trying to pull a stump with a government truck."

"What if we built a fire against the door?" she said.

John Péguy snorted as if to say "typical dumb idea from a woman" but McIntyre knew better than to say anything. Instead, he pulled off a mitten and felt the wood with his bare hand.

"Feels dry enough. Fire might be the answer. What say we take a couple of swings against the lower edge first, then maybe see if we could burn it down."

He and John got back to work with their battering ram. Hitting the door lower down was easier since they could swing the bar between them at knee level, using the weight of the steel and the inertia to do the hammering. After a half-dozen blows, they heard a splintering of wood followed by a pinging sound. Steel, falling on concrete.

"One of the lag screws from the bracket," Péguy said. "Sure sounded like it. Let's hit 'er again."

He was right: one of the two lag screws securing the steel bracket had popped out. On the very next blow the bracket gave way and the lower crossbar fell with a terrific thump to the concrete floor. They introduced the long bar into the gap and pried while Vi shoved in a thick tree branch to keep it open. Between the prying and the wedging, the upper crossbar finally splintered and broke in half. Péguy and McIntyre pushed the door open.

The inside of the blockhouse was dark as pitch. While McIntyre and Péguy dragged the steel bar out of the way and cleared broken wood from the doorway, Vi went to the truck for McIntyre's gas lanterns. She pumped up the pressure tanks on both and lit them.

"Okay," McIntyre said. "I guess we're ready. John, you stay out here. We need to be real careful in case there's footprints or anything."

"I think I hear engines coming," John Péguy said.

He did: even with muffling snow, noise carried a very long way through the silent mountain valley. Over the hissing of the gas lanterns they could hear two vehicles in the distance, coming toward the Betsy Mine.

"That'll be the sheriff and doctor," McIntyre said. "Vi, let's take a look around before they get here."

Careful to leave any footprints undisturbed, McIntyre and Vi went into the blockhouse and stayed close to the wall. The lantern light showed only one set of prints in the dusty, dirty floor. The tracks went every which way, to this corner and to that corner, toward the doorway, to the center of the tomblike blockhouse, back to the doorway again. Even though the dirt and dust near the entrance had been disturbed when they broke open the door, the footprints made it clear that the dead guy who was now lying next to the far wall had gone to the door more than once.

"I think he was trying to listen through it," McIntyre said.

"Those are all the same shoe prints," Vi said. "Almost new rubber soles, very flat heels. Snow boots, like the ones he's wearing."

"Agreed," McIntyre said. "I think he stood here beside the door for a long time. After running in here, probably to hide, he barricaded the door and then stood here in the dark, listening to hear whatever was out there."

"Maybe he was listening for a car engine," Vi said. "Maybe waiting until whoever was after him gave up and drove away."

"Or they were talking to him, through the door?"

"That's possible. Are you going to look at the body?" Vi asked.

"I guess. But keep your lantern pointed near the floor and watch where you step. Although it probably doesn't matter. His tracks are all over the place."

"Must've been scary," she said. "Cold, dark, smelly place. The only light he had came from that eight-inch stovepipe hole in the roof. Hey, maybe he had a candle with him! Here's a couple of burnt kitchen matches."

"I think John the scavenger dropped those down the hole."

"And what's this?" Vi was pointing at a piece of paper. McIntyre picked it up.

174

"Looks to be a page out of a pocket notebook," he said. The ranger held it in the doorway so they could read it.

"It's written in pencil. Says 'Dad, I killed them, so sorry, deserve to die, love, Richard.' "

"Seems to explain everything," Vi said.

"Except how he managed to print his letters so straight and even. In the dark. And look, the lettering is smooth, like he had a pad under the paper. Like the page was still in the notebook when it was written on. But I don't see any notebook like that. Maybe in his pocket?"

"Here's the pencil," Vi said, pointing at the floor near the corpse.

"Better leave it where it lies. I'll put the note back where we found it, too."

They didn't turn the body over or disturb it, but could clearly see that the dead young man was indeed Richard Leup. The blood smeared on his face was now dry, nearly black; the forehead showed a thicker, darker little circle of blood. The forehead showed a handprint as well.

"Bullet in the head," McIntyre said. "Look. He got shot in the forehead, put his hand up over the wound, like this. It must have hit a vein, the way he bled."

"Here's the gun," Vi said. She had stepped around to the other side of the corpse. "Okay to pick it up?"

McIntyre tore a half page from his own notebook and handed it to her.

"Here, mark the place with this and remember how it was lying. Which side up, which way it was pointed."

She held the revolver in the lantern light.

"H&R double-action revolver," she said. "I think it's the Victor model. The stamping on the barrel is smeared with blood. It's a .32 caliber, though."

"That's strange," McIntyre said. "Let me see it."

"How is it strange?" she asked. "It's a common enough caliber."

"William Leup said Richard had taken a Luger automatic. A nine-millimeter. He didn't take one of the .32 revolvers, or so I assume."

The ranger examined the .32 the way he might study a piece from a jigsaw puzzle. His mind recorded details of every part of the weapon, from the extreme holster wear on the muzzle and cylinder to the small crack on the left-hand grip. He took note of fresh scratches on the metal and cautiously jiggled both the cylinder and the hammer to see whether they were worn and loose, which they were. Everything about the pistol, in fact, spoke to its having been used and abused for a long time, a cheap gun that had become too worn out to shoot safely. It should have been turned into scrap metal.

They heard two cars drive up and stop.

"We'd better go greet the arriving troops," he told Vi. "Here, put this gun back the way it was. The sheriff will probably want to take pictures."

CHAPTER THIRTEEN:
A PUZZLING CASE OF SUICIDE

The two vehicles were the sheriff's black sedan followed by the county ambulance, which did double duty as a hearse. They parked next to McIntyre's truck and Sheriff Abe Crowell and his deputy, Sam Bartlett, practically collided with each other in their rush to talk to Vi Coteau, who was standing there looking like a model out of *Vogue* magazine. Whatever Ranger McIntyre had to say could wait.

The assistant coroner was a recently scrubbed youth with pale pink cheeks and pale blue eyes. Lugging a cumbersome camera box by its leather strap, he introduced himself to McIntyre. He was one of those young people who communicate in nervous, tentative, and generally questionable sentences.

"Ranger," he said. "I'm Howard Dobler? I'm Doctor Lipp's assistant? I don't think we've met?"

"Good to meet you," McIntyre replied. "Welcome to the Betsy Mine. I guess the first thing the doc wants is photographs. Right?"

"Yes, correct. I'm sure that's what he wants?"

Doctor Lipp gave McIntyre a quick nod of the head and went on into the blockhouse. He emerged a minute or two later to give Howard his instructions. While the young man got busy with tripod, camera, and flashlamp making photographs of the interior of the building and of the body, the others stood around Vi's campfire holding their hands to the heat.

"Straightforward to me," Doctor Lipp said. "You have looked

at the gun?"

"I did," McIntyre said. "It's an old, worn out H&R .32 caliber. Fully loaded with one shot fired."

"We'll find that bullet lodged above the right eye," the doctor said. "That's where the only wound is. I won't say for certain until we clean away the blood . . . not much light to see by in that place . . . but there seem to be powder burns on the face. The door was barricaded from inside?"

"That's right. We had to break it open."

"Straightforward. A clear case of suicide. That's how I'll write it up. I saw his footprints in there. They match his shoes. Didn't see any others except for the ones your clodhoppers left. And this pretty young lady's neat little impressions. So, nobody else was in there. Has to be suicide. Pretty straightforward."

"Why?" McIntyre said. "I mean, why would Richard Leup shoot himself? And why do it here?"

"Not my department," Doctor Lipp replied. "I do the how. Cops and lawyers can do the why."

"There's a couple of things I notice don't seem to fit the picture, though," McIntyre persisted.

Sheriff Crowell touched Vi's arm.

"Miss Coteau," he said. "Can I offer you a little advice? Don't ever share a meal with this tree cop. You'll ask him if the meat's okay and he'll say yes, it's fine, but there's something funny going on with the mashed potatoes. Drive you nuts."

"Thanks for your warning," she said, endowing him with a smile, "but I'm afraid it comes too late."

Howard joined the group at the fire. "I'm all done?" he said. "I want to report a gun. I turned the deceased over. Like you said? To take a picture of the torso? I saw another pistol sticking out of his coat pocket. It's a Luger automatic?"

"Thanks," Sheriff Crowell said. "Okay, 'Captain' McIntyre. Let's have your objections to the suicide ruling and then we'll load the kid into the ambulance. My feet are freezing. Sam, take off your mittens, get out your notebook, and write down the ranger's objections to the coroner's ruling."

"Speaking of notes, let's make sure he didn't have a notebook with him," McIntyre said. "As for objections to calling it suicide, the first piece that doesn't fit is that there's no sign of how Richard got here. No car, none of his foot tracks in the woods or along the road, nothing. It's as if somebody drove him up here and left him. Then there's the matter of the gunshots."

"Shots?"

"Yeah. You've met our friendly local metal collector? For some ridiculous reason I got aggravated when he aimed his shotgun at me. I took it away from him. Then I unloaded it by pointing it into the air and pulling both triggers."

"So what?" the sheriff said. "That's got nothing to do with this case."

"Wait a minute," McIntyre said. "A little while after that, here comes William Leup walking out of the forest. His story was that his car had gotten stuck on the road and he decided to keep hunting for Richard, anyway. He heard the two shots and smelled the campfire. He came to investigate, naturally."

"I'll say it again. So what?"

"William Leup also told us that on the day before he had heard two other distinct shots, sharp-sounding, like a pistol or rifle."

"One of those shots," Doctor Lipp said, "is probably Richard shooting himself. And you account for the second one how?"

"That's the problem. I can't account for either one," McIntyre explained. "If you fired off a .32 pistol inside that blockhouse with the door shut, there's no way anybody at a distance would hear it."

"If I know you, Ranger," Abe Crowell said, "you're about to come up with one of your theories. You're going to tell us how a murderer brought young Richard all the way up here to this mine to shoot him in the head. But he didn't die right away. With a bullet in his brain and blood running down his face, Richard returned fire with his own gun, then hurried into the blockhouse where he would be safe, closed the door, put both bars across it, then laid down and died. So those were the two shots. The one that killed him and the one he fired back."

McIntyre thought it over. He picked up a stick, broke it in half, and put both halves into the fire.

"Doc? Possible? Could you go into that place and put two heavy bars across the door while you've got a bullet in your forehead?"

Doctor Lipp was lighting a cigar with the glowing tip of a stick from the fire.

"Impossible, I won't say," he said, "it's how I don't see. Maybe with a sharp piercing wound above the eye, like an awl might make, maybe he could manage to close the door and barricade it. But it would be dark in there. There have been cases, men in accidents having a piece of steel driven through the skull and brain and able to walk for help. One was using a steel rod tamping blasting powder down a hole when it blew up and sent the rod through his forehead. Two weeks he lived and could walk and talk. But that's a slow-moving chunk of steel. Your lead slug, that's another thing. There you've got the lead deformed from striking the bone of the skull, which means the wound inside the brain is going to be ragged. There's also the trauma, the shock of the bullet hitting bone. And think about your evidence, if he managed to close and bar the door after being shot. There'd be blood drops, lots of blood on the floor next the door. Blood on the bars. Blood marks leading into the building. See? Except you managed to stomp all over the snow outside and messed up the dirt inside when you bashed the door open."

"Anything else?" the sheriff asked.

"One main thing," McIntyre said. "It's the gun. He was carrying a nice deadly weapon like a Luger, so why use a worn-out revolver? To shoot himself, I mean. Let's pretend, just for the sake of argument, you want to commit suicide. Let's say you planned carefully how to come all the way up here without a car, how to lock yourself in, how to shoot yourself. In the dark. Don't forget the dark. The best thing would be to use an automatic. That way if you only wounded yourself with the first shot you could take another and even another without having to fumble around recocking the weapon. Of course, the H&R is a double-action gun. All you need to do is squeeze the trigger a second time. But it takes more deliberate effort to squeeze off a revolver than it does an automatic."

"Often think about how to shoot yourself, do you?" Sheriff Crowell asked.

"Also, where did he find the .32?" McIntyre went on, ignoring Crowell's quip. "It's a beat-up piece of junk, really. He couldn't even rely on the thing going off. He takes one of his father's prized weapons, the Luger, which might make sense if he meant to give ol' dad a lesson by killing himself with it. But with a fine Luger in his coat pocket, he used a junky unreliable little two-dollar pistol instead? Which brings me to probably the most significant thing."

"Care to share?" Vi Coteau said sweetly. McIntyre tried to ignore her.

"The cylinder on that .32 we found. The cylinder rotates clockwise, right? So how come the only empty cartridge isn't under the hammer? In fact, the empty is two stop notches past the hammer. Richard—or another person—turned that cylinder after the gun was fired."

"Another person, McIntyre?" Sheriff Crowell said. "What other person? We've pretty much established that there was nobody inside the blockhouse except for Richard. With that door barricaded like you said, it'd be pretty near impossible."

"Okay," McIntyre said. "I agree. Nobody else could have been in there. In which case it was Richard who turned the cylinder after the gun was fired. Which says to me that it wasn't his gun. Let's say he was there in the dark, nothing but a little shaft of light coming through a hole in the roof, and he finds a revolver lying on the floor. The natural thing to do is to pick it up, take it over to the light, and flip the cylinder open to see whether it's loaded or not. And it is loaded. You've decided to kill yourself, and now you've found a loaded revolver. You put it to your forehead and pull the trigger. Now you're dead. And the hammer of the revolver has to be resting on a fired cartridge."

"Let me see," said Doctor Lipp, studying the glowing end of his cigar, "if I'm hearing what you are saying, you think your hypothetical other person shot the boy with that gun? Then he opened the cylinder to see how many shots were left, closed it again, and dropped it next to the victim?"

"Might be. That would explain why the cylinder had been turned after the shot was fired."

"Then this killer of yours, who didn't leave footprints in the dust, who didn't take the murder weapon or anything valuable from his victim, he contrived to close the door and slide two crossbars into place to lock it? From inside? Maybe you're going to think this is a dumb question, but why lock the door from inside? For that matter, how could he? Maybe you'll tell us he stood outside and used string to pull the bars into the brackets?"

Sheriff Crowell had been examining the .32 revolver.

"Odd you should say 'string,' " he remarked. "There's a little bit of white thread caught under the grip. Maybe the gun snagged on it inside his pocket."

"I noticed that," McIntyre said. "It doesn't quite look like thread. Looks to me like a bit of strand from a string. A white cotton string."

"String, no string, revolvers, automatics, dead men who bolt the door after they're dead, killers who look to see if a gun is loaded after the killing, killers who walk through solid walls," Doctor Lipp said, "all of which I have said before is not my business. Me, I've got a dead boy to take to the morgue and I've got a family to inform and that's what I'm paid for. Now I am thinking that Howard and I need to be going. You policemen can stand here with feet freezing and exchange theories if you want. But we are going."

With the morgue ambulance and its melancholy cargo on its way down the snow-packed mountain road, the others conducted another meticulous search of the scene. Deputy Sam Bartlett had a good idea, which was to find an undisturbed patch of snow and have each of them put his or her footprints in it. He then recorded the prints with his pocket Kodak.

"Just in case a footprint shows up on the coroner's photos that we can't identify," he explained.

They looked at the ground, they looked at the walls. Using the gas lantern, McIntyre went over every square inch of the inside walls in case there might be a concealed opening, like a loose block or a movable section. He scuffed the floor everywhere, hoping to find a trapdoor leading into a mine tunnel.

"Nothing," he reported to the others.

"Try the roof?" Sam asked. "Winter snow can bury a building up here in the mountains. Sometimes they put an escape hatch in the roof."

"Solid concrete and stone," the ranger said. "It's as if the miners built it to hide in. Maybe they felt threatened, maybe thought there could be an avalanche or a forest fire. Or maybe they had plans to dig through the back wall and into the side of the mountain but never got around to it."

"Maybe that ghost you saw in the mine scared them into hiding," Vi Coteau offered.

John Péguy took his leave, carrying his gunny sack and dragging the metal bar as he went, walking into the shadows of the trees the way he had come. Abe Crowell and Sam said they should make their way back down to the main road before it got any darker or any colder, and McIntyre reluctantly agreed. They packed up their gear, closed the blockhouse door and fastened the hasp, then started up the vehicles and drove slowly away.

"Well," Vi Coteau said cheerfully, blowing on her hands to warm them and then holding them in front of the truck's heat vent, "that was sure good fun. Don't think I'm being critical, but I prefer our first picnic to this one. What a gloomy place!"

"Gloomy's the word," McIntyre agreed, shifting down a gear to keep a good distance between his truck and the sheriff's car. "Perfect for our killer, I think."

"Tim, I think you think too much. Aren't you thinking about supper? I know I am."

"Supper? There's probably a law against what I would do to a juicy steak about now."

"See?" she said. "Let's go find supper. But why did you say 'perfect for a killer'?"

"I'm working on the three bullies theory again. The bullies had 'knuckled' a victim's chest, then one bully ends up with his chest crushed in a stamping mill. They 'canned' a victim, then another bully ends up suffocating head-down in an ore bucket. They locked one in a dark coal cellar until he wet his pants, and now the third bully is found dead in a building with no windows and no light. Wouldn't you say the killer had pretty much performed the hat trick?"

She held onto her door handle as the truck skidded around an icy turn in the road.

"Does this mean he's finished? There won't be any more killing?"

"I don't think there will be," McIntyre said. "He must be awfully pleased with himself."

"How's that?"

"Saving Richard and the room without windows for last. I doubt if he planned it that way. Probably planned all three at the same time and then took his opportunities as they came."

"Am I hearing you correctly?" she said. "You don't think Richard shot himself in the blockhouse?"

"Nope. Didn't shoot himself in the head, either."

"Don't be cute. If he didn't shoot himself, how did it happen?"

"I haven't worked that one out, not yet. But for the killer it makes a beautiful ending to his revenge drama. Look at it this way. Who was the one who read about Dunraven's hidden treasure and got the others all crazy to find it? Probably Richard. Who was 'The Little Man Who Wasn't There' when the other two got killed? Probably Richard."

"What's 'The Little Man Who Wasn't There'?" she asked.

"A children's nursery rhyme, but never mind that. Who was it who might be able to talk Winston into crawling down into the ore bucket? Who might have had access to an antique Irish coin?"

"Probably Richard."

"Who might be able to persuade Charles to lie down under the Big Horse stamping mill?"

"Okay, Richard."

"Now our killer realizes how perfect it is to have Richard and the dark room for last. If he can make it look like suicide, it will look as if Richard fell into a state of remorse about killing the other two boys and killed himself in a similar manner. It would be very Shakespearean, wouldn't it?"

"Oh, very."

"As an added benefit, Richard's suicide will cause deep grief to William Leup. The killer no doubt holds William partly responsible for Richard being a thug and a bully. When we figure out who the killer actually is, we might find out that he has a grudge against William, maybe involving money or a career. But it wasn't suicide. I'd bet on it. The suicide theory works out just swell for the killer. But it doesn't account for three things: no car, the rotated gun cylinder, and the Luger that Richard was carrying. I don't think the killer knew that Richard had a pistol."

They arrived at the intersection where the forest road met the main road, known to villagers as "the new road," where McIntyre stopped to remove the tire chains. Stepping out of the warm truck cab into the chill of the late afternoon, he realized that he had been running off at the mouth the whole way down the hill. And he had pretty much said that he would figure out how Richard was killed and who had done it. And he wished he had kept his mouth shut. The mere presence of Vi Coteau on the seat next to him seemed to turn his mind into a blithering mess.

Not that he minded.

By the time they reached the village, Ranger McIntyre and Vi Coteau had come to an agreement concerning how they would spend the evening. He would drop her off at the Pioneer Inn, then he needed to continue on to his cabin to feed Brownie and change out of uniform. Meanwhile she could clean up and change "and do all those other mysterious things we women do," and she could order supper for the both of them.

McIntyre returned an hour later and found that Charlene—or Mari, or both—had once again put two place settings on the small table near the fireplace. Logs crackled in the fire. Two floor lamps softly illuminated the corner of the room.

He had scarcely sat down when he had to stand up again, for Vi had come down the stairs. She had changed into a floor-length garment of Oriental design, a kind of flowing wrapper or dressing gown in silk with exotic designs. Her dark hair had been brushed until it shone in the firelight and she was wearing just enough fresh lipstick to make a man given to flights of imagination ask himself if his breath smelled bad.

"Wow," the witty ranger said.

"Nice, isn't it?" Vi replied. "Mari loaned it to me."

"Wow," he repeated.

Supper turned out to be Charlene's Irish stew accompanied by homemade bread in thick buttery slices and a platter of peeled carrots, celery sticks, and radishes.

"Sorry there's no steak. Be sure to eat all your vegetables," Charlene told McIntyre. "That's the last of the celery in the cold room and I don't know when I'll be able to find any more carrots. Be respectful and eat them all."

"You have refrigeration?" Vi asked.

"Just the walk-in cooler in the kitchen. And an icebox on the porch. But down in the cellar there's a dark room that stays cold all summer long."

"Oh, boy!" McIntyre said. "Darn!"

"Anything wrong with the stew?" Charlene asked.

"No, no. When you said 'cold room' it made me think of Fall River Lodge. I promised Minnie that I'd check the rat traps every couple of weeks. With all this murder and treasure business it slipped my mind. The stew is fine."

"Well," Charlene said, "Fall River Lodge had better slip back into your mind, and you'd better slip up there and have a look around. If Minnie should come back in the spring to a lodge full of rodents, I hate to think what she might do to you."

"Tomorrow morning. First thing. Priority Number One."

"I'll come along and help," Vi suggested. "I don't have to leave for Denver until after lunch."

With supper finished and the table cleared except for two steaming cups of coffee, McIntyre went to the bookshelves and returned with a new jigsaw puzzle. While he dumped it out and began to turn pieces right-side up, Vi put a fresh log on the fire and slid one of the floor lamps nearer the table. Charlene, having cleaned up the kitchen, decided to call it a night. Before retiring to her rooms, she peeked through the kitchen door to see if the ranger and the FBI woman were okay, thinking she might see them cuddling and necking on one of the couches. But they were sitting on opposite sides of the table in the light of a single floor lamp, their two heads nearly touching over the jigsaw puzzle.

The puzzle box showed the jigsaw picture labeled *Construction of the Acropolis*. A fanciful artist had made it look like an old woodcut engraving. One side of the Acropolis was mostly obscured by scaffolding; a primitive lifting crane resembling a hay derrick was prominent in the foreground. With the blocks of marble and the sections of column lying scattered about, it made for a challenging assortment of straight dark lines and shadows.

"I wonder how they make these things. How do they cut out all these pieces?" Vi said.

"I don't know. Maybe use a stamping press. Not a printing press. The kind that presses a knife blade down. Maybe it's a roller-like thing with blades in it that rolls across the cardboard."

"Pieces of two different puzzles would be interchangeable, like parts of a gun," Vi suggested.

"Maybe. Speaking of which, I hope Doctor Lipp recovers the bullet that killed Richard. I hope it's in one piece. I'd like to look at it."

"I'm sure he did."

"It's that gun, see? I was thinking about that gun when you came in to supper."

Thanks a lot, she thought. But "Oh?" was all she said.

"The way it's all worn out. Stands to reason the inside of the barrel is just as bad. Probably corroded, pitted. Rifling all worn down, I imagine. The bullet might prove it was fired through a worn-out barrel."

She picked up a puzzle piece she had been studying and slipped it into place.

"You're still pushing the idea that the .32 didn't kill him? But Tim, look at the evidence! We only found two guns, the .32 and the Luger. But the Luger was in his pocket. Even if he had used it to shoot himself, and had put it back in his pocket, we would've found the empty shell casing in the blockhouse. Plus, the Luger would have been cocked when we found it, being an automatic. Besides, Mister Ranger, a nine-millimeter bullet from a Luger would've gone right on through the boy's head. There would be an inch-wide exit wound, and a bullet hole in the wall behind him."

McIntyre had matched three pieces of puzzle. He set them into the frame.

"I don't know how the revolver's cylinder got turned, that's all."

"Well," she replied, "you yourself said that the stop notches were badly worn and the cylinder was loose. Maybe when Richard fell to the floor and dropped the gun the cylinder skidded on the concrete and just turned all by itself. Hmmm?"

"Maybe."

"Except you want to believe in a different version, right? C'mon, admit it. In your picture, a killer forces Richard into the blockhouse. Then he shoots him at close range, then for reasons we don't know, he opens up the revolver to look at the cylinder for remaining loads before he tosses it down beside the body. Then he leaves the blockhouse and magically locks it from the inside by sliding two thick crossbars across the door."

"I think Richard was in that place quite a while before he was shot," McIntyre said. "All those footprints seem to prove it. I think the killer wanted him to feel the fear of being locked in a dark place."

"Oh, goodie!" Vi said.

She might have said it because she had found a piece she wanted for the puzzle, or she said it to make fun of McIntyre's theory.

"Let me see if I understand clearly," she said. "Richard is inside. Hiding, maybe. From his killer. So Richard barricades the door. But the killer figures out a way to enter the locked building and shoots Richard. And leaves the gun. And escapes from the blockhouse without opening the door. Oh, say! I've got it! Look at this bit I've just finished! See how the builders of the Acropolis are using a crane to lift that huge slab of marble? I bet your killer had a way to lift the roof off the blockhouse! Or maybe one of the blockhouse walls is fitted with secret hinges to enable the whole wall to swing open! What do you think?"

He looked across the table and into her beautiful eyes.

"I think," he said, "it's funny that you're the one who called me a silly ranger."

CHAPTER FOURTEEN:
SHOOTING COTEAU TO MAKE A POINT

Gingerly so as not to scald his fingers, Ranger McIntyre lifted the brandy bottle from the pan of warm water, carried it to the table, and tipped it over his pancakes. He was fairly certain that it was contraband, although Rocky Mountain National Park was so new that nobody really knew whether or not foraging for food was illegal. New regulations were being handed down every day, it seemed, but so far no one had said anything about rangers gathering berries, catching breakfast trout out of season, or stealing honey from wild bees. One warm spring day, while he was investigating an illegal campsite, McIntyre had come across a bees' nest sagging with wild honey. By lucky coincidence there was a discarded brandy bottle, empty but corked, at the site. Obviously, it was fate: Mother Nature intended for him to have some honey.

Whoever had left him the empty bottle had good taste in illegal cognac. He remembered the brand from his time in France, and the price as well; squadron members joked about spending a month's pay on a single bottle. A couple of the fellows tried to scheme some way to purchase a full barrel, take it back to the States after the war, and become rich by bottling and selling it.

After breakfast he was wiping the last dish and wishing he hadn't filled the place with the smell of frying bacon, when his ears caught the unmistakable sensuous throb of the Marmon roadster coming along the road. Coming quickly along the road:

191

one of these days, McIntyre thought, smiling his wry lopsided smile, I'll be forced to give that girl a speeding ticket. He looked around the cabin to be certain that nothing was out of place. Should he offer her a chair? At the table, maybe. Coffee, was she expecting him to have fresh coffee? Would she find the cabin too warm? The woodstove gave off an awful amount of heat.

McIntyre hoped that one day he would be able to get over fretting about what Vi Coteau might think or what Vi Coteau might do. Each encounter with her was a lesson toward that end: little by little he was learning, as she usually said, "not to worry about it."

He heard her steps on the porch. When he opened the door, she swept into the cabin with a cheery "good morning!" and it seemed as if the brilliance of the sunlight on snow and all the glory of a Colorado winter morning had streamed through the doorway with her. Before he could say "let me help you with your coat" she had divested herself of both coat and gloves. She dropped them on the bed, took a mug from the pegs, poured herself a coffee, and sat down at his table. So much for worrying about it.

"What a morning!" Vi said. "I felt like driving on forever! Did you sleep well? Did you figure out how Richard ended up in that horrible dank blockhouse with a bullet through his head?"

"It is a great morning," he agreed. "I felt like throwing the saddle on Brownie and galloping through the snow. Yes, I slept reasonably well, and no, I didn't figure out how Richard was killed. But I can't accept suicide. Whenever I woke in the night there seemed to be a detail nagging at my mind about that place although I couldn't quite see what it was. Ever have the feeling when you woke up that you had just had a vivid, realistic dream, an important dream, but you can't remember any of it? Like that. But you're right, it would be a great morning to be riding or hiking. Even chopping wood, that would be great on a morning like this."

"Tim?"

"Yes?"

"You seem to be babbling. How much of this cowboy coffee have you had this morning?"

"Too much, I'd say."

She cradled the warm mug between her palms and sipped from it. McIntyre sat down at the table but wisely decided to forgo any more of the stuff. The two of them continued to chat like old pals, finally deciding to take the Small Delights pickup to the lodge, rather than drive the Marmon, because the last half mile of road from the highway to the lodge would likely be unbroken snow and the pickup had tire chains. Besides, as he pointed out, it was only a couple of miles and he had already put the gas lanterns and flashlights in a box in the back of the truck.

"We need flashlights?" Vi asked.

"The place is all shuttered for winter. Dark as the inside of your hat. And cold, I don't know why a closed-up building always feels colder when you're in it. We won't be long, though. Most of the rat traps are in the kitchen and dining room. A couple are on the stair landings. And I'll have a peek into the cellar while we're there."

"Do you really have rats up here?"

He laughed. "Not the kind you're thinking of. Not those city rats. We've got what they call wood rats, or pack rats, much bigger than mice. Almost the size of a ground squirrel. When they move into a building and start nesting, they make an awful mess."

The layer of unbroken snow on the approach road to Fall River Lodge was no more than half a foot deep. The pickup's narrow tires left a set of parallel tracks that looked as if they had been made by a skiing giant.

"The Marmon could have handled this," Vi said. "She can plow through this much snow at fifty miles per hour."

"That's what I was afraid of," McIntyre said.

He pulled around to the back of the building and stopped at the kitchen door. The garbage cans had been upended with heavy rocks on them and were undisturbed. There were no entry marks on the window or door, no sign of any problem whatever. When he unlocked the door and they stepped inside, Vi saw that he hadn't been exaggerating about the darkness of the place. The few tiny shafts of sunlight leaking through cracks and knotholes in the shutters seemed only to accentuate the gloom.

McIntyre lit the two gas lanterns. He and Vi Coteau made their way to the front door, which was secure, and they had a look at the reception desk. The trap behind the desk had been sprung by an unlucky field mouse: McIntyre unceremoniously dumped the dried-out little corpse into a paper bag and reset the trap. Another trap behind the electric refrigerator held a dead pack rat. The one in the pantry had been sprung, but was empty. McIntyre reset it.

"No bait?" Vi said.

"Old mountain man trick. You use bait to catch a big one first, then cut out his scent glands and wipe the scent on the trap triggers. Rodents can't resist sniffing at it."

"I see. And do you always have this much fun all winter?" Vi asked sweetly.

"No, not always," he said, "sometimes it's boring up here. Not like down in the city with gangsters firing machine guns at each other and bootleggers smuggling hooch."

When they reached the pantry area at the far end of the kitchen, McIntyre remembered the day when Minnie March pushed him into the little storage room and told him to take off his pants. The memory caused him to chuckle out loud.

"What is it?" Vi asked.

"Oh, nothing. Remember my tux, the one from Mike?"

"Remember your tux? It's an indelible memory. Every woman at that dinner probably wanted to take you home to meet her butler."

"Very funny. Was that a compliment? Anyway, I was chuckling because Minnie made me go into that dark room there and take my trousers off so she could make the alterations."

"Lucky Minnie," Vi said.

McIntyre set his lantern on the table and stood there, his arms crossed, a crease forming between his eyebrows. He was studying the dark doorway and the small square hole in the wall. The thick wall.

"Have you got your gun with you?" he asked.

"Sure. Why? Did you see a man-eating wood rat?"

"Take it out," he said.

Vi discreetly turned her back while drawing her pistol from its hiding place. She kept it where only she and God could see it. And God wasn't supposed to look. McIntyre, meanwhile, rummaged in the kitchen drawers until he found a ball of twine. He broke off ten feet or so and held his hand out for the gun. The warmth of the weapon was a surprise to his bare hand. He forced himself not to think about that warmth. Not at the moment. He definitely would think about it later.

A pile of chair cushions had been stored on top of a cabinet. McIntyre took a couple of them and used them to pad the floor inside the dark little cubicle of a room, just under the square hole.

"Now," he said. "You stand here in the storage room. I'm going to go out and shut the door. Imagine you're Richard inside the blockhouse. Somebody was after you and they chased you in here. You've realized it's the person who killed Charles and Winston. Now, pretend you're Richard and you've rushed into this place. You've barricaded the door. You're waiting. You're listening."

Ranger McIntyre looped the string through the trigger guard of Vi's pistol. As he got ready to shut the door, he looked at Vi standing there with her lantern, a look of patient curiosity on her face. McIntyre held up his fist with his thumb and forefinger extended.

"Almost forgot," he explained. "This is my own gun, see? Let's pretend it's the same caliber as yours. Okay?"

"Fine," she said. "Your fist is a loaded firearm and your finger is .38 caliber. I understand. Shut the door."

McIntyre closed the door and made a loud shout.

"Bang!" went McIntyre. "That was me shooting your gun into the air, okay?"

"No, it wasn't. It was you yelling 'bang!' "

Carefully, silently, he reached up and put Vi's pistol through the eight-inch hole in the wall. He held one end of the string and fed the other end until he felt the weight of the gun come to rest on the chair cushions inside. Then the pulled the string back, leaving the gun inside the room.

"Okay," he said. "Pretend you're Richard. What did you see and what did you do?"

"Well," she answered from inside the room, "there's a little bit of light coming in that hole and I saw . . . this is all kind of childish, Tim."

"Sure it is. Go on."

"All right. I saw a pistol come through the opening. A pistol on a string."

"And?"

"And what?"

"What was your reaction?"

"I picked it up. Oh, right! I see what you're thinking! Well, you smart cookie you! You're thinking I've never seen this gun before. I don't know where it came from. My natural reaction is to open the cylinder and see if it's loaded. Okay. Now I'm putting it on half-cock. Which turns the cylinder. Now I can open it. When I close it, the cylinder turns again. Now to take it off half-cock I need to fully cock it and gently lower the hammer. Which turns the cylinder once more. The spent cartridge is three chambers past the hammer. If he found the gun when he went into the blockhouse—sure! He would probably put the Luger in his pocket and then check to see if the revolver was loaded. And that's how the cylinder came to be turned past the empty shell."

"Right," McIntyre said.

"On the other hand, if it's true that he shot himself with it, then he had to have cocked it at least twice after shooting himself in the head, which doesn't make any sense at all."

"That's the idea," McIntyre said. "As for finding the gun in the blockhouse, remember the stovepipe hole? In the blockhouse roof? And do you remember the little white thread snagged on the .32's grip? I think he locked himself in, and then a loaded revolver appeared out of nowhere."

"And he shoots himself with it, then cocks it twice. Brilliant. Can I come out now? It's cold and dark in here."

"No, stay there. You're still Richard. There's one more thing. The most important piece of the puzzle. Now, be really quiet. Remember, you're Richard. I'm the killer. You're listening at the door trying to hear what I'm doing out here, right?"

"Okay, right."

"And don't forget. My fist is my own gun, same caliber as the one you're holding."

McIntyre pulled a chair close to the wall and stood on it. He put his hand to the small opening, his forefinger extended like the barrel of a gun. He whispered into the hole.

"Vi?"

"I'm Richard."

"Okay. Richard?"

He whispered very softly, so softly that she could barely hear. Vi Coteau stretched up to peer through the hole.

"What?"

"Bang!"

Vi came out of the disused storage room wearing an expression of mixed belief and disbelief.

"The killer was on the blockhouse *roof!*" she said. "To make it seem like suicide he needed an empty cartridge in the gun that he dropped through the hole. So he fired a shot off into the air. Before lowering the gun into the blockhouse."

"That was the first shot William Leup heard," McIntyre said.

"Except the killer didn't figure on Richard opening the gun to see if it was loaded. Anyway, the killer, he took out a second revolver, also .32 caliber, and whispered down the stovepipe hole. Richard, trying to hear what he was saying, looked up through the hole like I just did. And blam! Right in his forehead."

"Which would be the second shot William Leup heard."

"I'll be . . . darned."

"If the bullet in Richard's head doesn't match the revolver we found in the blockhouse, we'll have pretty good proof that it wasn't suicide."

"Let me take care of that," Vi suggested. "I'm sure the sheriff won't mind if I take the bullet with me and examine it. I'll photograph it under a microscope. What a new wrinkle this is! We've had lots of cases where we matched a bullet to a particular gun, but I don't think we've ever tried to prove that a certain bullet did not come out of a certain gun. Interesting. Gosh, Ranger, I'll say this much for you: you occasionally know how to show a girl a really good time."

They resumed searching the lodge for mice and pack rats

murdered by Minnie's traps. Down in the cellar it was even more dark, cold and spooky. Up on the second floor the hallway floorboards creaked underfoot. It was with a feeling of relief, a sensation of finally being able to breathe normally again, that they left the building and locked the door behind them.

"Lunch?" Vi suggested as she closed the valve on her lantern and pulled her gloves from her coat pocket.

"Got it right here," McIntyre said, holding up the paper bag with the deceased rodents in it. "Pack rat stew."

"You need to remember something, wise guy," she said. "I'm packing a gun. All you have is a finger you think is a gun. Now please dispose of that bag."

"Yes, ma'am."

McIntyre upended one of the garbage cans, dropped the bag into it, then weighed down the lid with a large rock.

"What's the name of that café in the village?" she asked. "Something about cats?"

"Kitty's Café," McIntyre said.

"Is the food any good?"

"Kitty's is usually open," McIntyre said. "That's what the locals say when anyone asks for a good place to eat lunch. They say 'well, Kitty's is usually open.' "

On the ride back to his cabin to pick up her Marmon, Vi Coteau finally said what McIntyre wanted to hear.

"I can't seem to think of anything wrong with your stovepipe theory. It even explains the powder burns on Richard's face."

"Thanks. Maybe I should come work for the FBI."

"Don't let's be too ambitious. One thing puzzles me. The condition of that .32 revolver. You said it was a piece of junk, really."

"Puzzles me, too," McIntyre said. "I don't think it came from William Leup's gun collection because he wouldn't have bought or kept such a thing in the first place. One of the college boys on a tight budget might have bought it at a pawn shop, but I doubt it. One thought I had . . ."

"Yes?" she asked.

"I thought maybe our metal scavenger, John Péguy, might have picked it up. Found it in an old cabin or mine site. Maybe kept it for salvage. But the problem is that it doesn't show the kind of rust you'd expect from a gun found in an old cabin. The bluing would be more faded, the grips would be dried out, cracked. Or missing."

Small Delights came around the final bend of the road, turned up the short approach road to McIntyre's cabin, and there sat the Marmon roadster. To McIntyre it suggested a crouching panther ready to spring. His Small Delights pickup truck, by contrast, seemed almost to be apologizing for itself as it came to a stop next to the Marmon.

"Did I see a bottle of French brandy in your kitchen?" Vi asked. "We could celebrate your murder theory."

"Honey."

"Are you getting fresh with me, Ranger?"

"Nope. Found the bottle empty. I keep honey in it."

"Ah, phooey," Vi replied. "In that case, while you remove your tire chains why don't I dash on into the village and reserve a table at Kitty's Café."

"Great," McIntyre said. "You could go ahead and order from the wine list. And maybe give the orchestra leader the names of your favorite songs. I'll just slip into my tux and be there before your motor cools."

She stepped into her Marmon, pressed the electric starter, and the heavy engine throbbed into life once more.

"You're still a silly ranger," she called to him over the roar. "You should know that I almost never let my motor cool."

Then with a spray of snow and exhaust, the roadster was gone. McIntyre stood looking after her. How she did enjoy life!

He wanted to tell her to slow down. But she must never learn why her speed and energy frightened him. She must never learn how his heart twisted into a knot when he saw her racing down a highway. Let her enjoy, he thought. He would not permit the other woman, the one whose car he found smashed and smoldering at the foot of the sheer embankment, he would not allow her ghost to rob Vi Coteau of so much as a minute of joy.

The snow had begun to fall again by the time the two of them had finished lunch. Reluctantly they said their goodbyes. Vi left the ranger with a kiss on the cheek and a squeeze of the hand even though the sidewalk in front of Kitty's Café was one of the most public places in the village.

"Take care," she said. "If you don't mind, I'd like to suggest that you keep your hole-in-the-roof theory under your big flat hat for the time being. If you're right, and I think you are, a killer is loose. And probably feeling cocky. If I were you, I'd drop the whole Dunraven treasure business and do something else for a while. He might be out there looking for the hoard, and I wouldn't want you to run into him."

"Suggestion understood. I'll be in touch," he said.

"I know," she replied with a smile.

Once more he watched until her roadster was out of sight.

He would need to drop in at the gas station and grocery store before driving back to his cabin. If the storm kept up all night he might be snowed in for a few days.

The following morning proved the wisdom of McIntyre's precaution, for the first thing he was aware of when he woke up was the tomblike silence. A deep, deep hush enveloped the cabin as if the Winter Giant had draped thick quilts over the roof. Inside, the place was as chilly as an icebox. Bravely, heroically, McIntyre silently counted "one . . . two . . . THREE" and pushed the blankets aside. He jumped from the bed, hurried to the stove, and got the fire going. His hands shook as he dressed himself and pulled on his heavy coat and mittens.

He went out into the silent white world. Before doing anything else, he needed to shovel a path to the stable and move snow out of the way in order to open the pasture gate. Brownie waited impatiently while he shoveled snow and tugged at the gate. When the opening was wide enough, she nosed him aside and dashed out into the unbroken snow like a little kid on winter holiday from school. She trotted the entire perimeter with her head high, looking out into the forest as if to let all other animals see that she was the queen of the national park.

McIntyre shook his head at her and went to prepare hay, grain, and water for Her Reining Majesty. The sky remained cloud-covered and gray, but since the snow had stopped falling, he decided he would dig a few more paths before fixing his breakfast. It was lucky that Assistant Ranger Jamie Ogg was using the official national park pickup truck while McIntyre was on furlough: it left room for his Small Delights pickup to stay dry under the shed, which had room for only one vehicle. The shed was not warm, but it was dry. At least he wouldn't have to dig the pickup out from under a pile of snow.

After breakfast McIntyre washed the dishes and put them away. He went about the cabin straightening the bedclothes, stacking the magazines neatly, hanging clothes in the cupboard. He wanted to keep the place looking as tidy as Dottie and Charlene had left it. He sat down and wrote two letters, which he would post the next time he was in town. He shaved, brushed his uniform, and polished his boots and gun belt.

Around noon the cloudless sky was an endless deep blue and the sun was as high and as warm as it was going to be. He saddled Brownie and went for a fast trot up along the river trail. Before long the muscles of his back and thighs were telling him he needed to spend more time in the saddle. He paused beside the stream at a spot where an underwater ledge of granite created tumbling rapids and the churning of the water kept it free of ice. There would be trout down there. Large ones. There would be oxygen in the bubbling water and insects and worms caught in the swirl. A man could use a sparsely hackled small fly resembling a dead nymph. With a tiny weight of split shot on the line, maybe twelve inches above the fly to carry it down to where the trout were. They wouldn't be feeding as actively as in summer, but they'd be there.

Brownie heard the ranger's deep sigh and flicked one ear. She took it as a signal that he had decided to end the ride and return her to her stable and a fresh pail of grain. If it had been summer, he might have dismounted with his fly rod and left her to sample the moist grass growing tall along the water. Damp, fresh, wild grass beside a mountain stream was all she knew about fishing and it was all she cared to know.

The ride back up along the stream served to solidify one idea in McIntyre's mind. After putting Brownie back in her pasture and a few slabs of firewood in the stove—and setting the coffee pot to warm—he went to work on it. First, he took sheets of writing paper and cut them into fourths. Then on each square he wrote one fact about the killings of the three boys. Next, he wrote down all the remaining questions, including those concerning the so-called "hoard" of treasure. He made a square for the name of each person who was connected to the puzzle. Finally, a mug of coffee by his elbow, he sat down at the table and started sorting the paper squares into patterns.

The telephone rang at midmorning of the following day. The weather was still pleasantly sunny and clear; the snow had begun to melt enough to drip from the eaves of the cabin roof.

"Lonely up there?" Vi Coteau asked.

"Heck, no. Crowds of people coming and going. The family of marmots who hibernate behind the truck shed, they've even been complaining about the noise. How about yourself? I bet you're keeping busy at your typewriter, huh."

"You're not far wrong," she said. "Things in Denver have been pretty quiet, but Agent Cannily still manages to find stacks of reports to file and letters to type and statistics to correlate. But I did have time to take that bullet to the guys in the lab, after Sheriff Crowell posted it to me."

"What'd they say?"

"I hope you're listening, because you may never hear me say this again."

"Say what?"

"That you were right."

"I was?"

"That slug in Richard's forehead? It never came out of that .32 revolver we found beside his body. The point of it was smashed until it looked like a mushroom, which is to be expected when a bullet hits bone, but the tail of the bullet showed very clearly that it came out of a nearly new gun barrel. The rifling grooves were sharp and deep."

"I'll be darned."

"No doubt you will. The lab boys fired the .32 into a water tank—twice—and compared the slugs. Inside the barrel of the gun there was a corroded gap in one of the rifling lands. One of the slugs showed that gap. Ned—that's the lab guy—he said the barrel was so worn out that a bullet would actually wobble as it went down it."

"Okay," he said. "I really, really appreciate you for doing that. One more thing? Can you ship the gun and bullets back to Sheriff Crowell, along with a formal-looking report from the lab? About the bullet not coming from that gun?"

"Boy," Vi said, "between you and Agent Canilly, a gal hardly has time to go shopping for clothes. Sure, I'll see to it."

"And . . ." Ranger McIntyre added.

"And?"

"I'd like a couple of phone numbers," he said. "One for that 'Beeky' kid at the library, maybe his home phone number, and one for that mining engineer, that inspector named Beauchamp. As soon as I can organize it, I'd like to maybe set up a little trap and maybe catch our killer in it."

"Wouldn't that be illegal?" she asked sweetly. "I wouldn't want to visit you in prison."

"Think of it as fishing. I'm thinking of using the Dunraven Hoard as a lure, see."

"You still believe in it? I thought you came to the conclusion that it was a myth."

"No, I'm pretty sure it isn't. In fact, one of my jobs this week is to find out. Either way, it'll make a pretty good piece of bait."

CHAPTER FIFTEEN:
THE SCENE WITH SUSPECTS
GATHERED IN A LIBRARY
(OR, MCINTYRE RUNS A BLUFF)

When this is all over, McIntyre thought, I'm sending my phone bill to William Leup. Supervisor Nicholson sure as heck won't stand for it. Besides, Leup probably has more money than the Park Service has.

He picked up the telephone one more time and asked the operator to connect him with Sheriff Crowell. With any luck at all, this could be the last of the phone calls.

"Abe?" he said. "This is Tim, up at the Fall River ranger station. I think everything's been arranged. The librarian said we could use the small conference room in the Special Collections section. 'Beeky' agreed to gather up any documents the boys might've looked at. Beauchamp will drive down from the School of Mines, and I've persuaded the young lady at the scrap yard to give John Péguy a message that he ought to be there, too. She's been seeing a lot of him lately, or the other way 'round."

"What about the two families? Of the dead boys? Or Mr. Leup, for that matter."

"I don't see any need to trouble them. As for Mr. Leup, we know where to find him. He wouldn't be interested in the 'hoard' idea, anyway. But I'll let him know, or let his secretary know. If he wants to be part of the discussion, fine."

"Okay, Tim," Abe Crowell said. "I'll be there. I'll bring my deputy. Might even bring Judge Walker along, if he's free. He and I had a long chat the other day. He's mighty interested in the whole case. He's also a fisherman. Wants to pump you for information about good spots in the park."

And that was that. Everything arranged. Ranger McIntyre pushed the phone to the far side of the desk and stretched his legs. What he needed now was a warm day, green grass, and a fly rod in his hand. Either that, or an especially fine breakfast.

He paced the cabin. He took the little squares of paper he had sorted and stacked them in a shoebox. He thought of saddling Brownie and going for a long ride; however, when he looked out the window and saw Brownie standing in her stable, her head drooping almost to the ground, practically asleep, he knew how she felt. He felt the same way. A ride seemed like too much bother. With a sigh of self-pity and a brave shrug of his shoulders, he sat back down at his desk and took out his fountain pen. Before the upcoming cockamamie "conference" about the Dunraven case, he needed to write himself a script, including all the probable questions, all the possible answers.

Ranger Tim McIntyre in full uniform and looking and feeling very official was at the library when the doors opened that morning. Mr. Pipple recognized him, as did Mr. Pauling, the librarian in charge. "Beeky," they told him, wouldn't be arriving until ten o'clock. And yes, they had no objection whatever if Beeky wanted to leave his duties long enough to participate in an informal meeting. The room in Special Collections was prepared. Would the ranger care to wait in the librarians' lounge where he could help himself to coffee and rolls?

The ranger would. In order to make it to the early meeting in Denver, he had skimped on breakfast.

Sheriff Crowell was next to arrive, accompanied by deputy Sam Bartlett. Like McIntyre they were dawn-rising men. Sam helped himself to a mug of coffee. Sheriff Crowell declined, explaining that the thousands of gallons of coffee he had drunk during years of law enforcement had given him a pretty dodgy stomach.

At ten o'clock they went into the Special Collections room and discovered Beeky hard at work copying index cards.

"I don't know why people cannot wash their hands before riffling through the indexes," he complained. "I'll bet I copy these cards ten times per year. Look at these smudges!"

"Did you find out anything more about the Dunraven thing?" McIntyre asked.

"Not much more. After you phoned, I went looking for any other journals or letters connected to the English Hotel but other than a few lines in a book written years later by Dunraven's personal physician there seems to be nothing. I'm ready to summarize for everyone, as you asked."

"Mind if I look around while we wait for the others?" McIntyre said. "Old books really fascinate me."

"Yes, but please don't remove anything from a shelf without telling me. Whenever a person reshelves a book in the wrong place it can take weeks to find it. The documents behind the glass doors are off limits, of course. Need to be handled with gloves."

McIntyre was pleased to see John Péguy, scrap metal collector, come through the door. Péguy had shaved, combed his hair, and donned a jacket and tie. The apparent reason for this transformation followed him, both of them looking a little unsure of whether they should be there. It was the young woman from the scrap yard, she with the unforgettable blue eyes and ungovernable curls of red hair.

"Okay if she stays?" John asked.

"Sure," McIntyre said, offering her his hand. "I'm Ranger McIntyre."

"Claire Candler," she said. "You were at the metals yard earlier."

"Guilty," he said with a smile. "C'mon in. We're going to use the conference room back there, if you want to find a chair and make yourself comfortable."

When John Beauchamp arrived, McIntyre studied him closely, and not only to confirm that the mine engineer was a husky-looking outdoorsman, strong enough to move a human body if he needed to. He also wanted to watch how John Beauchamp greeted Beeky. They shook hands furtively, very formally, very stiffly.

When Vi Coteau came sweeping into the room John Péguy jumped to his feet like a man in search of a way to escape.

"Don't worry," Vi said, gently pressing him back into his chair. "I'm just here to watch what the ranger does."

Vi extended her hand to the young woman with the red hair.

"Vi Coteau," she said, introducing herself. "I'm afraid I pointed my gun at your friend once. He's a little uncertain about me."

"Claire Candler," the young woman replied.

Ranger McIntyre and Sheriff Abe Crowell stood talking to each other. The others, except for Vi Coteau, were sitting stiffly at the table, uncertain as to what it was all about. The ranger seemed to be waiting for one more participant to show up.

On the pretext of browsing the shelf of books behind the table, Vi covertly gave each person in the room a visual inspection. Very casually she made her way over to McIntyre and whispered in his ear.

"Your scrap collector's lady friend is carrying a pistol," she said softly.

"You sure?"

"She keeps patting the pocket of her slacks to assure herself it's there. And I caught a glimpse of the outline through the material. A small automatic, I'd say."

"I'm not really surprised," McIntyre said. "Working in scrap iron, she must run into any number of rough men. Probably carries a good bit of cash, too. Anyway, I've got a gun, too."

McIntyre's final guest appeared in the doorway, an athletic-looking young man wearing a varsity sweater over his shirt and tie.

"They told me you were here," he said.

"Here we are," McIntyre said. "I'm glad you came. Hope we didn't pull you out of classes?"

"Just a lab. I can make it up."

"Everyone," McIntyre said, "this is Bruce Jones, formerly of the Fifteenth Field Artillery, secretary of the fraternity house where the three unfortunate boys lived."

Bruce Jones found himself a chair, Vi and the sheriff took chairs next to each other, and Ranger McIntyre went into his prepared script. To tell the truth, he would rather face a charging grizzly than do any kind of public speaking.

"Uh . . . gentlemen, ladies," he began, "you probably don't know everybody. So as not to beat about the bush, each of us has a connection to the poor kids who met with these bad accidents up in the mountains. Mr. William Leup—father of Richard, the young man who died in the blockhouse—he asked me if I would try to figure out what happened to Winston and Charles. Richard was a longtime friend of theirs and he thought the least he could do was make certain the families weren't left with any questions about the accidents."

"Speaking of which," John Beauchamp interrupted, "I don't see Leup or any parents here."

"I didn't see any reason to put them through it. The pain of talking about it, I mean," McIntyre explained. "And I'm sure they don't go around talking about it with friends and neighbors. I thought we might all kick some ideas around, exchange thoughts and questions, generally see if we can get a clearer picture of everything that's happened. I'm also here to ask you folks about how we can hush up all this talk about a hidden treasure. Dunraven's Hoard, they call it. I don't know who first put the bee in their bonnets about it, but according to Mr. Beeky here, the three young men showed up to search the collection for journals, articles, diaries, anything connected with Lord Dunraven's enterprise. Apparently, they found certain information in an old journal whereupon they started skipping classes and went prowling around various abandoned gold mines on the edge of the national park. John, you do a lot of exploring up there. How dangerous are those places?"

"Awful dangerous," John Péguy said. "A man can trip and fall down a shaft or a pit. Old tunnels can have deep sumps in the floor, to drain the water from underground springs. Some of those you could drown in. The miners laid beams across the holes but those beams can rot out. Man steps on a rotten one and down he goes."

"Mr. Beauchamp," McIntyre said. "What about machinery?"

"I've got to agree," the mine inspector said. "Old rivets can rust, those corroded cables can break, maybe a sturdy-looking headframe can give way without warning. Well, like we found out, even a rusty ore bucket can trap a man and suffocate him. It's dangerous to encourage people to poke around that stuff."

"Is that what you were doing at the Big Horse Mine, when you were hammering on a support beam inside the tunnel? Testing to see if it was safe?"

"Uh . . . yes. Yes, testing."

"There's another hazard," McIntyre explained to the group around the table. "Let's say the mine inspector here had been pounding on tunnel braces to see if they were sound, and he accidentally knocked one loose enough—accidentally—that maybe the next curious person who came along would touch it and cause it to collapse and trap him inside a dark tunnel with no way out. Maybe."

"Could happen," Sheriff Crowell added. "It might seem far-fetched but you wouldn't think so if you've ever seen one of those supports collapse. The whole tunnel roof can come down."

"Here's another thing," McIntyre continued. "If our hypothetical explorers are searching for Dunraven's Hoard, let's say they came into a tunnel and saw fresh marks on a support. Or maybe recent marks on the tunnel wall from a miner's pick. Wouldn't they be curious and try the same thing? Kind of like people who see a sign saying 'Wet Paint' and can't resist putting their finger on it to see. But we're straying off the track here a little."

"Yeah, what is the point, exactly?" John Péguy asked.

"Just this. Other than the families of the three boys, all of us in this room are the ones who have been closest to these tragedies. What I'm saying, John, is that we can be kind of a citizen's committee to try and keep it from happening again. Now you, for instance. What's the most extreme thing you could do to help keep people from prowling around those unsafe old mines?"

"Well," John said thoughtfully, looking at his blue-eyed friend, "ever since you and I had that chat up at the Betsy Mine I've been considering changing locations. Find me a regular house. It's not much of a life for a man, living all alone and scrabbling around for junk to sell. I guess the very most extreme thing I could do would be to haul away all my metal scrap, burn the shack to keep anybody else from using it, then close the road I made through the woods. Cut down trees and let 'em fall across it. I could make it harder to drive a car to the Big Horse, anyway."

"Sheriff? What about you?" McIntyre asked.

"Me? Most extreme thing I could do?" Sheriff Crowell replied. "Let me think. Like John said, I guess we could block off any roads going to old mines. We could print signs warning people not to enter any tunnels or climb on any old equipment. Maybe I could ask the Forest Service boys to block the roads and pull down any old headframes, maybe dynamite the old tunnels."

McIntyre turned toward the fraternity house secretary.

"How about it, Mr. Jones?"

"I see where you're headed with this, Ranger. The most obvious thing, I mean in my world at least, would be to alert the heads of all the Greek houses on campus. We meet once a month. The heads, I mean. I'll warn them to be on the lookout for any members—especially young ones, pledges and sophomores—getting worked up over some scheme or other. We have had boys come up with fantastic schemes to build a distillery in the frat house garage, or find a roulette wheel for the rumpus room and make money running a gambling den. We've had young men taken advantage of by slick-talking salesmen who con them into buying huge lots of vitamins to sell door-to-door, or encyclopedias. And, of course, there was the 'treasure' furor where each boy thought he could be a hero by hiking up into the mountains and coming back with a treasure. I think you're right. Us Greek leaders need to take a more active part in discouraging such stuff. One good thing about college types is that they lose interest pretty quickly if you shut them down fast enough."

"Good," McIntyre said. "Very good. See? This meeting of ours might save a life or two. Now for Miss Vi Coteau. I'm not going to put her on the spot with the same question. A couple of you know that she's administrative assistant to Agent A.T. Canilly at the Denver office of the FBI, but the FBI doesn't have a role in this situation. Other than the fact that all three mines are on federal land, of course."

"I don't like to disagree with you," Vi Coteau said sweetly, and insincerely, "but there is one thing to consider that might discourage treasure hunters. It's the ownership angle. As you pointed out, the abandoned mines are on federal lands. Most of them once operated under federal mining permits. If anything of value should be discovered, you see, then the question of ownership comes into play. Technically speaking, it would be illegal to remove anything from the national forest without permission—firewood, rocks, old buildings . . . and artifacts such as scrap metal. The government doesn't have the resources to track down and prosecute everyone who does it, of course. Lucky for Mr. Péguy, you see. However, if a hoard of money and valuables happened to be discovered, the government would undoubtedly claim it. To take it away without declaring it would be illegal. And if you were allowed to take it away, there would be taxes to pay on its value."

"Sounds discouraging," McIntyre said. "I'm glad I turned that old Irish penny over to Sheriff Crowell for safekeeping."

He looked around the room as he said it, hoping that the mention of the Irish penny had caused a reaction. No one, however, with the exception of the sheriff, seemed to know what he was talking about.

McIntyre asked Sam Bartlett, the sheriff's deputy, for suggestions and questions. Sam was a deep-thinking man, and a slow-talking man, and by the time he had finished considering and explaining, the others were starting to squirm in their chairs. He wasn't done, either. Having slowly described every detail of every piece of evidence, Sam went back over it again to make sure they hadn't missed anything.

"Thanks," McIntyre said at last. "How about you, Mr. Beeky? I don't want you to think I've forgotten about you. Anything to add?"

Beeky was an easy person to overlook. With his thin frame and drab suit, he seemed to blend into the bookshelves. He cleared his throat—a nervous habit, like adjusting his spectacles on his beak-like nose—and spoke. Evidently, he had spent the past hour rehearsing what to say; when he started to speak he sounded as if he had mentally translated his sentences from the German.

"I am," he began, "I am not privileged to deny access to this collection of documents to any person qualified. Nor indeed to any resident of the state of Colorado or any person engaged in any legitimate occupation within the city limits. I know all of you are thinking that I should not have let those boys rummage within the collection. They discovered documents which they were clearly not qualified to interpret properly. I suppose my 'most extreme' action would involve supervising persons who conduct research in the collection, although I'm certain that many would consider it unwarranted invasion of privacy were I to look over their shoulders, in a manner of speaking, while they examined documents. As for the three men in question, I shall adamantly refuse to accept any and all responsibility for their deaths. I am not a very husky fellow, as you can see, and when three athletic college men demanded access to the shelves—which they had every right to—I had no way to deter them whatever."

"I understand," Ranger McIntyre replied, "I also understand that you knew the three varsity gentlemen from way back? In high school? I only bring it up because it helps explain why you couldn't stand in their way. Even if you didn't like them, maybe resented them for picking on you when you all were younger. Right?"

While speaking to Beeky, McIntyre had been keeping an eye on the others, particularly John Péguy and John Beauchamp. Those two were becoming more and more fidgety as the hour dragged by and as the discussion became more and more pointless. McIntyre would later explain to Vi Coteau that it was like hunting rabbits. The animals would freeze motionless in the grass and become virtually invisible; however, if the hunter remained calm and kept on pretending to be indifferent to them, sooner or later one rabbit would twitch an ear or shift a foot.

John Beauchamp spoke up.

"You're still wandering off the point," Beauchamp said. "If you even have one. I don't know about the rest of you, but I've got better things to do than sit here chatting about keeping secrets. But I got a question I'd like answered, Ranger."

Gotcha, McIntyre thought. "What's that?" he said.

"I heard . . . I mean, somebody said . . . or maybe I read it somewhere in a newspaper . . . you or the sheriff or somebody thought these three boys were, you know, killed by a third party. Murder. What's the official stance on the thing? Accidents? Or murder? Or have you made up your mind?"

"Sure. Except maybe it would be better if Sheriff Crowell addressed that issue. It's under his jurisdiction. Sheriff?"

"No," Sheriff Crowell said. "You go ahead. You're better at sticking the pieces together than I am."

"Somebody do it!" the mining engineer huffed. "Make up your minds! Hell, I wish I hadn't asked! This whole so-called meeting is stupid, if you ask me."

Good, McIntyre thought. The rabbit's getting edgy.

"I'm glad to talk about it, then," McIntyre said. "I'll try to boil it down as quick as I can. First off, when they found Winston dead in that old ore bucket everybody thought it was an accident. Except what nobody could figure out was why he was there alone in the first place and how he got there. To the May Day Mine, I mean. It was almost like somebody he knew had said something like 'Hey, Winston, I was up at the May Day the other day and found these old coins and you and I ought to drive up and look around for more and then . . .'"

"Then what?" John Beauchamp demanded.

"Then left him there alone, see. And he got stuck in the

bucket while trying to retrieve an old coin he saw in there. End of story. Then Charles was found lying under the stamping mill with his chest crushed and the same questions came up. How did he get there and why was he there? When I began poking around, it seemed like he might have driven up there in his own car and there was confusion over whether John here had just 'found' the car or if Charles had sold it to him. But then how did he figure to get home again if he left the car with John? The obvious answer is that there was somebody else up there at the Big Horse, somebody he could ride back to town with. I think maybe he went there to meet that person. Seems odd that he'd go there alone. It seems more likely that someone he knew said something like 'you know, Charles, I was at the Big Horse Mine the other day and found a really old arrow carved into a tree and it points toward the tunnel, and maybe you and I ought to meet up there and look around.' "

"I didn't see anybody else," John Péguy volunteered. "I was up there scavenging when I heard the kid's car come up the road and stop. When I went to see who it was, I seen he had a handmade 'For Sale' sign in the window so I asked him how much and we dickered a little and I paid him cash. He gave me the keys and the title and I drove back down the road and then up to my place. Never seen nobody else."

"Okay, okay," John Beauchamp said. "You're saying somebody lured those two up to the mines to accidentally kill them."

"I think the first one was accidental. Meant to frighten Winston, but it killed him. Maybe it was the same with Charles, although with that stamping mill there was a much greater risk that it could actually kill him."

"Then who did it, if anybody? If the boys weren't just messing around with the equipment. That's why I've been commissioned to inspect those places, you know. To keep stuff like this from happening."

"Richard Leup maybe did it. That's what it looks like, doesn't it? I guess we can all figure out how it could happen."

Beauchamp now appeared even more nervous than before. He seemed to regret having brought up the whole issue.

"What I mean is," McIntyre calmly continued, "the finger points toward Richard. It makes sense to think that he was the one who . . . what was your word for it . . . 'lured'? Who lured them up there."

"Why?" John Péguy asked.

"That's the part that had me puzzled. But then I realized what had happened. Richard and his pals stumbled across this reference to the Dunraven Hoard, right? They then learn—from the college librarian—that there's more information at the Denver library. And who do they run into there? The boy they used to call 'Beeky' and used to torment something awful. The boy who dropped out of college because of them. The boy who would have become an engineer if it wasn't for them. Who was still afraid of them. Richard, who apparently was the more mature of the three, he begins to feel regret. Or remorse. Anyway, he feels bad about what they did to ruin Beeky's life. When they find him working at the library, Richard's two pals start right in bullying him again so he'll help them. Richard, who probably realized by now that all the treasure hunt stuff was pure bunk, he comes up with the idea of giving his pals a little taste of their own, see? Teach them a lesson. Help them grow up. They 'canned' Beeky in school, therefore Richard sees the ore bucket and has the cute idea that he might 'can' Winston to show him what it was like. Charles used to 'knuckle' Beeky's chest until it was all bruised. Richard says okay, I'll smack him in the head and he'll wake up with fifty or a hundred pounds of steel pushing down on his chest. And here's another motive for Richard wanting to silence Charles: Charles might figure out how Winston actually died and tell the police. Maybe he said 'remember how you used to torture Beeky, same could happen to you,' and like that. But things go wrong again and both boys end up dead and Richard realizes that he's the obvious suspect. He's scared, he's full of remorse. He takes a .32 revolver from his father's collection, locks himself in the dark blockhouse, just like they used to lock Beeky in the dark coal cellar, and he shoots himself. He's killed his friends, his father's life will be all upset when it turns out his son is a killer, and to top it off . . . and here's where I feel guilty myself . . . there's a snoopy ranger hired by his father to find out all the facts. What's the only way out? A bullet to the head. I apologize for being long-winded, but that's how we're supposed to see the whole situation."

"Supposed to?" Claire Candler asked. McIntyre turned his attention toward her and missed John Beauchamp's quick move to slide his gloves off the table and into his jacket pocket like a man preparing to leave.

"Yes, supposed to," McIntyre said to Claire. "You've worked on jigsaw puzzles? You know how some pieces don't seem to fit anywhere, almost like they got into the box by accident?"

"Sure."

"In Richard's case we've got a couple of pieces like that. How did he get to the Betsy Mine? It's almost like whoever 'lured' Winston and Charles also enticed Richard into a car and drove him up there, then left him. The next piece that won't fit is this: why did Richard barricade the door? You'd think he would want people to open it and find him. Suicides usually want to be found, or so I've heard. No, I think somebody, maybe somebody with a gun, was chasing Richard. I think he ran into the blockhouse and threw the bars across the door for protection. Ask yourself why Richard would be carrying a Luger automatic, if he didn't have anything to be afraid of? Then there's one more really puzzling piece. The gun. The one we found lying next to Richard wasn't the one that killed him. The gun we found is old and beat up, a real piece of junk with a badly corroded barrel. The bullet in his brain, though, it came from a nearly new and well-maintained gun."

McIntyre rose from his chair and looked across the table at John Beauchamp.

"Just one more piece that bothers me," he said. He was smiling, but he didn't mean it.

"And what would that be, Ranger?" Beauchamp asked.

McIntyre nodded toward "Beeky."

"How come you've never told us that Beeky is your son? Your son Melvin. You know, 'Beeky' being a kind of nickname for the way your name is pronounced. 'Beecham'?"

"None of your business," John Beauchamp growled. "But if your next damn question is whether I'm glad those bullying bastards are finally out of his life, such as it is, the answer's yes. I am. If you ever had any kids, you'd know what I mean."

"As a matter of fact," McIntyre said, "for my next question I was going to ask where your rucksack is. The one you had with you when we ran into each other at the mine sites."

"It's in my car," Beauchamp said.

"Sheriff," McIntyre said, "are you a gambling man at all?"

"Been known to lay down a bet now and then."

"I'll bet you that if you were to lay hands on Mr. Beauchamp's rucksack and look inside, you'd find three things. You'd find a camp hatchet, just the thing for cutting green wood into wedges. You'd find a surveyor string, a ball of twine with knots tied at two-foot intervals, used to measure approximate distances, like how wide a mine tunnel is, or how high a headframe is. Probably thirty feet of string, or more. And you'll find a shiny, well-oiled, nearly new .32 pistol, probably a revolver."

"Is that all?" Sheriff Crowell asked.

"That ball of twine, it's going to be white cotton like the little strand we found stuck under the pistol grip. I'd bet on that. Heck, I'll go out on a limb and bet on one more thing you'll find in the rucksack, probably in one of the side pockets."

"Being?"

"Being a pocket notebook like surveyors and inspectors always carry. There'll be a page torn out, which we'll compare to the edges of the supposed 'suicide' note. Did you bring a warrant to search Mr. John Beauchamp's car, like I suggested?"

He had tipped the sheriff a quick wink of the eye and Crowell instantly picked up on it.

"Sure," he said, patting his jacket lapel. "Got it right here."

"That's fine. I'm one hundred percent certain we can tie that rucksack to the killing of Richard Leup. Stake my badge on it."

McIntyre was a hunter, and McIntyre was a horseman. In both pursuits his nerves had learned to read an animal's intentions from the way it tensed its muscles or in the way it cocked a foot a certain way that meant it was about to run. Or attack. Now he watched Mine Inspector Beauchamp carefully.

However, he didn't speak to the suspect. Much to Vi Coteau's surprise, McIntyre turned away from Beauchamp and focused on Beeky instead. The ranger's voice came low and deliberate and there was nothing but seriousness in it.

"What I'd like to know, Mr. Melvin Beeky, is how you managed the physical part of killing Winston and Charles. I tried hoisting that ore bucket and I tried raising one stamping rod on the crusher and I could barely move them. And I've got twice your weight and muscle. The car, too. I need to know about the car you used to take the boys up to the mines, after you showed them the 'documents' you had discovered in the library collection. You don't own a car—I checked on that—which makes me guess that you persuaded Winston and Charles and Richard to use theirs. You may not have become an engineer like your dad wanted, but you're a lot more clever at things like that than you look. I think your dad is right. I think if it hadn't been for the bullies, you could have earned your degree and become an outstanding engineer."

Sheriff Crowell shifted nervously in his chair. Trying to follow which man in the room was McIntyre's murderer was starting to give him a headache.

"Wait," the sheriff said. "You're trying to tell us that it was young Beauchamp who caused those deaths? Including Richard's? You think he borrowed his dad's gun and hatchet and string and stuff? What did he do, make up that whole story about Dunraven's Hoard so's he could tempt the boys into going up to the mines? How the heck could he shoot Richard and then bar the door from inside?"

There was a moment of silence in the room, followed by the scrape of John Beauchamp's chair as he stood up.

"Ranger," the mine inspector said, "could I talk to you in private? Maybe just step outside for a minute, have a word with you? Won't take long. I'd sure appreciate it."

"Sure," McIntyre replied. "Sheriff, if you'll keep everyone here just a little longer? Mr. Beauchamp and I, we'll go down the corridor by the fire exit. Be right back."

Beauchamp led the way, walking slowly as he and the ranger went to the end of the library corridor. To McIntyre the sadness and resignation in the slump of Beauchamp's shoulder looked somewhat exaggerated, a bit too dramatic. When they got to the end and the engineer turned to face McIntyre, his face was blank and staring.

"Listen, Ranger," he began. "You've got to understand about my boy. I think those bullies caused him a kind of brain damage. Back in high school, I mean. He never talked about it much. His mother told me he just came home from school most days and went to his room and she heard him crying and sobbing. He told me the boys picked on him but we never knew how bad it was. What I'm saying is, if you'll take care of him . . . I mean, none of this is really his fault, you know. Don't let the law go too hard on him. That sheriff, he asked about the Dunraven Hoard story? I know that part's true because Beeky told me how he uncovered the journal and then the letters. God, I don't know what's to become of us."

McIntyre put his hand on Beauchamp's shoulder.

"Don't worry about your son," he said. "He'll be fine. Given enough time. Kids have a way of turning into responsible adults if you're patient. He likes his job, they like him, he'll be fine."

"What do you mean? Are you telling me that he's not going to jail?"

"Nope. You are."

Believing that McIntyre suspected his son Melvin of the killings had been John Beauchamp's straw upon the water, something a drowning man would grab for, but now it was snatched away.

The tired slump of his shoulders and the weary resignation in his face were gone in one instant.

Beauchamp ducked away from McIntyre's hand, slamming his elbow into McIntyre's stomach. John was strong and tough; the sharp elbow to the gut brought out a "whoof!" like a ruptured inner tube, causing the ranger to double over in pain. McIntyre stumbled, caught himself, and reached out to grab hold of Beauchamp but was too late. Beauchamp rammed his shoulder against the fire exit door and before McIntyre could straighten up, the man was down the metal stairs and running for the parking lot.

CHAPTER SIXTEEN:
CAR CHASE AND TREASURE

Those in the conference room heard the noise of the hallway door crashing open and then McIntyre yelling to Beauchamp to stop. Beeky was the first to make a move, but he had hardly reached the hallway when Sheriff Crowell and Vi Coteau dashed past him with guns drawn. They got to the exit door in time to look down the fire stairs and see Ranger McIntyre vanish around the corner of the building.

The sheriff turned to the others who were standing open-mouthed in the corridor.

"Sam!" he shouted. "Sam! Down the stairs! Start the car! I'm right behind you! Go! Go!"

There was a clatter of heels on metal steps. Vi Coteau was more than halfway down the fire stairs and moving fast.

Vi caught up to McIntyre at the parking lot, where he stood scanning the parked automobiles. Beauchamp was nowhere in sight. It was obvious that he had gotten into one of the cars, but which one? The sunlight glaring from windscreens made it next to impossible to see. Then without warning, they heard the whine of a self-starter and jumped out of the way as a dark touring car shot out of a parking spot and came at them.

McIntyre turned toward his pickup truck. But Vi Coteau caught his sleeve and spun him around.

"We'll never catch him in that truck of yours!" she said. "Besides, my Marmon is closer. C'mon."

McIntyre had to take long strides to keep up with her. How

could she move that quickly in high heels and skirt?

"Beauchamp's car," she said, "it's a Studebaker. A Big Six, I think. Sounded like a six. But the Marmon can still catch him. He's not the only one with six cylinders."

When they got to the roadster McIntyre said "I think I'd better drive."

Vi laughed and pinched her finger and thumb together as if holding an imaginary coin.

"Here's a dime," she said. "Have yourself another think."

Before McIntyre could do much thinking at all, they were into the car and accelerating toward the parking lot entrance.

"Which way?" Vi shouted.

"Probably east. If I was him, I'd be heading for the nearest state line. Kansas."

Vi swung the Marmon eastward on Colfax Avenue. McIntyre's guess was right: the Studebaker was going up the hill by the capitol building, moving in the direction of faraway Kansas. Vi glanced in her rearview mirror.

"I think the sheriff is behind us," she said. "He might be catching up with us, but not for very long."

Her stylish high heel shoe punched the clutch, her slender manicured fingers slid the shift lever into third, and McIntyre saw parked cars and telephone poles begin to blur as they flew past. Just over the crest of the hill she had to swerve into the oncoming lane to avoid another car, then brought the shift lever down into fourth.

"Too fast for you?" she shouted over the sound of the engine.

"Yeah, a little!" he returned.

"You told me once that you went this fast in your airplane," she said with a laugh. "On the ground, too! Takeoff speed?"

"Yeah," McIntyre said through clenched teeth. "But with takeoff speed you sort of assume you'll be airborne before you hit anything!"

Vi kept the roadster in fourth gear, dodging slow-moving delivery trucks, forcing oncoming automobiles into the curb, blaring the horn at any pedestrian about to cross the street. All the while she was closing the distance between the Marmon and Beauchamp's Studebaker, leaving Sheriff Crowell's sedan further and further behind. When they sped across Josephine Street, Beauchamp nearly collided with a milk wagon, which Vi avoided with an adroit twist of the steering wheel. The Marmon rocked and tilted, but all four tires stayed on the pavement. At Colorado Boulevard they zipped around a Model T that was sideways on the pavement, probably owing to Beauchamp's dash through the intersection. On they raced, through the neighborhood of private homes, between the new apartment buildings, overtaking all traffic in their path. Oblivious to honking horns and shouts of drivers, Vi whipped around each car they passed as if it were standing still.

"Try a shot!" Vi called out. "A slug through his windscreen or a tire should slow him down!"

"Nothing doing!" Ranger McIntyre replied. "Too many cars and people! If I hit him, he might swerve into parked cars, maybe through a front porch!"

"Nuts!" she said. "Okay, in a minute or two we'll be out in the open farm country. Then I'll close the distance and you can shoot him. Hang on."

"You think I'm not already hanging on?" he replied.

Vi was right. In the next moment the Studebaker shot across an unpaved cross street, zipped past a small farmhouse with silo and barn, and they were racing across an open prairie. Instead of homes and parked cars, the highway was now bordered by fields of stubble where snow still lay in the furrows. She cautiously edged the roadster forward, never taking her eyes off the Studebaker's taillight. Beauchamp might be desperate enough to brake unexpectedly in the hope of having her ram into him and damage her radiator.

"That's it," she called to McIntyre above the howl of the engine and the shriek of the wind. "No closer!"

Ranger McIntyre needed to push his door hard in order to open it against the slipstream. He squeezed himself out of the car and onto the broad running board where he could hold on to the doorframe with one hand while drawing his .45 service revolver with the other. He tried for one of Beauchamp's tires but missed. The second shot also missed the tire. The cold wind was making his eyes water and the Studebaker was a moving blur.

"Ah, to hell with tires," McIntyre muttered. He took aim just to the right of the oval rear window and sent a .45 slug ripping through the canvas and on through the windscreen. Beauchamp's brake light went on and he pulled the car off the side of the road. Beauchamp was an outdoorsman tanned from long days in the sun, but when he gingerly stepped out of the car, he looked pale white. He held both his hands high in the air but he wasn't looking at McIntyre. He was looking at Vi.

Vi Coteau was out of the Marmon. Her small revolver had once more materialized out of nowhere and was pointed at Beauchamp.

"When the sheriff joins us," Vi said to McIntyre, "I think he'll have grounds for searching Mr. Beauchamp's car even without that warrant you claim he has."

"That's a good thing," McIntyre said. He sat down on the Marmon's running board, for his knees were shaking something awful.

During the entire trip back to the library, Vi kept the roadster reasonably close to the posted speed limit, for which McIntyre was grateful. He was also thankful for the Marmon's good heater, which worked far better than the one in his pickup. In their dash to catch up with Beauchamp both of them had left coats, gloves, and hats in the conference room.

"Where shall we have lunch?" Vi said brightly.

"Your choice," he replied. "I don't know Denver that well."

"Okay. There's a good chop suey joint on Champa Street. After we pick up our coats at the library, we'll drive down there. I thought Mr. Beauchamp seemed absolutely eager to spill his story to Sheriff Crowell, didn't you? Like he was relieved to be able to talk about it. When he told the sheriff how the first two deaths were accidental, I nearly believed him."

"In my experience with engineers," McIntyre replied, "it's really hard for them to admit they made a mistake. And when they do admit it, if they can't blame it on someone else, they always seem to need to explain exactly how it happened. That bit about Winston suffocating because he didn't have enough body weight to tilt the ore bucket in order to back out of it, that was a good example. Or the stamp mill, the dry Colorado air making the wood shrink? So the iron rod dropped? That was pretty far-fetched. Personally, I think he convinced himself that the deaths weren't totally his own fault."

"Just wanted revenge on the boys for bullying his son, is that it?"

"That's it. Up in the mountains inspecting old gold mines, he probably got the idea. If he and Beeky talked to one another about the mines, I can imagine Beeky saying something like 'there's a coincidence, because I was reading about the English Hotel owners stashing valuables in an old mine' and maybe that put Beauchamp's mind in high gear. Like every father, he wanted his boy to be strong and smart and successful. But here's this skinny kid that everybody picks on. Must have preyed on his mind. For years. How to get even. Then one day he's got it on his mind and happens across the ore bucket that looks like a giant-size waste paper can. He starts working out the mechanical details of canning one boy, knuckling the chest of another, locking the third one in a dark room. Get them out of his son's life, and for good."

"Did your father want you to be an army airplane pilot?" she asked. "Or a ranger?"

"Dad? Heck, no. No, the only thing he wanted for me was to put distance between myself and the farm. He and Mom ran a dairy farm. He always said having forty cows was like being married to forty women. Sunrise to sundown, feeding them, cleaning them, milking them, worrying about them, never able to leave for even a day. He always hoped I would leave the farm and have a better life for myself. He thought maybe I should be a teacher and have two or three months' vacation every year."

"And here you are," she said, smiling, "being paid to ride around in the mountains and go fishing whenever you feel like it."

They reached the library parking lot. Vi set the parking brake but didn't shut off the engine. With its canvas top up, the Marmon was very cozy.

"Beauchamp already had an old Irish coin, then. And the beat-up .32 revolver?"

"Yeah. If he's like most men, he decided one day that he needed a new gun but couldn't bring himself to toss out the old one. Probably doesn't even know that William Leup collects .32 revolvers. Or coins. I think he resents Leup, mostly because Leup has money and the money spoiled Richard, but he didn't set out to incriminate him. You know who I feel sorry for? The fraternity house guy, Bruce Jones. The house is going to be pretty dismal and gloomy for the rest of the year, I'm thinking. Three members dead, killed by the father of a kid that the fraternity had rejected. Wow."

"Yeah, wow," Vi repeated. "You said it. Let's go get our coats. Oh, wait. Tell me one more thing. You told me the librarian thought the boy's name, Beauchamp, reminded him of chewing gum."

"Sure," McIntyre said. "That librarian had never seen it in writing. He had only heard it. So to him it was Beeman, or Beecham."

Back inside the conference room they found that Bruce Jones, former army sergeant, had assumed command. He had John Péguy, Claire Candler, and Beeky write brief statements of how they were connected to the incidents, including addresses and phone numbers where they could be contacted. They were more than willing to do it, if it meant they could leave and go to lunch.

"You'd make a swell assistant detective," Ranger McIntyre told him, "if ever a man agreed to do detective work again. Which at the moment he doesn't think he will."

After Jones and the others had gone, McIntyre and Vi picked up their gloves and hats and left Special Collections without a backward glance.

"Okay, Detective Ranger," Vi said with a mischievous smile, "what was Mr. John Beauchamp hammering on the mine support for?"

"Curious thing to do, wasn't it? Especially for a mine inspector who would know it was dangerous. But do you remember the arrow on the tree, the one that looked like it was carved fifty years ago? Pointing at the mine?"

"Sure."

"I think he's going to tell us that he was considering using the mine to trap Richard Leup. Maybe he was going to tell Richard he had found another clue to the hoard, drive him up to the Big Horse, show him the arrow in the tree. He would rig up a way to pull down that weak support beam, maybe a rope to his car bumper, maybe hide a heavy sledgehammer or a miner's pick in the mine and knock it down when they were inside. Anyway, I bet his plan was to trap Richard inside a dark place with no way out. Either that, or . . ."

"Or what?"

"Or Beauchamp already had the bright idea of using the blockhouse for Richard's punishment. If that was the case, then I think he was testing the mine supports because he was looking for the hoard. In the library there's a letter, or a copy of one, to Lord Dunraven from his foreman. In that letter he says that he and the workers from the English Hotel have 'secured' the valuables for the winter 'well-hidden by the same thick timber supports which I showed to you.' "

By this time, they were driving toward Champa Street and the chop suey palace. Vi Coteau was keeping her hands on the wheel and her eyes on the busy Denver traffic.

"Whoa a minute," she said. "Is there a Dunraven Hoard, or isn't there? I thought I heard you call it a story made up by the locals, just another 'lost treasure' legend. Dunraven's money buried in a mine, or hidden behind a wall in a tunnel."

"It's real enough," McIntyre told her. "Boy, am I hungry!"

"How do you know?"

"Because I can feel my belt buckle digging into my backbone."

"No, nutty ranger. How do you know the hoard exists?"

"I've seen it."

"When?"

"Last week. I went back up to the Big Horse Mine and there it was. But there won't be any way to share it with the families of the victims the way Richard wanted."

"Where did you find it?"

"Near the tunnel entrance. Under the floor of the tunnel. The miners who dug the mine started to excavate a vertical shaft there, probably following a little vein of ore. There's a damp hole, like a cold cellar. When they gave up on the idea of a shaft, they built a floor of timbers over it and went on digging their horizontal tunnel into the mountain. Don't know how Dunraven's crowd found the hidden pit, but it was perfect for what they needed. Remember the water in the tunnel, how it disappears into the floor?"

"Yes."

"That's where the water goes. It runs down the rock walls of the pit, then seeps out downhill and emerges from the hillside where that stand of aspens is, near the little creek. Makes a terrific icebox. It's a natural cold cellar. Those old miners might not have hit a good vein of gold but they sure did make a swell place to keep venison and vegetables. I used my shovel to pry up two of the timbers—and boy, were they ever heavy!—and made enough room that I could lower a lantern and have a good look."

"Would you please stop teasing?" Vi said. "I don't care about pits and veins and cold cellars. Tell me what you found!"

"I can't."

"You can't tell me what it is? Why not?"

"Because you're FBI and if I told you what it is, the FBI would confiscate it. Nobody can have it, not until Congress repeals the Eighteenth Amendment."

"Booze?"

"I didn't say so."

"Say. Or else you don't eat."

"Blackmail? From the FBI?" McIntyre replied. "What next? Okay, it's booze. Jeroboams of wine, kegs of brandy, cases of real Scotch whiskey, all keeping very damp and cold in that mine pit. That's what the Englishmen didn't want to leave behind in a hotel storeroom. They didn't trust the locals not to break in and help themselves to their expensive hooch."

"What are you going to do about it?" Vi asked.

"I put the timbers back and covered them with dirt. But . . . John Péguy is pulling up stakes and he'll be moving to Longmont. He owes me a favor. Before he goes, he and I are going to plant blasting powder above the mouth of the Big Horse Mine and start a little precision landslide to bury the entrance to the tunnel. So nobody will wander in there and meet with an accident, you know. At least that's what I'm going to tell John."

"Cute," she said.

"Thank you."

"Not you. Your landslide scheme. Let's have lunch."

CHAPTER SEVENTEEN:
BY WAY OF AN EPILOGUE

Beams of light from the electric chandeliers of the William Leup mansion struggled with the stifling darkness of yards and yards of black crepe draped along the walls and around the windows of the dining room. Neither did the black silk runner down the center of the dining table do much to cheer the atmosphere. Leup's dinner guests had finished with the main course; as the dishes were being removed in preparation for dessert, people conversed in hushed tones.

Ranger McIntyre remained respectfully quiet and serious, although inwardly he was feeling quite smug. He had managed to get through another formal dinner without selecting the wrong fork or resting his elbows on the table. He had eaten soup without slopping it and had been pretty darn adroit at handling the slippery buttered string beans. Moreover, he accomplished this social triumph under what seemed like constant scrutiny from a dozen pairs of female eyes. Maybe Mr. Leup's high society ladies had never seen an outdoorsman wearing a tuxedo.

Dessert was a challenging dish of runny cherry pie topped with melting ice cream—the hostess had some kind of French name for it—that a person had to eat with a little flat spoon. It was a relief when the servant finally reached around him to take the dessert dish away. Mr. Leup snapped his fingers at another of the servers, whereupon, as if by sleight of hand, a crystal champagne flute appeared before each guest. Three servers

234

entered the room carrying ice buckets.

"Now," Leup said, a sly look on his face like a teen boy smoking a stolen cigarette, "a special, special treat. My lawyers tell me—and Miss Coteau here might confirm it—that the Eighteenth Amendment does not prevent one from owning alcoholic beverages. Only buying or selling or transporting same. I've been saving these bottles of champagne for a special occasion. I regret to say that the supply is limited. And I have no idea where a person might obtain anything approaching fine wine. Or brandy or whiskey, for that matter."

McIntyre felt Vi's elbow poke him in the ribs.

"I think we know," she whispered with a little smile. "Right?"

"No idea what you're talking about," McIntyre whispered in return.

William Leup lifted his champagne flute and looked up and down the table at his guests.

"I would like to ask you to raise your glasses in a toast to my—to our—departed son Richard, and to his lifelong friends Winston Dole and Charles Monde, whose lives flared like bright torches in our midst all too briefly, only to be tragically snuffed out. May we be up to the task of carrying their dreams for them until such time as we, ourselves, are called to join with them in God's own hereafter."

He drank. The somber assemblage drank. Then Leup put a hand on McIntyre's shoulder.

"I would now like to formally recognize two persons who have been most instrumental in investigating the tragic, tragic fates of our young people. All of you know who they are and I'm sure you've all heard the story. I present to you Ranger Timothy Grayson McIntyre, late of the Second Aero Squadron in France, of the United States National Park Service. The lovely lady at his side is Miss Violet Coteau, executive administrative secretary to Agent A.T. Canilly of the Denver Office of the Federal Bureau of Investigation."

"Whew!" McIntyre whispered. "And all in one breath, too!"

"Shut up," Violet hissed.

"Ranger McIntyre graciously agreed to use all of his own furlough time, all his vacation time, to discover the cause of these senseless homicides and place the culprit in the hands of the law. He will not, or cannot, accept a reward; however, I want to say, and I want all of you to be witness to it, that if ever there is any kind of reward that can be given, in keeping with official policies, I shall gladly give it. As a matter of fact . . ."

He put his hand on McIntyre's shoulder again and grinned like a favorite uncle giving his nephew a new pocketknife. Oh, oh, McIntyre thought. What's the man gone and done?

". . . as a matter of fact," Leup continued, "I have used my influence—which as you all know I rarely use—to persuade the National Park Service to extend Ranger McIntyre's furlough, to let him have another two weeks of vacation time beginning immediately. To make up in a very, very small way for the time he has spent uncovering the facts of our son's death."

"Oh, God," McIntyre whispered to Vi. Not two more weeks. Fishing closed for the season, no new jigsaw puzzles, nobody at the cabin to talk to except a smart aleck horse and maybe the occasional blue jay. He wanted to return to work, that's what he wanted.

And there was going to be even more generosity from Mr. Leup. As the evening dragged to a close and the guests filed out through the front door, receiving hats and coats from the servants and an overly exuberant parting handshake from their host, McIntyre and Vi hung back. As special guests they did not want to look overly anxious to leave. Instead of joining the line of departing diners they stood, making mostly meaningless small talk with the hostess, Mrs. Leup. When the last of the guests had left, William Leup joined them.

"Ranger," he said.

"Thank you for a nice evening," McIntyre said. The tuxedo seemed to make him speak formally. Like that.

"One more thing," Mr. Leup said. "I want to do you a favor."

"Oh? No, sorry," McIntyre hurried to say. "No rewards. Glad to help. Really, it was flattering that you asked me. I'm just sad and disappointed it turned out the way it did."

Vi Coteau put her arm through his and gave him a subtle squeeze. William Leup put his hand on the ranger's shoulder again. He was wearing that benevolent uncle expression again.

"Look at it as simply one man helping another. A grateful citizen saying 'thanks' to a soldier. It's nothing special, something you'd probably want to do for me, if our situations were turned around. It's that I happened to notice your truck, that's all. I was thinking 'now, what could I do to show Mr. McIntyre my appreciation?' and I noticed the truck with 'Small Delights' still painted on the door."

"Name of a tourist lodge," McIntyre explained. "I got the truck after the lodge closed."

"Yes, Miss Coteau told us that story. Well . . . I'm a businessman. And investor. I own a number of Denver businesses. A dry cleaner, a small hardware store, that kind of thing. I also own a repair shop on Federal Boulevard. Steve's Auto Body and Radiator Repair."

"I don't really need any dry cleaning at the moment," McIntyre said. "And the pickup doesn't need any body work, unless it got hit while we were at dinner. Dinner was excellent, by the way."

"Thank you," Mr. Leup replied, "but what I mean to say is, I would like you to take your truck to Steve's and let the boys paint your doors. My treat, anything you want done. While they're at it, they might as well paint the whole truck, give it a shiny new paint job. Maybe you don't want a whole paint job, but at least have them cover up the bit that says 'Small Delights.' As a favor, one guy to another."

McIntyre's mind searched for a way out. Mr. Leup's insistence made him think of being in Minnie's little storeroom with no trousers on.

"It's really fine of you to think of it," McIntyre said. "Not many people would be so . . . well, so considerate. You know what? Maybe a new color! Gosh, there's an idea! Let me think about what color I might like."

"Good, good!" Mr. Leup said. "Then I'll have my secretary tell the body shop to expect you and whenever you're ready for that new paint job, you just take your truck to them."

He gripped McIntyre's hand as if they had completed an international exchange agreement.

"Glad we could settle it!" he said.

Vi and McIntyre emerged from the Leup mansion to find themselves all alone in the whole city of Denver. There was not a single person to be seen on the street, no sound of motorcars, no indication of life anywhere up and down the boulevard of expensive houses. Vi clutched her fur-trimmed cape closely against the winter chill as they walked toward her car. McIntyre wished he had brought his overcoat from the pickup even if it was army olive drab and hardly the thing to wear with a tuxedo.

"Small Delights" was parked nearby, but the two of them got into Vi's Marmon. She started the engine and turned on the interior light and the heater. *I should go on back up the mountain,* McIntyre thought, *and let her go home to bed. Trouble is, I want to go on being with her.*

"What about small delights?" she asked.

"Pardon?"

"The paint job. Are you going to take him up on his offer?"

"No, I don't think so. I'm sort of getting used to having that sign on the doors."

"How about a midnight snack?" Vi suggested. "I know a little all-night diner. It's down by Union Station."

"Not really hungry," McIntyre said with a grin. "Not after that dinner. They had enough food to feed a village for a week. I could probably stand a cup of coffee. Probably need it for the drive up the hill. Otherwise I might go to sleep and slide off the road."

"I've been thinking about that," Vi said. Her dark eyes reminded him of those of a mountain cat, looking at him from under her fur hat and with her fur-trimmed cape wrapped high around her neck. "You have tomorrow off, don't you?"

"I guess so. Sure. Lots of days off, apparently."

"Have you ever seen our Denver zoo?"

"Nope. Never have. Is it open in the winter?"

"We could find out. If not, there's always the natural history museum. Very interesting exhibits."

"Okay."

"What I was thinking, Tim, is that . . . well, that here we are again."

"Here we are again? Not sure I follow you."

"We've been here before, remember? Too late at night for one of us to drive home? In this case it's you. It's late to be searching for a hotel room. It's a long, long ways back to your log cabin. But I've got oodles of room at my place. And I'll have you know that I make a doozy of a breakfast."

"Got no pajamas," McIntyre said. "Nor a toothbrush."

"Silly ranger," Vi replied. "I've got extra toothbrushes."

Ranger McIntyre followed the twin red taillights through the dark streets, careful to keep them in view even though there was no chance at all of losing them in traffic because there was no traffic. The only cars moving were his pickup truck and the Marmon. He found himself humming a popular song, then singing the lyrics.

"I'll be with you in apple blossom time . . ."

What the heck? he asked himself. *Why in hell do I have that tune in my head?*

He slowed down because the Marmon's taillights had turned into a broad driveway. *Why the hell would I even care?* he thought.

ABOUT THE AUTHOR

James Work was a small boy when his parents moved from Denver to Estes Park, where they had purchased a rustic cabin camp on the edge of Rocky Mountain National Park. He attended grade school and high school in the village, but as soon as classes were dismissed, he could be seen with his fishing rod, heading for Fall River, or on his bicycle on his way to the nearby ranger station. All through high school he and his pals hiked the trails of Rocky Mountain National Park, climbed the peaks, and fished the lakes and streams. He also had summer jobs with the trail crew and worked for the U.S. Forest Service fighting fires and tending campgrounds.

James holds a Ph.D. in Victorian poetry from the University of New Mexico. He is currently professor emeritus at Colorado State University and lives in Fort Collins with his wife, Sharon, and an independently minded Westie terrier named Duncan.

In addition to his definitive anthology of Western American literature, *Prose and Poetry of the American West* (University of Nebraska Press), he has published more than eighteen other books including mysteries, westerns and personal essays. His latest project is the Ranger McIntyre series, *Unmentionable Murders, Small Delightful Murders, Dunraven's Hoard Murders, Stones of Peril* and a work in progress, *The Case of the Missing Bierstadt.*

The employees of Five Star Publishing hope you have enjoyed this book.

Our Five Star novels explore little-known chapters from America's history, stories told from unique perspectives that will entertain a broad range of readers.

Other Five Star books are available at your local library, bookstore, all major book distributors, and directly from Five Star/Gale.

<u>Connect with Five Star Publishing</u>

Visit us on Facebook:
  https://www.facebook.com/FiveStarCengage

Email:
  FiveStar@cengage.com

For information about titles and placing orders:
  (800) 223-1244
  gale.orders@cengage.com

To share your comments, write to us:
  Five Star Publishing
  Attn: Publisher
  10 Water St., Suite 310
  Waterville, ME 04901